" Meet Spikez, a hedgehog hero for those who want more out of life than to run, jump, and collect golden rings. Armed rather more offensively than the traditional covering of prickles, he is the result of some fast-track evolution from Professor Windar - and is called upon to risk everything in defence of his woodland home.

Close to the surface of lasers and computers is another story, one that will easily leap out at any reader, young or old. And that is, nature is pretty amazing in its own right. I believe that the best way to get people hooked on the natural world is to tell them great stories - and this is such a story.

So dive deep into the world of Spikez and his friends and next time you are out in the wilds, see if you cannot magic up a little of the techno-whizz yourself."

Hugh Warwick, ecologist & author, A Prickly Affair:
The Charm of the Hedgehog (Penguin).

D0488741

523 173 10 1

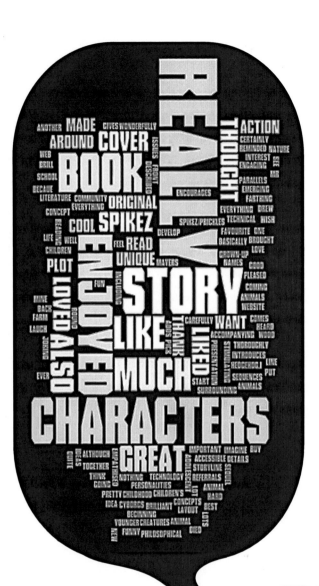

Author's Note

I have two questions for you. Firstly, what do hedgehogs do?

Until recently I'd only seen three live hedgehogs in my entire life. They were either wandering around aimlessly at night looking for food, or hiding in places that we humans like to clear out. There is a certain mystery and charm surrounding these wonderful creatures and, given their ranking on the UK endangered list, a rarity of seeing a healthy one alive.

The second question is this - what happens to all the roadkill?

It's a disturbing figure, but an estimated 10 million animals and birds are killed by motor vehicles on UK roads each year. Now, I've never met a person who officially counts roadkill, but that figure could be nearly double. I've seen more rabbits, pheasants, hedgehogs and other rare British wildlife dead at the side of the road than alive. Some of it is really badly squished into the ground, but some looks untouched at the roadside, almost as if the creature were dozing. Perhaps it's carried away by scavengers, or are there people or organisations that collect it? (Sorry, that's three questions!).

Photo taken by Jacke Burke, Leighton Buzzard Hedgehog Rehabilitation

My thanks go out to everyone that has helped bring Spikez to life. This wouldn't have happened without the love and support of family members, especially: Sally, Dad, Amelie-Rose & Ruby for their biased enthusiasm.

The credits are endless, so I've broken it up into categories.

1) Team Beta - Without their time spent proofing and critiquing the early drafts, Spikez might still be on a hard drive and never have made it to testing phase. I'd like to give thanks again to (in no order of preference) Sue Anderson, Bethany Thomas, Neil Parsons, Jackie Pigott, Amanda Mayers, Michael Cox, and Fran Barnard. **2)** The Academics - Due to the scientific and sometimes techy nature of the book, I'm very grateful to Dr David Dewhurst, Secretary of The Cybernetics Society; Dr. Mohammad Majid al-Rifaie, Researcher at Goldsmiths, University of London and Committee Member in the Society for the Study of Artificial Intelligence and the Simulation of Behaviour (SSAISB); Dr. Colin Johnson, University of Kent; and Fiona McNeill, for all their advice. **3)** The Creatives – A big thanks to John Burton for being so stupid and agreeing to work with me on the project for so long; Stefanos Efthimiou for his exciting musical scores that enhance Spikez. **4)** The Schools – Several schools across Hertfordshire and London, both primary and secondary, have allowed me to either visit and share my vision of Spikez, or allowed the Beta Copies to sit on their library shelves and get read by the most important people of all: the students. Special thanks to Jenny Bishop, Vicki Johnston and Edward Gaynor at The Astley Cooper School for organising focus groups; to Fallon Ismail at Townsend School for giving me huge audiences, twice! Thanks also all the librarians, teachers and students at (in no order of preference): La Sainte Union Catholic Girls' School, The Raglan School, William Patten School, St Columbas College, Loreto College, St Albans Girls' School, Verulam School, Mount Pleasant Lane Primary School, Nicholas Breakspear Catholic School, Tewin Cowper C of E Primary School, Henlow Middle School, Highgate Primary, Bishop Hatfield Girls' School, Monks Walk School, Hammond Academy, Aycliffe Drive School, Maple Grove Primary School, Beaumont School, Loxford School, Holtsmere End Junior School. You know who you are. **5)** Hog Lovers - My thanks to Hugh Warwick, for his support and fab foreword; Jacke Burke, for allowing me to get so close to these amazing creatures; Fay Vass, British Hedgehog Preservation Society.

www.spikez.co.uk

Spikez

Written by **Richard Mayers**
Illustrated by **John Burton**

Throughout the novel we've included secret QR codes that link to enhanced content.

"The fox has many tricks,
and the hedgehog only one,
but that is the best of all"

Archilochus Greek Poet and Mercenary

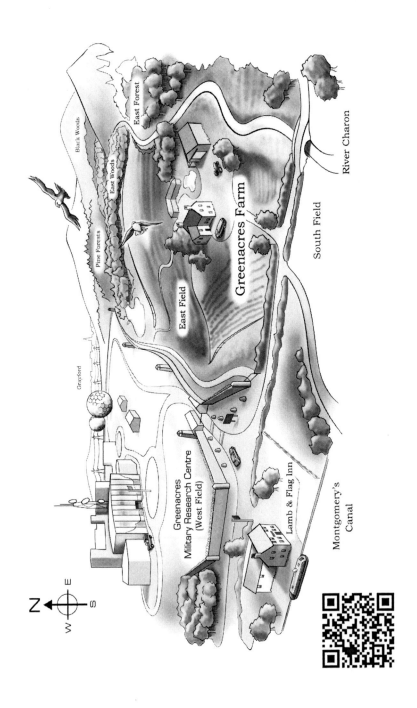

Black Woods

East Woods

Pine Forests

East Forest

East Field

Grayford

Greenacres Farm

Greenacres
Military Research Centre
(West Field)

Lamb & Flag Inn

Montgomery's
Canal

South Field

River Charon

N
W E
S

Prologue

G reenacres Farm used to be a fertile, unspoilt haven set in the heart of the English countryside. Farmer Cullem had lovingly managed the land for over forty years.

As harsh economic times swept the nation, the farmer faced rising costs and increased competition from foreign produce. To guarantee a comfortable retirement, Farmer Cullem sold a large portion of his territory to the British Ministry of Defence.

Before long, machines arrived and began developing the West Field. As the seasons passed, a large tower constructed of metal, concrete and mirrored glass commanded the countryside; warehouses, offices and satellites were also assembled, secured by a thick wire fence. In contrast to this, Farmer Cullem's buildings began to crumble, livestock were neglected, and agricultural equipment was either sold or left to rust as he enjoyed his new found wealth.

The Greenacres Military Research Facility was joined to the outside world by a winding black road; when the sun shone upon it, the surface glistened like treacle. Many of the animals and birds that ventured beyond it never returned – most of the woodland creatures believed that it was cursed.

Chapters

Part One: **Creation**

Part One: **Creation**

1: Crash

"I'm not leaving here without a meal!" scowled Fagin, blood glistening along his jawline. He slowly rose from the ground, sizing up his opponent.

Spikez stood upright on his hind legs, his front claws extended, ready to fight the beast.

Fagin studied the hedgehog's face. "Wait a minute, I know you. But . . ." he ducked his head, inspecting the mechanics beneath Spikez' mass of erect spines. "You're dead! I watched you die!"

Spikez did not respond. He had taken a wire-frame analysis of Fagin's face and processed it against all his past and present memory files, and it had triggered something.

The words echoed in Spikez' head: 'You're dead! I watched you die!'

It matched the same menacing tone that had been locked

away, buried in the deepest, darkest sectors of his brain - until now.

'I know you.' Fagin's sneering voice replayed again, again and again. 'You're dead!'

Frozen to the spot, Spikez wavered like a sheriff too drunk to draw as the outlaw prepared to attack.

'I watched you die!'

```
F:404 [SYSTEM ERROR] SPIK-3Z offline...
...
SPIK-3Z.exe has encountered a problem and needs
to close.
```

2: A New Threat

"**H**urry up, Rosie! We're going to be late!" snapped Henrietta, a rather plump hedgehog with a round, polished snout.

From beneath a dead hedgerow, a tiny ball of bristles and brown fur emerged. "My legs ache," whined Rosie.

"Now listen, it's not often that we have these meetings, but when we do the animal covenant states that *all must attend*."

"Whatever." Rosie sat and proceeded to groom her quills back into place with her claws.

Henrietta gave a disapproving snort. She turned and carried on walking across the farmyard with her muzzle held high.

Inside the dilapidated dairy barn, birds and mammals gathered together. Queen Eliza, a graceful sparrowhawk and chair of the Animal Council, was perched regally upon the central rafter. Beside her was Hercules, a mighty red kite and Eliza's most trusted friend. The raptors were motionless as they cast their yellow eyes at each new arrival.

In the dying moments of dusk, the farmer's last remaining flock of sheep congregated by the main entrance, pressed tightly together for warmth against the biting autumn winds. Protected against some corroded, iron sheets where the cows once stood, a family of field mice gathered by the webbed feet of the Geese, who were quietly honking to themselves.

More creatures convened in the shelter: rabbits and hares thumped along the wall in a flurry of brown and grey fur; finches, songbirds and pigeons lined the remaining rafters and added to the cacophony of chattering and chirping.

"Where's your father and brother?" Henrietta asked, pausing for breath at the barn entrance.

"Right here, dear," boomed Harold Hog. A bulk of dark copper spines and coarse, tan hair burst into the open. From beneath his large, wet snout a juicy worm writhed as he swallowed it whole. "Need to stock up before the soil freezes over. Isn't that right, Prickles?"

The lean shape of an adolescent hog with sharp, white-tipped spikes snuffled behind his father, no worm in tow. "If I ever get a chance," Prickles muttered to himself.

The farm building was now a hive of activity, feathers and fur united together. A full moon gave light to the proceedings through a gaping hole in the barn roof; watching everything, like the owl who trained his eye on a couple of field voles. But only on official occasions like this was there such an amicable relationship between predator and prey.

The hedgehogs sought refuge amongst a pile of logs. This was Prickles' and Rosie's first time at such an event, which occurred maybe once or twice in an animal's lifetime. The meeting was prompted by the devastating effects of the *black river*, which continued to affect the whole community.

Queen Eliza scoured the gathering to check attendance once more. "Make a note of who is not present," she instructed. "We are to begin."

A woodpecker started tapping violently on the corrugated metal roof. All the animals and birds silenced, giving their full attention to Eliza.

"Creatures of Greenacres, the council has convened to share our concerns about the increased activity of *man*."

There was a murmur of bitter chirps and snorts of disapproval at that *word*.

"What about the magpies?" a deep, wheezing voice yelled out. All eyes, heads and beaks turned towards Baldwin, a well-respected badger. He shuffled into the dusty light, coating himself in a halo of silver. Baldwin had survived man for generations and he had foreseen the military base before construction had even begun. Most of the younger animals believed him to be over a hundred seasons old.

"Magpies will be magpies," dismissed Eliza. "They are not our main concern."

"I'm afraid you're wrong about that!" he said, prompting gasps from council members at his boldness. "They're up to something - I know it."

Hercules' eyes tightened. Eliza flicked him a glance, for she valued Baldwin's comments, even though his tone was not always agreeable. "And just how do you conclude that a bunch of reckless *magpies* pose more of a threat to us than *man*? They are creatures of this land - they would never turn against us."

"You're wrong, my Queen."

"Enough!" bellowed Hercules.

"Hercules, my loyal friend," Baldwin retorted, "pardon my unrest, but you need to check on them before other corvids fall under their control. Let none of us forget the painful legacy of Morag." The badger paused, pawing at the earth in reflection. "They already have influence over the squirrels. And there is one magpie distinctly different to all others, to any corvid that I have ever known . . ." Some of the animals and birds nodded – Baldwin was on to something. "Big Mag."

Disgruntled whistles erupted from all the bird representatives.

"Big Mag is an overgrown thug, nothing more and nothing less. He will soon be overrun by another magpie, such is their nature. They pose no mortal threat," argued Eliza.

"No, he's right!" A pair of elderly starlings were perched on a rotting beam in the shadows, away from the other songbirds. Sadness strained their voices. "They took our young. The man-base has brought so much carrion across the land, yet they continue to feast on the healthy." The mother shielded her eyes as she wept. "They chattered brazenly at us as they carried them *all* away."

The rest of the starlings clicked their beaks in anger.

"Order!" yelled Hercules, silencing the dissenting birds. "You speak of murder."

"A balance has always been kept and must be upheld, the code of nature dictates this," continued Eliza.

"But they are not maintaining balance - they *are* killing for fun, and taking more than is needed to survive, thus exhibiting the same characteristics as man. Therefore, it is my firm belief that they pose a greater, more immediate threat to us all!" stressed Baldwin. "It is only a matter of time until they manipulate other creatures to support their efforts."

Eliza could not ignore the growing anger felt amongst council members. The thought of a creature behaving like man was a dangerous prospect and the raptors had learnt much from their epic fight with Morag many moons ago. "Very well, we will have words with their leader."

Rosie and Prickles had no say in the matter. As adolescents, they relied upon the direction of their parents, who were both busy scratching for insects.

"This is so boring," whispered Rosie. "I want to go and see the man-tower."

"We can't," said Prickles. "It's too dangerous."

"Chicken!" heckled Rosie.

"I'm not a chicken – I'm a hedgehog. I just don't feel it's safe to go there in the day. You've heard the rumours!"

"Yes, rumours. And anyway, who said anything about going in the day? I'm too tired then and there's too many humans wandering around. I want to go at night and see the man-moon with its flashing stars. I hear it's beautiful."

"Who told you that?"

"The rabbits – some of them have been and say the best dandelions grow beside the black river, which means lots of damp hiding places for luscious worms. We could have a feast!" she said excitedly. "Dad barely lets us have a look in."

They glanced over at their father; he was busy chasing woodlice, which rolled across the floor as he tried to suck them up.

"I don't know, Rosie. This meeting sounds important-"

"Then I'll go on my own," she snapped, flinging herself round to face the bleak wilderness.

"No!" Prickles cautioned. "You're my little sister. If you go, I go. You need me to protect you."

She butted her brother in the snout. "You're only older by a couple of minutes, and I don't need protecting."

"Yes you do - from *yourself!*"

Rosie smiled. "Let me work on mum, you back me up when I give you a signal." She trundled over to Henrietta with a mild limp and began feigning symptoms of hog flu.

"Whatever is the matter with you?" she grunted, sniffing her daughter.

Prickles sidled up to Rosie. "Sis, you look rough – and you smell pretty bad, too."

"Shut up Prickles, I'm not well. I think something bit me," Rosie inspected the soft, bronzed fur of her tummy and sneezed. "Mum, I want to go home."

"But we can't leave now, we've only just got here and we're about to eat dinner."

"I can take her back," suggested Prickles.

"Well, I'm not sure about that, I'll have to speak to your father. Harold!" she looked around for her husband. "Where is he now?"

"What is it, darling?" Harold's face poked out from behind the logs, his mouth stuffed with slugs.

As the young hedgehogs pleaded with their parents, Fagin watched them from the shadows. Cloaked in the corner of the barn by a stack of worn out tractor treads, the rogue had no interest in what was said at the council meeting, instead he saw it as an opportunity to groom potential victims - and the young hoglets would make a fine meal.

Harold began crunching on dried beetle shells, popping several into his mouth in one go as he spoke. "Well, he's nearly an adult now. I'm sure he can look after his sister."

"Okay, but you take Rosie straight home, and don't mess up the nest!" warned Henrietta.

"I won't let you down," said Prickles, leading Rosie away behind him.

Shifting back across the farmyard and into the hedgerow, Prickles could hear the names of animals being read out in remembrance.

3: A Hedgehog's Purpose

Rosie and Prickles made good time. As they rustled through overgrown brambles, chickweed and wood sage, they made jokes about their parents, betted against each other, and played games like they always did.

"What are you going to do after hibernation?" Prickles asked.

"I'm going to leave Greenacres," affirmed Rosie.

"Why? This is our home."

"Yeah, but it's such a boring place to live. All we do is go out looking for food with mum and dad, to the same spots - every night! I want to travel, go on an adventure and hang out with other hogs, like uncle Spyke did."

"Mum says he didn't go on an adventure. She says he left aunty Tiggy for another hog."

"That's rubbish! He told me he was going. Wherever he went to must have been better than here, otherwise he would have come back."

Prickles reflected for a moment. "I don't want you to leave, Rosie."

"Then come with me, it'll be fun – the two of us together, like always."

"It'll be dangerous."

Rosie sighed in frustration. "You're too cautious, that's your problem. But don't worry, bro – when the bugs get too big, I'll protect you!" she joked.

They walked some more, over a mound of earth and past several varieties of heather and valerian. Prickles remained in deep thought before he finally spoke. "What's our purpose in life, Rosie?"

Rosie stopped, turned and looked into her brother's eyes; they were round and fretful, shimmering in the moonlight. "What do you mean?"

"Well, we've got a comfortable existence. We're the only hedgehog family left in Greenacres and don't seem to want for anything other than . . . bugs. Aside from eating, what are hedgehogs supposed to do?"

She couldn't answer. "Well, what do you think they should do?"

"I dunno. Maybe they should have an active role within the council. Why should the raptors make all the decisions? Hedgehogs ought to have a say on what happens in Greenacres. I don't want to be like dad and just eat and sleep all the time. I mean, he wasn't even interested in what that old badger was wheezing on about. I want to make a difference!"

Rosie stared at her surroundings and pondered. Prickles desperately hoped that his words might have struck a chord, altering her views on life, but instead his sister began flicking her spines back into place. "That sounds like hard work. Wouldn't you rather become an explorer like me?"

"I don't know," he said, trying hard not to sound disappointed. "There are a lot of things on my mind right now."

Shuffling forward, Rosie nuzzled his cheek. "It's probably the cold weather getting at you. Let's wait until we wake in spring, that'll give you plenty of time to think. We need to enjoy now."

4: Another World

A steel tower stands above countless warehouses and offices, its red eye blinking rapidly as it hunts for movement. Shielding the military research facilities, linked by strings of glimmering lights, are several scallop-shaped satellites which gaze up at the night sky, listening for any signs of danger.

Three magpies were perched in rank order on the perimeter fence, watching. At the top sat Big Mag, the self-appointed leader of the pack, who was remarkably large for such a bird. Mag seemed to absorb the beacon's energy as his oily blue tail ticked back and forth like a paddle, ready to swat his deputies. Beneath him were Hood and Ringpull, adolescent magpies who - although smaller by comparison - were equally as ruthless as their idolised commander.

"That, gang, is where we shall all be one day," Mag boasted, his broad wing outstretched toward the man-complex. "Once we've taken control of Greenacres from the raptors, all the riches of the land will belong to us." He glanced down at the ground beneath him; squirrel foot-soldiers were busy depositing nuts and seeds in his newly conquered rabbit warren, preparing for the harsh winter to come.

"They will talk about us at the council meeting," fretted Ringpull.

Big Mag looked down at the young magpie. Despite wearing a fizzy-drink's tab on his head to appear more urban and menacing, Ringpull's feathers were lank and unkempt, and he looked malnourished. In Mag's opinion, the bird he'd fostered from a fledgling needed more confidence in his species' ability to lead.

"Let them talk. It's all Eliza and her kind can do. Wars were never won by chatting."

"Yeah, don't be such a songbird, Ringpull!" taunted Hood, a bullish magpie. Strands of old plastic bags shrouded the bird's head in darkness as he hopped erratically along the fence, gesturing at the base. "It's the humans you wanna worry about. They've got some serious gear - I'm talking big, metal machines that will crunch your bones and rip your feathers out."

"Yes, Hood. And like the humans, we will use this machinery to provide us with more tasty meat," declared Mag. "Then we can take over the farm. And we all know what lies inside the farmer's house ... don't we?"

The magpies squawked in unison: "Chatak-chatak! Lovely shiny things!"

A mob of carrion crows loitered behind the magpies in the cover of trees; they had heard many rumours about this corvid revolutionist and were keen to become part of Mag's master plan.

"Stick with me, gang, and you'll see why magpies were meant to rule."

The hedgehogs were only a few yards away from the boundary fence. The glow from the tower created a misty, red hue in the night sky; tiny droplets of water seemed frozen in mid-air and collected on the white tips of their spines as they crept closer. It was a world away from the woods they knew.

Prickles' heart thundered. "Maybe we should turn back. It feels too dangerous being here, so late at night and far from home."

"No," insisted Rosie, "we've come all this way. I want to see more!"

Dew gathered on their tummies as they shuffled over long, glistening blades of grass. Then Rosie was prompt to spot food, wriggling ahead of her on some gravel next to the fence. She quickly scrambled over and gobbled it up. It was the juiciest, tastiest organic worm Rosie had ever eaten in her short life; her father was good at finding worms for the family, but he always kept the best ones for himself.

Prickles watched his sister munch with glee. Knowing there was food nearby, he began to relax, and then he spotted it: a worm, even more succulent and fatter than Rosie's! He sprang towards it, devouring it messily. They had done a lot of walking and it felt good to replenish before investigating further.

After gorging on several more juicy treats, the pair came right up to the perimeter fence, resting their tiny front feet against the metal wire, which felt cold and had an unfamiliar smell. Beyond it they could sense that not all of the humans were asleep, distinguishing between voices and the sounds of machines grinding and whirring. The pair watched and listened in amazement.

They decided to track a little further to see if the worms would keep getting bigger, and to identify where the racket was coming from. Ahead, Rosie noticed a section of fence where an animal had been digging underneath it.

"Are you thinking what I'm thinking?" she asked.

"No, Rosie. I think we've done enough exploring. We should get back."

"But we've come this far, the worms are probably even fatter on the other side!"

"There's plenty of food here. You're as bad as dad!" scolded Prickles.

"Don't say that," she said, butting him in his snout. "Where's your sense of adventure gone?"

"I know what's through there," whispered a voice, tainted with menace.

Both hedgehogs spun round. Fagin slunk out from the shadows. The watchtower's red light reflected in his eyes, which burned like lava pools.

Rosie's lips began to tremble. Prickles stood in front of her, his body arched defensively. "We didn't really want to go through it," he explained, spikes twitching.

Fagin slowly shimmied forward into the light so that both hedgehogs could see him; mange had left him with patches of bare skin amongst his scraggly red fur. Stooping lower to the ground, the beast smiled revealing a sharp set of teeth. "Why not, you're small enough? I dug that hole for us all. You see, I'm good at digging. The humans don't know soil like I do."

Prickles and Rosie backed away. They knew of Fagin, and his reputation. He was suspected of luring numerous young rabbits and hares into his secret den, although nothing was ever proved - no bodies were ever found.

"Let me show you what's on the other side. You can come and feast with me in my underground house." On his last word Fagin leapt forward, his fangs protracted.

Rosie and Prickles coiled themselves up and rolled through the hole, past the verge and onto the road. The fox, who only missed Prickles' leg by a whisker, slavered frantically as he squeezed his scrawny orange body beneath the barrier.

"Hurry!" Prickles shouted, but he knew they could not outrun Fagin, they needed to find a ditch small enough for them both to curl up inside. He watched Rosie tumble into the middle of a smooth, cold looking surface; it was black and moist, glistening in the light. And then he realised where they were, the black river.

Rosie began to uncurl herself. She was still shivering with fright. Ahead, two glaring lights hovered ominously.

"Rosie, get away from there. Quick!"

The beams of light grew more intense, thundering towards Rosie. Paralysed with fear, all she could do was stand and watch in horror.

Fagin towered over Prickles with evil intent in his heart. "Two delicious hogs!"

Prickles quickly bounded over to his sister. "Go!" he barked, striking Rosie with enough force to roll her to the other side of the road and safely into a ditch. But now he was directly in the path of the approaching man machine, sandwiched between the safety of Rosie and the threat of Fagin. The gaunt fox was hesitant as the sound of the vehicle grew louder. He backed away from the road, torn between an easy meal or becoming roadkill himself.

Prickles looked up, transfixed by the lights about to consume him. Then he felt its touch and his world went black.

The car skidded to a halt.

Fagin crouched down at the roadside and watched as the driver's door opened. The villainous fox panicked, fleeing the scene as a human exited the vehicle.

Rosie slowly began to uncurl herself. "Prickles?" She waited eagerly for the sound of her brother's voice. "Prickles, what's happening?"

The car door slammed.

Rosie peered over the verge, searching for signs of her brother. She grew scared at the sound of feet clomping on tarmac. Then she caught sight of Prickles and froze. He lay motionless, his limbs contorted and crushed. An unbearable sadness made her whole body shudder uncontrollably and her stomach tumbled; it felt as though the worms were planning a revolt. She tried to call for her brother, but couldn't breathe.

A thin looking man, wearing brown shoes and odd coloured socks, lurched above the hedgehog's remains with his arms crossed, as if in deep thought. A nimble hand pulled out a small but powerfully bright LED torch from his left trouser pocket, which he then used to scour the roadside. He saw the fence and the hole that Rosie had so desperately wanted to go through. Fagin was nowhere to be seen. Then the light shone on Rosie's face and she mechanically coiled up into a ball as tightly as she could, rolling back into the protection of the ditch. The man hesitated for a moment before returning to his car to retrieve some surgical gloves, a bag and a silver canister.

Prickles was dead. A circle of light shone down upon him. The man's gloved hand reached down and diligently collected what was left of the young hoglet, sealing his remains tightly within the cylinder, which was then pumped with an inert gas.

The man returned to his vehicle, took two attempts to start the engine and then drove off towards the base.

Minutes passed before Rosie had enough courage to investigate again. When she did finally venture out to check on Prickles she found nothing. There was no sound of his gentle grunting, joking about how close a shave that was; no sight of his deep brown eyes beckoning her over to share a humble thought; nothing was there to greet her, except a deathly silence.

She quietly wept to herself. Her twin brother was gone.

5: Construction

There is a flash of brilliant white light. Prickles is momentarily conscious, lying on a cold slab of steel and staring up at several shimmering orbs of intense brightness. Something leans over him holding a syringe. He watches as his foot is lifted off the ground and injected with bright liquid, but he cannot feel it - he cannot feel anything. White slowly fades to black.

Bright blue and red pixels spark across the air. For a split-second the shape of a mouse appears, and then there is darkness again.

A rhythmic blip echoes in Prickles' head. Whirring noises reverberate across the confines of a laboratory. Prickles opens his eyes to see his hand lying on a small table, hooked up by wires to a silver box. He goes to reach it but he cannot move, instead he watches it twitch and shift by itself. Beyond, the silhouette of a man paces back and forth through frosted glass, and there's a glimpse of a mouse again.

A loud pip rings in Prickle's head and then the room turns fuzzy. Silence.

Blackness.

```
STOP: 0X000000008E(0XC0000090, 0X004B4BD8,
0XEE25885C, 0X00000000)
beginning dump of physical memory...
Loading...
fc-b{ref48b-mag} - connected to host: carrion.
sys
run SPIK-3Z.exe . . . loading (please do not
switch off during important updates)
```

He sits in a chair, the hand reattached to his arm. He raises it, studies it, what is it? He has no memory about what he is or who he was. He does not understand the concept of time or how long he has been in the lab; and there are no memories, feelings or emotions.

There is movement in front of him. His hand clenches into a fist as a creature appears: it is small with large ears and it has two motorised rubber tracks attached to its legs – it stops and looks at him, revealing two large incisors. He does not know how to respond. He looks back at his fist and unclenches it – what is it?

A sound resonates 3.84 metres away. He quickly identifies the source: it has two large white appendages with five pink claws at the end; its head has patches of fur missing from the top; and from its face, two glass rectangles balance on a small pink stub that protrudes from it. It is holding something, a strip of shiny material. The figure reaches forward and places the object over his eyes.

There is blackness again.

6: The Magpie Motif

Unable to talk of their loss, the Hog family had entered hibernation with emptiness in their slow beating hearts. During this time, Rosie suffered from terrible nightmares. In these dreams her brother kept calling her name, and when she finally found the courage to look at him, Rosie saw that Prickles' face was crushed and his limbs fell limp by his side. Every time the vision ended, watching as his contorted body was sealed in a silver chamber, he gave his final warning: 'Rosie, get away from there. He's coming!'

Their energy stores depleted, the hedgehogs were roused early from their winter slumber to find more bitterness in Greenacres. Big Mag had taken control of the forest. The squirrels, under his command, attacked other land animals over food supply lines, and for remaining loyal to the raptors. Birds and mammals that broke Big Mag's curfew were publicly beaten and driven from their nests by magpies. Seeds, berries and the shoots of young plants were being ripped up and taken away to a secret location, leaving the creatures of Greenacres to starve.

Big Mag watched, as he always did, his loyal followers execute their mischievous acts. And as he perched, thinking about his next tyrannical move, he formulated a plan to raid one home in particular and steal something special and shiny. Mag would often gaze at its beauty, waiting for an opportunity to come.

"In all my life," moaned Farmer Cullem, one afternoon, "I have never seen anything like it. These bloomin' magpies are getting into everything!"

"Get out there with ya shotgun," his wife replied, removing freshly baked scones from the oven.

"I wouldn't know where to start. So many of the damn things, I might as well just close my eyes and 'ope for the best."

"Stop moanin' and go wash yer 'ands - me programme's about to start."

Farmer Cullem removed his boots and waddled to the wash-room. He was a stout man who was nearly as wide as he was tall. He could only manage a few hours of light, manual work in the morning before retiring for the afternoon, watching repeats of his wife's favourite TV hospital drama, Admissions. Afterwards, if he had the energy, he would amble over to the Lamb and Flag Inn and enjoy a pint of cider - then moan to the landlord about the cost of it.

Mrs Cullem placed her scones to cool on a wire rack by the

kitchen window, which she liked to leave open. She was a skinny woman with excess amounts of loose skin that flapped below the sleeves of her floral dress, the product of several crash diets. After washing up she would join her husband in the living room, cranking the TV volume up to drown out his snoring.

It was just how Big Mag had predicted. The window was open just enough for him to slip inside, followed by Ringpull and Hood. They were silent, like masked assassins, as they stealthily bounced through the kitchen towards the staircase.

"You two wait here and stand guard!" ordered Mag, whipping his tail back and forth. Ringpull and Hood nodded as they watched their master hop upstairs to seek treasure.

Mrs Cullem had amassed a large collection of costume jewellery over the years, but when her husband prospered from the land sale she became more lavish with her tastes; pearl earrings seemed to be her favourite.

Big Mag's claws tapped against the walnut dressing table as he sprang back and forth, lifting trinket lids off with his beak and inspecting the contents. In the mirror he could see the uncultivated fields through the window, and then he caught a glimpse of what he was looking for.

The Magpie was not after a piece of jewellery, but a war medal that hung beneath the picture of, what looked like to him, a large mechanical, silver bird. Big Mag turned and examined the print in more detail; it was certainly shaped like a bird with sharp, bold lines; on the front of the object above its beak were two windows; and below its smooth, metallic belly were three legs with rubber wheels for claws. Mag angled his head, and his eyes twitched from side to side; he was fascinated by its abnormal features, yet deeply admired its sleekness and size.

Eventually, Mag's focus returned to the emblem attached to the frame. He would have to try and pull it off, not an easy feat even for the strongest and cleverest of birds. The magpie flew at the painting and grappled the medal with his claws, trying to pull it away, but instead his wings flapped fiercely and knocked items to the floor.

Ringpull glanced at Hood. "What was that?"

"Why don't you go and investigate?"

"You go and investigate!" Ringpull snapped, pacing towards the bottom step and looking up.

"I'm not the one that's scared," jeered Hood.

"Shut it, I'm not the one with a bag over my face!"

Luckily for the magpies, the Cullems did not stir.

Big Mag leapt into the air for another attempt, beating his wings frantically as he strived to pull the war motif loose. Nothing budged, except a small glass perfume bottle that smashed to the floor.

Hood nervously flicked his tail upwards. "Sounds like he's trashing the place."

Mag thought about his tactic once more. He remembered when he had first laid eyes upon the trophy one winter's morning. The magpie had been busy practicing aerial manoeuvres with some rooks across the farmyard, until he came to rest upon the bedroom's window ledge. And from that day on, morning or night, he would peer in and marvel at its splendour. If the curtains were drawn, Mag would tap at the window pane until one of the Cullems would open it in frustration and shoo him away.

The magpie hopped over to the other end of the bedroom and took one last look at the picture.

Mrs Cullem was engrossed, her favourite soap character (Mandy) had just revealed that she was having another baby. There was a drawn out moment of silence as the character's partner (Dr Sterile) kissed and hugged her, before asking if it was his. Even Hood and Ringpull peered round the doorway to watch Mandy's reaction.

Big Mag launched himself, an angry flurry of black and white feathers, and struck the picture with all his might, firmly clasping the medal as he ricocheted off the wall. The emblem came loose but so did the frame, crashing to the floor and shattering the silence below.

Mrs Cullem sat up. "Gerrup!" she yelled at her husband, "We're been burglarised!"

Farmer Cullem, who had been fast asleep in his special chair, jumped into the air at the clatter.

Ringpull and Hood looked at one another. "You create a diversion, I'll wait for Mag," said Hood.

"No, Mag asked me to wait for him here. Go flap your own wings and sing like a long-tailed tit!"

As the pair bickered, Mag hopped down the stairs with the prize in his beak. "We should leave now," he said, skipping past them.

Hood and Ringpull followed Mag into the kitchen as the

Farmer got to the doorway. They turned and mocked him, cawing wildly. Chatak-chatak! Farmer Cullem froze as he saw what the biggest magpie held: his antique war medal, gripped tightly in the mouth of an expert thief.

Ringpull and Hood both grabbed a scone in their beaks before escaping though the open window. Big Mag followed but stopped to glance round at the farmer. And in that moment, he believed that the magpie had winked at him before slipping out of sight.

The magpies flew back towards the forest in close formation, low to the ground: mission accomplished. They could hear the farmer's wife barking furiously at her husband to fetch his rifle. But as quickly as the winged miscreants had struck, they were gone; a pattern of behaviour masterminded by Mag that had brought them great success, instilling fear into the lives of many animals and now, it seemed, the Cullems.

7: The Royal Messenger

Big Mag had skilfully woven some Japanese knotweed though the medal. It now hung neatly around his neck as he watched squirrels busily hiding supplies gathered from the East Forest. Some of the rations were foods they didn't even eat, like wild mushrooms, fungus and vegetable shoots. Mag figured that the animals would be easier to control if there was a famine.

A sudden blast of wind ripped through the trees. All the squirrels and magpies stopped working and looked up at the sky. Through the sticks and twigs they saw the large outline of a shape gliding above. The birds heckled one another to get a better look. Squirrels scurried hastily up tree trunks, sensing real danger.

One squirrel quickly clambered high above the others, where the branches were thinnest. He leapt towards another tree, but something intercepted him. The rodent screamed with fear, his body clamped within thick, feathered talons.

Hercules landed upon a thick bough of the pine tree, mantled his wings and turned to address the magpies. The squirrel gasped for breath as its body was crushed; there were protests from his comrades all across the forest floor, shaking their tails in anger as the red kite's claws pierced the rodent's skin and slowly cut into his internal organs.

The magpies bunched behind Big Mag. "Do something," they cawed, "he could kill us all!"

"Magpies!" Hercules yelled, bringing a hush to the forest. "I bring you a message from your Queen."

Big Mag held his own, Ringpull and Hood sneered from behind each of his wings as he shifted towards Hercules. "She's your Queen, Hercules, not ours. A tough bird like you shouldn't be running errands for her! You should be out here mixing with the real hunters."

The red kite lowered his head down to Mag's level. "What do you know about hunting, magpie? You're scavengers. You need the support of all your gang to threaten and pillage from other creatures, feasting on the deceased. Come and visit my neck of the woods and I'll teach you a thing or two about hunting."

"But I wouldn't want to keep you from tidying the Queen's nest now, would I?" Mag replied. The magpies cackled wildly, much to Hercules' distaste. "Now, before you go on your way, you said you had a message for us?"

Hercules lunged towards Mag's branch until they were beak

to beak. "The council has had one too many complaints filed against you. Since a representative from your pack failed to attend the last meeting, you and your kind were unable to defend your actions or those of your furry little puppets below. Serious allegations continue to be made that you are hunting for fun, breaking the most fundamental laws of the natural covenant – you stand accused of organising and inciting murder!"

Mag shook his head. "My my, such rumours, Hercules. Now, please tell us what would happen if we were found to be breaking your sacred laws?"

"The code must be upheld," scowled Hercules. "It is the same law your father and forefathers followed. The animal world has always survived upon it - to break this code will be on pain of death. Those are the words of your Queen."

Big Mag sniggered. "Well, my dear Hercules, I'm sorry to have wasted your time. When you fly back to Her Majesty, I'd like you to pass on our regards and thank her for thinking of us. But you, your queen and her words no longer have a function in my neck of the woods."

Hercules grimaced. "Mark my words, magpie: actions speak far louder than words." With a swift snap of his wings, the red kite hit Mag into the pack. The up-thrust of Hercules' flapping propelled him graciously into the air like an angel recalled to heaven, dispersing all the wicked birds.

The magpies pecked angrily at each other in frustration. "If that was any other bird," spat Hood, "we'd have given him a good whippin'. How are we supposed to control the skies with him under the Queen's command?"

"He's given us a warning," whimpered Ringpull. "They know about our plan."

"Silence!" Mag hissed. "If we can control the forest, then Hercules can also be controlled. He was looking a little thin, don't you think? Must be hard to hunt songbirds when we've driven so many out. You all mark Mag's words - when I am King, raptors will have no place in Greenacres. I promise you that!"

8: Goodwill Gesture

Two pairs of well-polished, standard issue, black shoes beat purposefully across a long, brightly lit corridor. They are on their way to meet with a pair of brown shoes at the Research and Development Laboratory, the most secretive and closely guarded section of the Greenacres Military Base. The shiniest pair of black shoes belong to Colonel Flattery, the Operations Manager. They stamp heavier on the concrete floor than those of Commissioner Goodwill, of the London Metropolitan Police.

"I'm excited about meeting him," remarked Goodwill.

"Well, don't expect much of a conversation," said Flattery. "The man's a genius, but a bit of an idiot if you ask me. He's like the modern day equivalent of Alan Turing, but rather than immersing himself in complex mathematical theories, he surrounds himself with computers and dead animals. You can't help but wonder why he's somewhat lacking in social skills."

"Yes, I'm sure, but the new type of drone he supplied us with worked remarkably well. I don't know how he did it, but the images retrieved from that exercise surpassed all of our expectations. It would have taken hundreds of officers on the ground and in the air to track the same subject, yet we relied on one device to do the work of an entire force. It's just brilliant - he could save us a fortune!"

"Commissioner, I agree with you, but please remember that these devices don't come cheap." Flattery stopped as they reached the entrance to the laboratory. "And remember, it's just a prototype so let's not get too excited."

"It'd better be good. The PM has scheduled a COBRA meeting in Whitehall today at noon - we might need to use it."

Professor Albert Windar was in his laboratory, the culmination of over two decades of extensive research, making the final touches to his presentation. He was a pioneer in the field of neuroscience and robotics; very few scientists around the world had managed to seamlessly fuse the two together.

Prickles could hear his creator talking to himself. He watched the white shape traverse back and forth through a frosted screen. Every so often, he listened to mechanical motors circling above him, the scratching of claws, and the beating of wings. He felt numb, emotionless with no thoughts – reacting to the stimuli around him, recording the atmosphere of his new environment.

There was a succession of bleeps at 35.6db before the door to the laboratory slid open. Windar startled himself to life. 'They're here,' he hummed. Prickles replayed the voice in his head over and over, detecting patterns of stress: 'They're here! They're here!'

Colonel Flattery swiped his ID card and the secondary door to the lab opened, revealing the two men; Prickles sensed traces of animosity from one and physical signs of excitement from the other. Flattery, a solid looking man with an icy glare, stepped forward.

"Commissioner Goodwill, I'd like to introduce you to Professor Windar."

Windar extended his hand, which was as delicate and refined as the instruments around him. His grip was firm as he shook Commissioner Goodwill's hand. "You are most welcome," he said, sincerely. "Please, come in, I'm just about ready."

Although Prickles was shrouded in darkness, he had excellent vision and watched closely as Windar's limbs beckoned the men into the main part of the laboratory, recording the behaviour. He also detected a rise in body temperature.

Commissioner Goodwill was met by a proliferation of technology. Machines, cabinets and large spotlights formed a backdrop to the orchestra of test tubes, computer screens and sealed cases. Hazard symbols were stamped on vats of chemicals, which lined the shelves like tins of food and pots of spices; surgical tools hung like kitchen utensils. The whole lab was a military crucible.

"This way, please." Windar pointed towards a set of chairs next to a large, electronic whiteboard. Goodwill could hear the scratching of a bird and the sound of wheels whizzing about as he sat with Flattery, adjusting to his surroundings.

The lights dimmed. Windar began his presentation and the video screen flashed behind him, making the whites of his hair seemingly glow. Picturesque photos of Greenacres' countryside were displayed in super high-definition.

Prickles watched, his spikes twitching at the beauty of the open fields.

"For years I've been fascinated by nature, by all creatures great and small and their ability to blend in to their surroundings." Windar stepped aside and gazed at the image. "My whole life has been dedicated to unlocking some of her amazing secrets."

Classical music began playing. Flattery groaned and turned to Goodwill with apologetic eyes.

The image froze and Windar touched some grids on the whiteboard. It zoomed in to show the figure of a rabbit watching from the edge of his warren, then tracked to a bird of prey perched on a telephone wire above. "My research has taken me far beyond my wildest expectations, exploring the design and function of some of the UK's most common wildlife."

A carousel of screen shots appeared: pigeons and rodents

were amongst some of the species. The images then dissolved into a backdrop of an urban landscape, typical of a city at dusk; railway tracks, high-rise blocks, power cables and industrial bins framed the dying moments of a sunset.

"Even in urban environments, animals are experts at adapting to their surroundings." This time Goodwill and Flattery knew to search the picture. Windar tapped the board and the video zoomed in to reveal a fox lurking behind some wooden pallets.

Prickles felt his vision blur momentarily.

"When I was first approached by the military to work on Project Carrion, I was a bit puzzled as to how I could help. However, it soon dawned on me that they were looking for new ways to limit the loss of human life, supporting our forces at home and abroad. They wanted to create technology that could not only monitor the enemy, but help defeat them."

Windar tapped a button on his remote control. One of the containers, behind where the men sat, opened. A sprightly grey and green coloured Racing Homer Pigeon flew out and landed on top of the whiteboard. Her head remained perfectly still as she looked at them.

"To us", he began, "this looks and reacts like any other bird of its kind that you might find in the UK. But with one touch of this button . . . "

The professor clicked the remote and the video screen switched to the pigeon's point of view. Goodwill laughed at the surprised expression on his face as he saw himself in super HD, applauding Windar on his work; Flattery disguised his amusement.

"Allow me to formally introduce you to model PIG3-0N, or Pigeon if you like. She's one of the most advanced specimens I've created to date. Contained within this wonderful creature is the technology to capture and broadcast images to multiple locations. She's also fitted with several surveillance devices and is capable of discharging small electro-magnetic charges, which can be used to disable enemy technology - such as mobile phones, computers and even some vehicles."

"Excuse me," Goodwill queried, "is this the same device we piloted in London last week?"

"The very one," replied Windar, beaming.

"Brilliant!" he exclaimed, "Just brilliant."

PIG30N flew onto Windar's shoulder and bobbed her head forward. 'Thank you' said a computerised voice. Flattery managed a half smile.

"They can speak?"

"Not quite," Windar remarked, "we're a long way from cracking that code."

Goodwill was captivated. "Professor, that's the most realistic looking robot I've ever seen."

"Oh, it's not a machine," he replied, pulling up an x-ray image of the bird on the screen. "All my creations are cybernetic organisms, a symbiosis of living tissue and robotics." Windar coaxed PIG30N onto his hand and placed her on a stand. "Since I made the breakthrough, the opportunities are endless. A combination of simple, surgical procedures to insert my revolutionary nano-chips into the brains of creatures is just the start of something much bigger."

Flattery piped up. "Professor, the commissioner is a little pushed for time – we were hoping to see your latest conception."

"I've a few questions, before we do," countered Goodwill. "My force has just ordered several surveillance drones. What makes your devices a better alternative?"

"There are several. The main advantage of using my technology over drones and other AI based machinery, is that they have the natural ability to merge with changing environments without human intervention – complete autonomy. The level of programming required for a drone to do the same is not quite there yet. My creations can behave and act like normal creatures, but with the flick of a switch they can carry out mission protocols, which make these specimens the perfect solution."

Flattery muttered. "Yes, although a little costly I might add."

Windar continued. "My ultimate challenge was to develop something that could survive without natural threat in both rural and urban locations. Pigeons are regarded by many as vermin, a pest or scavenger, and so their capabilities are restricted by reputation and their ability to defend themselves against more dominant birds." Windar clicked his remote control and an image of a pigeon being attacked by magpies flashed up on the screen, followed by footage of another racing homer being caught mid-air by a swooping peregrine falcon.

"What I'm about to unveil to you represents the next generation of intelligent spy drones, it's capable of blending in brilliantly to the environment, whilst being more robust and versatile. Gentlemen, I would like to introduce model SPIK-3Z, or as I like to call him . . . Spikez."

Prickles, now operating under the guise of Spikez, felt his limbs convulse. He stood up in his cage.

Flattery and Goodwill turned in their seats and looked towards Spikez' cage. The door slowly slid down revealing a shape lurking in the shadows. "Come on," Windar beckoned with his arms.

Spikez understood Windar's behaviour, tracking the motion of his creator's arms, and emerged from the darkness of his cell into the light. Every part of his underneath had been rebuilt and strengthened with a titanium alloy, including new arms and legs. His round, hazel eyes were shielded by the neatest of opaque visors, which allowed him to see, in infinite clarity, the colours and heat signatures of the room.

Standing at the edge of his cage, five feet below him was nothing but solid tiled floor. His natural instinct would have been to retreat back into the cage, but those brain signals were filtered. Instead he leant forward like an Olympic diver, spinning and then uncurling his body as he landed effortlessly on his robotically enhanced legs.

Goodwill raised an eyebrow. "Well, I certainly wasn't expecting that."

Flattery was less impressed by Windar's genius, he didn't know whether to applaud him or scoff at his outrageous creation – a robotic hedgehog, whatever next?!

Spikez shimmied across the ground, running towards Windar. He didn't know why he was doing it, but felt compelled to weave between chair legs and in between cables and computer desks.

For a hedgehog he was super-fast and did all of this silently. Windar wheeled a tall platform into place and instructed Spikez to climb it.

"Impossible," snorted Flattery.

As if by intuition, Spikez understood the professor's words and began to ascend the leg of the platform effortlessly. His hands and feet fluently gripped the table, even upside down. Once at the top he stood and faced his private audience, glazed in bright light.

"Spikez, standby," commanded Windar. Spikez remained fixed in one spot, as though control of his limbs had been turned off. The hedgehog watched as the two men got out of their seats and came closer, hesitantly, for a more detailed inspection. He remained neutral, mapping their facial features.

"Windar," remarked Flattery, "I won't lie to you. You know how I feel about your roadkill creations, but this time I think you've gone too far."

"No, this is most impressive," challenged Goodwill. "But I can see where the colonel is coming from. How do you suppose a hedgehog can help us win the war on terror?"

The human odour of pessimism began to fill the room. Flattery continued. "You rebuilt a dead hedgehog, but to do what - climb up and down a pole?"

"Allow me," replied Windar, directing them to the screen. "What you're seeing is an x-ray image of what lies beneath Spikez' exterior." A skeletal outline of model SPIK-3Z rotated on the screen, clearly highlighting the complexity of the robotics and wires contained within him.

"As you know, the hedgehog is renowned for having one of nature's greatest defence systems. Grafted onto his skeleton, I have fused a hybrid-titanium alloy capable of withstanding extreme forces of pressure and heat."

The two men gazed at Spikez' muscles as he stood on parade. Finely interwoven beneath real fur was solid, armour-plating.

"The spikes," Windar added, "which form part of the hedgehog's unique protection, have also been significantly strengthened – and modified. In addition to this he will also have the added benefit of being able to move whilst curled up. Allow me to demonstrate." Windar stood back and asked the men to part. "Spikez: sequence alpha-one."

Spikez felt his body tighten into a ball. He projected himself off the table and onto the floor without sound, gathering exceptional momentum. Flattery and Goodwill watched in astonishment as he reached the other side of the laboratory in seconds.

"Now, observe Spikez' most lethal attribute," said Windar, holding up a red target in his hand, a disk half the size of a DVD. He tossed it towards the corner of the lab.

Turning his head to the side, Spikez tracked the object and then, with a flick of his spine, fired one of the spikes from his back, cleanly hitting the target in the centre.

Both men gasped, then applauded. "Windar, maybe you are a genius after all."

"Spikez has many other functions and abilities; including his excellent array of tools, neatly tucked away within an internal utility belt - not to mention his exceptional night vision, supported by thermographic technology. And then there's the multitude of potential upgrades."

The two men had seen enough. As the professor droned on, the general consensus was no longer 'what can we use in the war on terror?', but 'when can we use Spikez?'.

The hedghog was an automated, expendable asset, fixed in the corner of the room awaiting new instructions. But it was Windar who was now being bombarded with directives.

Goodwill pulled Flattery aside. "Professor, could you give us a moment?"

Windar nodded and strolled over to Spikez, who remained poised. He felt totally at ease with his creator; he had no fear – but how could he? That feeling had been wiped from his memories. The hedgehog remembered nothing; he didn't even know what he was. All he knew was life inside the lab.

"Come on, little fella," said Windar, putting on a set of thick gloves. "I think you've had enough fun for today." He scooped him up in his hands and returned him back to his cage, connecting him to a glowing pod at the rear of his enclosure. Windar then slid a wire mesh down which locked in place.

Spikez listened to Goodwill as he whispered. "Colonel, Spikez could be exactly what we're looking for. I'd like to use him, I've the perfect mission."

"Hold fire, Commissioner, he's just a prickly prototype. We should really do some tests first."

"But PIG30N worked brilliantly. Look, I know it might seem

like a bit of a daft idea, but I believe in this man. You need to let me have the hedgehog!"

Flattery leant forward. "I agree that he needs to be put to use, but there's lots at stake if something goes wrong - this technology isn't cheap. However, if it's not being used effectively then our budgets will be cut, just like all the other frontline services. Windar says he's still working on protocols, but leave it with me – I know how to work him - you'll have your hog."

The professor was led away from the laboratory, a man either side of him. Their hands were massaging ideas into his shoulders, pressing for ways to use their new secret weapon.

Usually, the professor would have shut Spikez down and let him electronically hibernate, but not today. He sat there, alert but idle. He searched the laboratory for signs of movement or visual stimulation – there was none, not even a flashing light; instead he focused on the sounds of scratching and cooing and the hum of electric tracks traversing above him. Maybe he had heard them before?

9: A Migrant's View

Every year the Redwings made the gruelling journey to Greenacres with the sole purpose of settling down to breed. They had stumbled upon the area by accident, after severe Siberian winds had blown them off course from their original migratory route. It was how Arim and Mira both met, at this very place, and they had remained together ever since. However, their arrival was met by some resentment from native wildlife; Mira was ignored by the other songbirds and Arim found work hard to come by.

In the seasons they had spent together at Greenacres, the pair had only yielded one egg. But for some inexplicable reason, the egg never hatched and the couple never quite recovered from their ordeal.

This year the Redwings were more hopeful. The couple had their egg, but life in the woods had changed for them and every other bird. They were tormented daily by the squirrels or heckled regularly by magpies. Food was scarce and there were often scuffles between other birds and mammals around them. Mira was often stressed, and worried that she would be too weak to raise their fledgling, if it were to even hatch. Arim worked his hardest to support her, but found food and wood in short supply, leaving their nest open to attack.

The Redwing's story was just a snippet of the misery that beset all the inhabitants of Greenacres, but like the migrant birds there were other creatures who persevered nonetheless. Many sought refuge underground to avoid aerial attacks or a good kicking and biting from the feral squirrels that patrolled the woods. It was here that a resistance movement was formed.

Baldwin, whose prediction had come true, began planning a counter attack. But the badger's numbers and resources were limited against the sheer might and magnitude of the magpies, who had brought reinforcements from other woods and enlisted the support of the swift and agile jackdaws. His last remaining hope was that a message would get through to Queen Eliza so that she could instruct Hercules to forcefully remove Big Mag from power, but with Mag's army monitoring the skies and the squirrels watching the forest floor, no communication could get through.

10: Protocols

Several hours had passed and Spikez had not moved from his pod. He had not craved worms or hog affection, nor sought to play or rummage through leaves. He thought of nothing, except the noises around him – recording and playing them over and over in his head.

The laboratory door opened and Windar strode in, rubbing his head frantically. In his hands he carried official documents from Cobra and direct orders from his superiors at the base: to deploy Spikez and the rest of the team for the first time. Human lives were at stake.

Windar opened Spikez' cage and removed him, standing him on a long open desk. Soothing, ambient blue lights lit up around him as Windar gathered the rest of the team. PIG30N landed beside the hedgehog, her head bobbing forward to formally greet Spikez. Windar returned with a small blue rodent in his hands and placed him on the surface with the rest of the team.

Spikez stared at the creature. Its feet and lower part of his hind legs had been replaced by small tank-like tracks. Balancing above its nose, and an impressive set of large incisors, were thick, clear goggles that made his eyes seem oversize and bulbous. The mouse moved forward and Spikez instantly recognised the noise.

"Call me Trakz," he squeaked.

The hedgehog did not answer.

"Having problems with your memory?" he asked, rolling closer.

Spikez still did not answer - he didn't know how.

Trakz peered right into the hedgehog's face, his fine whiskers brushing against Spikez' visor whilst his jellied eyes searched for any hint of social intelligence. "I guess not," he guffawed.

The lights dimmed and the large whiteboard glowed. Windar sat at the console desk and instructed Trakz to link Spikez and PIG30N into the system. Trakz zoomed over to the edge of the table and collected two black and silver fibre-optic cables. He returned and positioned himself behind Spikez, inserting the cable into one of his many artificial bristles.

Spikez felt a stream of energy buzz around his body, causing his muscles to twitch. He studied his hand and claws, clasping them back and forth as he watched Trakz hook up PIG30N, who cooed and flapped her wings.

"Sorry, wrong hole!" said Trakz, wiping his goggles and trying again.

Windar began reading out his directives aloud, as though the creatures were somehow able to understand him (which they couldn't). During this process, classified content, protocols, maps and GPS data was downloaded onto their internal hard-drives. "The carrion unit has been called into action for the first time. This is a real exercise and not a drill! What you are about to see is a blueprint of the building you are to infiltrate, a warehouse in the Docklands area of London."

An image of a disused factory appeared on the screen. In the backdrop of the picture was a bar chart of luxury flats and banking offices. As Spikez felt the data trickling towards his brain, his real eye twitched.

"This is a covert operation. There will be no immediate human assistance since the threat to human lives is considered to be too great. You will enter the building by any means neces-sary, gather enough evidence so that we can assess the danger, and disable their security systems."

The screen dissolved into some shots of severe looking male faces. "The building is likely to be occupied by members of the Red Dawn terrorist group. Study their biometric data and stay out of their sight. They also have a guard dog who will alert them to any intruders."

A powerful looking Rottweiler came up on the screen. Even though the picture had been taken from a distance, it was clear to see that the dog was looking directly at them, through the camera-lens and into their eyes. Spikez felt a mild tingle in his spine, as if a fragment of fear from a lost memory was drift-ing through his bloodstream, trying to remind him of his past mortality.

"I'm uploading all the mission protocols as I speak. We leave in two hours."

Windar clicked the monitor off and walked across the lab. Download complete: Spikez and PIG30N had all the necessary schematics and programs installed to complete the tasks.

Trakz removed the cables and returned them to the edge of the table. "Don't worry," he said, returning to Spikez' side. "You'll both do just fine."

11: Docklands Diffusion

Windar's team of cyborgs had been shrouded in darkness for over four hours, listening to a soundtrack of engine noise and van parts creaking. For the whole journey, neither PIG30N nor Spikez communicated; they were awaiting directives to allow them that right. Trakz, on the other hand, was different; he was in control of his thoughts and words, even if his mechanical legs sometimes had a mind of their own. Spikez had recorded eight instances when Trakz randomly careered into a wall or reversed rather than went forward.

The van steadied to a stop. Spikez heard the driver's door open and then slam shut. The sound of heavy footsteps followed; he identified them belonging to a male carrying approximately 210 pounds in weight, limping on his left side. The rear-door unlocked and opened, revealing the driver's silhouette against a backdrop of orange streetlights. Spikez watched as he leant forward and grabbed their respective cages, pulling them out into the chill of a frosty night. Spikez quickly surveyed his new surroundings, identifying his location on a map using GPS: they were being deployed from an alleyway close to the target.

Windar sat in the back of another van two blocks away, monitoring his creations' vital signs. Seated beside him were commanding officers from the Met Police and an expert in bomb disposal. They watched as live video feeds appeared on their screens, transmitted by Spikez and PIG30N. Satisfied that everything was in place, Windar gave the driver a signal to release his drones.

Stubby fingers tapped in a code on each cage. Spikez heard them unbolt and watched the gates flip open. He observed PIG30N promptly fly upwards, arcing towards the target, leaving him the challenge of making it there on foot.

Spikez was faster than a normal hedgehog, especially when he built up enough momentum to travel in a ball, rolling through the shadows. He made good time catching up with PIG30N, who was already perched on a streetlight and recording footage of the warehouse. Her data was streamed directly to him, helping him plot probable access routes and identify threats. There was no sign of the dog.

The warehouse was quiet - too quiet.

Trakz' voice came over the intercom. "This is your in-mission mouse speaking. I'll be monitoring your stress levels and helping you enjoy your first assignment. The emergency exits are everywhere around you, except for that big warehouse thingy in front of you."

Cautiously, Spikez began making his way towards the building.

"Okay," continued Trakz, "the tenants have installed their own surveillance devices. Look out for trip alarms, infra-red cameras and pressure pads - they are all linked to a computer in the main room. You need to find a way in undetected and neutralise it fast."

PIG30N gained entry though a broken skylight in the warehouse's roof. Silently, she swooped down and found somewhere to balance and monitor the activity below. Beneath her were three men, one big sleeping dog and lots and lots of explosive components linked together by wires. PIG30N slowly extended her leg, activating an inbuilt directional microphone in the base of her claws, giving the crew in the van audio to accompany the video footage.

Spikez shimmied along an outside wall. Waste paper, rubble and shards of broken glass were just some of the many obstacles he had to overcome. He was searching for the air vent which, according to the blue prints of the building, would funnel him towards the target. The hedgehog gained access and headed towards the target.

Two men were playing cards on an old tea chest whilst the other slept on a decrepit sofa. The dog, a bulky mass of black and tan coloured fur and muscle, dozed by the doorway. Spikez could see them through the metal grills of the vent and took a biometric profile.

"That's all of them. We really should have knocked," Trakz commented. "Whatever you do, don't make a sound."

Spikez began silently removing the screws to the vent grate with one of his many inbuilt tools when a loud shriek came from behind. It was a rat, horrified by what it saw.

"It's always the rats!" Trakz said ashamedly.

The Rottweiler woke, rising to his feet to investigate the noise. The two men glanced up from their round of poker.

The rat scurried away, disappearing through a crumbling gap in the wall. Spikez quickly followed as the dog scratched, panted and sniffed at the vent.

One of the men looked to the right of his hand, a pair of aces, at the loaded gun - ready to be used if necessary. "Rats," he hissed to himself in a thick Russian accent, watching the Rottweiler whine.

Spikez remained still. He had to get rid of the dog, but how?

Trakz radioed in. "Okay, you're going to have to find another way in. Head back to the courtyard - you can go in via the basement."

Sensing Spikez scramble back along the tunnel, the Rottweiler gave a loud snort, shook his fur to life and left the room.

The hedgehog re-emerged near a set of redundant sewage pipes, outside in the yard. Carefully, he manoeuvred along the wall, abseiled down some old phone cable and darted towards a basement window. But he became distracted. A sensation tingled in his spine; he had felt the very same way back in the laboratory. Then he froze, for Spikez had clearly underestimated the predatory skills of the Rottweiler. The hedgehog turned to read the name Maximus clearly etched on the dog's collar, its body hunched above him. The security light from adjacent offices coated the dog in a menacing orange haze. Maximus slobbered, the beast had found a new toy to play with.

Watching on his monitor, Windar sat up, alarmed at the dog's proximity. But before he could relay defensive protocols, the dog leapt at Spikez.

The hedgehog instinctively curled into a ball, which triggered one of his many defence mechanisms. A tranquilliser spike shot out from his back, burying itself into the underbelly of the Rottweiler. Maximus gave a small yelp for a big dog. He landed, crumpling awkwardly to the floor, his mighty paws bumping Spikez aside. The canine attempted to get up, seething with rage and drooling over broken tiles, but by the time Maximus had watched Spikez uncurl himself, the dog collapsed into a torrid mound of muscle.

"Good work, Spikez," muttered Windar, under his breath.

"I've never seen a drone react so fast," remarked an officer. "Total autonomy!"

Windar smiled. "It's not a drone."

Spikez studied the results of his swift actions. The dog lay on the floor, its tongue stretched out, flapping with each deep breathe it took.

"Okay, so that was impressive," Trakz said. "We can do a hi-five later if you like, but right now there's that pressing matter about a very large bomb we need to diffuse. Judging by the shape of Maximus, I'd say he's not the kind of dog to take long walks – you need to hurry!"

The basement route led Spikez beneath the main room. He entered a disused gas pipe and clambered upwards. He was fortunate enough not to encounter any rats, or any other rodents for that matter.

Peering into the room he surveyed the targets. One man was asleep next to the bomb, snoring quietly; a small remote device was cradled in his lap. The other two men continued to play cards and drink clear liquid from heavy glasses. Using PIG30N's footage from above, Spikez weaved his way round obstacles to avoid detection until he arrived behind the table where the bomb sat. Unable to climb the leg, he removed a small grapple hook from his utility compartment and fired it upwards, hooking the table edge so that he could ascend towards the target.

Windar watched with the team of experts as Spikez relayed video footage. The mechanism was much more complex than initially thought: a series of thin, faintly coloured wires, linked to a small computer and the black casing which housed . . . radioactive material.

The bomb disposal expert cursed his luck and frantically consulted his handbook to identify the trigger mechanism. Other members of the task force stood up and made urgent calls, their worst fears were confirmed: a dirty bomb.

Spikez remained idle; poised and ready to react to his commands. Apart from listening to the men playing cards, he could hear Trakz eating over the intercom.

Another pigeon, a scrawny male with lank grey and brown plumage, found his way in to shelter from the wintery night.

PIG30N gave a quick glance to assess the threat, but did not intentionally flutter her natural eye at him - this was a reaction to the video signals she broadcast. The pigeon, however, was instantly love-struck and started to coo. He then began to court her, dancing along the beam with lustful intent. PIG30N attempted not to show interest at this display of amorous affection as he made deeper cooing sounds, flowing from his loins to the tip of his scabbed beak.

The two men grew distracted by the noise. "Another damn bird, I'll be glad when we're finally out of this dump, Uri. They're putting me off my game!"

Uri, a portly man with acne scars and cold grey eyes, took another swig of his drink. "Relax, Rasto, don't blame your run of bad luck on them. Twist or stick?"

"Stick!"

The explosives officer had identified the bomb's trigger device. He accessed the necessary computer files and gave them to Windar, who uploaded them to Spikez' database. "Sequence, Bravo-Delta-7. . ."

Spikez reactivated and located the casing screws in accordance with the data he had received, unscrewing them with a tool from his pouch. Silently removing a small metal plate, he saw three wires: red, green and blue.

"Spikez, disconnect the blue wire first," instructed Trakz. Spikez chose the wire and effortlessly snipped it in half. "Now, cut that fat, juicy red one." But the hedgehog had already done all three with a flick of his claws. Trakz' voice faltered for a moment. "Impressive work for someone who's supposed to be colour-blind . . . now let's see if you can remove the trigger that fast."

Spikez searched for the component.

Windar looked to the bomb disposal expert. "Where is it?"

"It must be located on the front of the device."

"But he'll be in clear view!"

PIG30N was still being harassed by the shameless male pigeon, whose head bobbing and cooing had increased in speed and volume significantly. She sensed that there was a problem below and decided to act. As he made a pass for the umpteenth time, PIG30N looked up and acknowledged his advances with a fluttering of her eyelids. He stopped and looked at her, amazed that his vigorous efforts were starting to pay off. She gave another blink at him. He nodded and winked back. She bowed her head towards him slowly, raising her tail feathers ever so slightly. He tottered forward some more and bobbed his head, cooing deeply. PIG30N continued to flutter her eyelids until the forlorn male was within pecking distance. He fluffed up his scrawny chest feathers. She slowly extended her wing. He leant in for a kiss. By this time, PIG3ON's wing had become fully armed. She tapped it against him, zapping him with an electrical charge.

"Oh, Pidge," laughed Trakz, "That was cold!"

The stunned pigeon crashed down into the lap of Rasto. "Damn birds!" he yelled, flinging the disorientated ball of feathers away from him. "Where's that damn dog of yours?"

Uri could not contain his laughter. "Eating rats, I imagine."

"I'm going to get him. We need protection in case there are any more crazy animals lurking around in here."

Uri sighed, took a deep puff from a yellow cigarette, and watched Rasto leave the room, giving him enough time to put some more playing cards up his sleeve.

The opportunity had come - Spikez could now access the trigger. Cautiously, he tiptoed round to the front of the device and got to work unlocking the mechanism, which was the size of a stereo speaker.

Rasto lit a cigarette and surveyed the derelict courtyard. "Maximus!" he shouted, his breath mushrooming into the night sky. There was no response. He put two fingers into his mouth and whistled loudly. The noise ricocheted off the crumbling walls and into silence. "Damn dog!"

Spikez carefully removed the last of the screws and accessed the trigger device. Inside there were another four different coloured wires. "Okay, Spikez," said Trakz, "Why don't you go ahead and snip that red wire." Spikez went to cut it when he heard a scream from outside.

Uri stood, his gun cocked. Rasto came running into the room with his weapon raised, shaking. "Someone's poisoned Maximus, he's out cold!"

The third man, Lukaz, woke as the two men shouted in Russian. He went to turn and tell them to be quiet, but he couldn't. In front of him he saw a hedgehog, diffusing their explosive device. He rubbed his eyes wildly, trying to focus on the agile

62

ball of spikes with sharp claws slicing through wires. Lukaz'
jaw quivered as he tried to find his voice.

"Smotret!" he finally shouted in Russian.

Uri and Rasto stopped and looked over at him. Lukaz
gazed back at them with wide eyes and pointed at Spikez. The
other men gasped, could they really be seeing this?

In the control van, Windar and his crew froze. There were
just two more wires to cut and Spikez' cover had been blown.

"Kill it!" screamed Uri.

Reassured that what he saw was not a figment of his
imagination, Lukaz stumbled to his feet and picked up the
closest solid looking object he could find, which unfortunately
for Spikez was a ten kilo sledgehammer.

"You might want to hurry up a little," suggested Trakz.

Spikez snapped into active AI mode, full autonomy - his
decisions were now based on a combination of defensive
logic and natural instincts. He tracked the hammer as Lukaz
lifted it above his head. In the time that it took Lukaz to angle
the sledgehammer and strike, Spikez had turned and cut the
last remaining wires. And at that precise moment, just as the
angry Russian was about to swing it down upon him, he fired
another tranquilliser dart from his back.

The speed of the drug was instantaneous. Lukaz' hands
and arms immediately loosened and the hammer dropped,
hitting the top of his head with a dull thud.

Uri watched his comrade crash to the floor. Enraged, he
went to fire his gun at Spikez. But PIG30N, who had been

watching from above, had already anticipated this and excreted a glowing pod the size of a large jelly bean.

Spikez back-flipped off the table and used his utility wire as a sling shot, propelling him towards the safety of the gap in the wall as Uri fired off a barrage of bullets, which whizzed past the hedgehog.

Rasto gawked as he caught sight of a flashing pellet, watching it ricochet off the floor with a metallic din. Both men now directed their attention at PIG30N above as she escaped through the broken skylight. Rasto went to fire, but before he could pull the trigger the EMP pod exploded. A great flash of light blinded both men and took out the remaining security systems. The men howled, clutching their eyes and pulling their heads into their chests.

Windar received the confirmation he had prayed for: objective complete, security systems disabled. The bomb disposal expert radioed for his unit to storm the building.

Spikez escaped out into the courtyard and ran for the gates, where he saw a black van screech to a halt. He counted a dozen well-armed men burst from it, charging towards the warehouse. Spikez' instincts told him to keep running.

Overriding AI mode, Windar ordered Spikez to halt, but the hedgehog failed to react. A flicker of interference waved across his monitor - the professor stood up. "He's not responding!"

Trakz radioed in, sensing something was wrong. "Hey buddy, if you like long distance running I can let you have a spin on my wheel when we get back to the lab."

Spikez didn't listen. He was compelled to keep going. 'Get to the road . . .' He made it past the courtyard rubble, through the gates and onto the pavement. He flicked his head to see another van approach at speed. 'Keep going', he thought to himself, leaping out into the road, 'Go! Get to the other side'. He sped to the middle and turned to face the vehicle head on, becoming mesmerised by the two luminous disks of light that enveloped his scope of sight.

'Rosie . . . where's Rosie?'

```
404 Error
SPIK-3Z.exe has encountered a problem and needs
to shut down. . .
0X000kbs(3488) memory failure - bad sector.
Restart carrion.sys in safe mode. . .
```

The wheels ground to a halt, centimetres away from where Spikez was rooted to the spot, idly entranced by the bright halogen light bulbs.

The side door of the van slid across and a pair of brown shoes, complete with odd coloured socks, exited and walked towards the hedgehog. Windar leant over and cupped him gently in his gloved hands before returning to the vehicle with his cyborg.

12: Memory Loss

Spikez awoke naturally the next morning, before Windar arrived at the lab to 'restart him' manually. He felt as if his brain had been freed from the clutches of some terrible dream. A glimmer of sunshine streamed through narrow windows at the top of the laboratory walls, giving the hedgehog the opportunity to study his new surroundings. He held his hands up into the warm light and examined them, they felt rigid and his claws seemed polished and sharper than he remembered. Spikez suddenly glanced down at his feet in shock – he was standing upright on his hind legs. He steadied himself against the cage door, peering deep into the laboratory. 'Where am I?' he asked himself.

"You're in Professor Windar's lab."

Spikez turned to see the shape of a mouse wheel himself into the light, peering in at him from the adjacent cage. He stared at

Trakz' custom made spectacles, fixed above his long twitching nose. Spikez raised his claws up to his face, running them along his muzzle towards his brow until they tapped against a visor, which fitted snugly around his worried eyes. "Who are you? What am I doing here? What's happened to me?"

"Ahhh," Trakz gave a pained expression; he remembered those very same feelings from months ago, seeking answers about how he got his tracks and perfect vision. "Maybe we should talk later, after breakfast when you've had time to adjust."

"Breakfast? Adjust to what? How long have I been here?"

"Questions, questions and more questions - look, don't worry," assured the rodent, "you're safe here, that's all you need to know right now." With that, Trakz returned to the middle of his roomy cage and began chewing on a large stick.

Spikez' eyes hunted across the lab for answers, at all the sharp silver instruments and shiny metal machinery that was sprawled across a conveyor belt. Above him, a soft, simulated coo came from another cage. The hedgehog was comforted by its gentle sound, as if to reassure him that the mouse's words of comfort had been genuine. He was safe. Answers would come.

Precisely 8am. The doors glided open and Windar bounded in with excitement clearly visible on his face. He logged on to his computer before skipping over to his kitchenette, where he prepared himself a strong black coffee.

Spikez was transfixed, recording every detail of the professor's mannerisms: vocal tones, heat signatures and, when he dropped his spoon, reaction times. A light flickered on above his head and the cage door slid down. He continued to watch as Windar interacted with an electronic tablet, vocalising his thoughts.

Minutes later, Windar walked over to the cages and examined his team of animal cyborgs. Trakz, familiar with the routine, eagerly anticipated being carried over to the examination desk in the middle of the lab. The professor then collected Spikez with equal diligence, placing the two cyborgs side by side, in front of the large screen. PIG30N flew down and joined them.

"I want to show you the product of your excellent efforts last night." Windar clicked an icon on his monitor and a slideshow began. Images of the previous night's operation rolled across the screen, dissolving into newspaper headlines and live feeds from TV news stations, which were all reporting on the same story: DOCKLANDS BOMB PLOT FOILED; TERROR PLOT DEFUSED; and CAPITAL AVOIDS NUCLEAR MELTDOWN. Windar left one of the news channels running as he went to fetch breakfast. Spikez listened to the speculative commentary about how the operation had been a joint venture between the police, MI6 and a division of the British military – no mention of robotic hedgehogs and hybrid pigeons.

As Windar rustled together some food, the lights above the laboratory door flashed from red to green, then opened to reveal the shapes of two highly decorated army officers. Colonel Flattery strode in first, followed by an older man. Windar came to meet them.

"Professor Windar," said Flattery, formally, "I'd like to introduce you to General Grievance."

Windar quivered before motioning towards them both. "It's a pleasure," he replied, extending his hand.

A thick, bear-sized hand clasped itself tightly around Windar's. "No, the pleasure is all mine," said Grievance in a growly voice, a side effect from years of shouting and smoking cigars. "I wanted to meet you personally. Your creative involvement was deeply rooted in the success of last night's operation. A lot of human lives were saved, thanks to you."

Grievance looked past Windar at the parade of robotic creatures. "Amazing!" he remarked, advancing towards them. He leant forward and inspected them all closely. His eyebrows rose and his moustache twitched in approval at Windar's craftsmanship. "My god, the way you've manufactured these things is remarkable, you'd barely recognise the difference between these and the real thing."

The general reached out and lifted Trakz with his fingers, chortling to himself as he examined the mouse's robotic prostheses. He replaced the mouse and then went to touch the underbelly of Spikez, who instinctively huffed and snapped himself into a ball, presenting an array of solid metal spikes. Grievance's hands quickly recoiled. Flattery drew breath; Windar went white, about to apologise profusely - but before he could, Grievance erupted with cavernous laughter.

"Yes," he said, "I like this one - a real fighter! He knows how to defend himself."

"Hedgehogs have the best self defence mechanism of any

land creature I know."

"Hmm . . . yes, quite." Grievance continued to pace round the laboratory proudly. "Can you believe that I've run this base for over a year and never once set foot inside this room?"

"Windar," Flattery butted in, "the General and I would like to talk to you about where we take Project Carrion from here. We need more machines like Spikez, but what's really needed is an aggressive aerial device. The pigeon you enhanced is excellent at reconnaissance, but you said so yourself – not the perfect model for all missions."

"The British army needs a more fearful, bolder motif for their new division of drones," remarked Grievance. "Pigeon's don't quite do it for me,"

PIG30N shot them both a blank stare.

"Well, I have been developing some exciting modifications for Spikez, I'd be happy to explore these with you-"

"No no, hedgehogs can't fly, Windar - and no-one wants to see them do so either!" stated Flattery. "We need stealth and force combined in one, an adaptable predator that can be found all across the UK. We're giving you the opportunity to create some-thing totally new. There's a meeting scheduled this lunchtime, Commissioner Goodwill will be there, along with several other representatives from Cobra."

"As will you," ordered Grievance. He had completed his circuit of the lab and stood staring deeply into Windar's eyes. "Profes-sor, we can get you all the funding you need. Imagine - an endless pot of money to sustain all your wonderful research and development. Come to the meeting with some ingenious new ideas."

Flattery gave Windar a hard pat on the shoulder and then a knowing wink to General Grievance. The professor remained still, defeated by the bureaucratic ambush as he watched them exit the laboratory.

Spikez was no longer stood, idle and awaiting commands, but sat eating a rich, blue jelly; a combination of essential nutrients and amino acids needed for optimum cell growth and regeneration. Trakz and PIG30N watched Windar pace around the room. Occasionally the professor would smile and laugh to himself, excited at the prospect of developing a whole squad of unique creations like Spikez; then he would stop and tut, traversing the lab whilst shaking his head. 'Is this really what I want?' he would say. In four hours' time, his future at Greenacres, and the longevity of Project Carrion, would be decided.

Trakz empathised with the professor and began to whizz across the table in circles.

"What's the matter?" Spikez asked.

"What is it with you and questions?"

"Isn't that a question?"

"Very good, Spikez. Perhaps it's all starting to come back to you."

"What is?"

"Never mind." Trakz sniffed the air - he could smell the faint aroma of a cheese croissant as it toasted. "Hedgehogs don't usually function so well in the day, that'll probably confuse you even more. Finish your breakfast and we'll talk some more then."

"Did you say hedgehog? Is that what I am?"

Trakz gave a pained laugh and looked at PIG30N, who also shook her head. "That's right, and I'm a mouse and this feathered chatterbox is a pigeon. That agitated looking human over there is called Windar, he's the guy that put us all together again."

Spikez lingered in deep thought for a moment, and then looked fretfully at them both. "What do hedgehogs do?"

13: How Trakz got his Tracks

Two hours had passed. In that time, Trakz had attempted to explain to Spikez what hedgehogs do, which didn't seem like much. In between questions, Spikez watched Windar sketch designs and complete an audit of his lab tools and parts; he had also concluded that PIG30N was unable to talk, other than to coo if she liked something or bob her head towards the ground if she was troubled; but Spikez was particularly fascinated by Trakz, watching the mouse steer himself around the table as he completed his morning exercises.

"How long have you known him?" Spikez asked.

"Windar? Oh, many moons – the problem is that I don't get to see the moon very much anymore, so I can't tell you precisely. These things attached to my legs aren't very adaptable to the outside world."

"You mean those aren't your original legs?"

"Boy, you really are something else, Spikez."

"You keep calling me Spikez, but I don't think that's my name."

"True, it's model SPIK-3Z, but Spikez is what everyone knows you as round here."

"No, I have another name . . . " Spikez flicked through his memory files, but Trakz was right – every time he processed this thought, 'SPIK-3Z' flashed up inside his augmented reality visor.

Trakz tried to offer some reassurance. "You know what - it'll all come back to you eventually. Boy, did I get a shock when I woke up in this place."

Spikez walked over to Trakz. "Tell us about it," he said, desperately seeking answers. The headlights from the van had triggered some reminiscences of his former life; perhaps some rodent insight would reconnect more neural pathways of his brain and help him find answers.

"Well, I've known Windar my whole life," began Trakz, "since I was a young buck." PIG30N warbled forward to listen to his story. "So he starts setting up loads of equipment all over his house, a bit like what you see now. He was just as messy, too, which meant that we got to go exploring a lot as a family. He also had a wife back then, a big lady who was always at home cooking. If we were lucky, we found enough scraps for three meals a day. My dad used to bring home leftovers of meat, vegetables, oats and even cream cakes!"

Spikez sat bemused, watching Trakz make mad gestures with his little arms and jig from side to side.

"One day Mrs Windar starts screaming something terrible

- going crazy! Every day she's shouting at Windar, more and more. Of course, we didn't realise that she wanted him to get rid of us - we just thought that she wanted him to tidy up a little."

It was a long time since anyone had told Spikez a story – the feeling unlocked some small but delicate memories; an image of a female hedgehog drifted in his mind, she had a soft, soothing voice. He could see dirt all around him amidst the comforting smell of damp grass and the feeling of dry leaves tickling his belly.

"So anyway, one day she gets a whole load of people in with these crazy sounding pipes and stinking wet rags on sticks and they start attacking the whole house. By the end of it all, there's nothing left to eat on the floor. Dad gets worried and goes out to find some provisions, but I want to go with him. 'Course he won't let me – says I'm better off with my mum and brothers."

"You had a large family?"

"Sure," Trakz wavered for a moment. "So, he's gone for a long time. When my mum turns her back, I decide to sneak out and go find him. It's dark and everyone's asleep. I go looking everywhere, but there's no sign of him. Now, my eyesight was never great, but I eventually turn this corner, and do you know what I saw?"

Spikez and PIG30N shook their heads in unison.

"Boy, I still remember that feeling when I laid my little eyes on a big lump of heaven. I'd do anything to relive that memory. The smell was out of this world, I felt so overjoyed - I had found enough food to feed my whole family. It's just sittin' there on this strip of old wood. I get closer and I can't help but want to nibble on it. My nose is twitching like crazy just looking at it. I go forward to collect it, when suddenly I hear my dad's voice. I look over to the other end of the room and see him calling my name, telling me not to touch the . . . "

"What?" Spikez was engrossed; PIG30N cooed impatiently.

"That's about all I can remember. Next thing I recall is darkness and the sound of my dad crying." Trakz paused, sighing heavily – he had been so excited about telling the story that he suddenly felt vulnerable. A tear, magnified tenfold by his glasses, appeared in the corner of his eye. Spikez watched as it fell, barely bigger than a dew drop. "I never got to see him again, or any of my family for that matter."

Trakz wheeled himself towards the edge of the table and looked down at the solid porcelain tiles. "The next thing I remember was a brilliant white light. I could hear Windar's voice - feel his breath against my bare skin. I couldn't feel anything, but I wasn't scared any more - all I could do was focus on the amazing white light." Trakz nodded towards the contraptions fused to his joints. "The first thing I noticed when I woke up was that I didn't have any legs. Sometimes, when I get distracted or emotional, I can't control them."

The mouse turned round and gave them both a toothy smile. "I think I was Windar's first success – I'm happy, and he treats me well, but I'm not like you guys."

With those words Trakz motioned forward and tipped over the edge of the table.

Spikez and PIG30N howled in unison: "Nooooo!"

Silence.

Both creatures waited fearfully for the unearthly clamour of his body cracking against the floor. Neither of them could bear to walk near the edge; they had never known an animal to willingly end its own life. Spikez felt his eye sting and it began to leak.

"Relax," said Trakz, reappearing at the opposite end of the table. Spikez and PIG30N swivelled round and gave a deep sigh of relief; Trakz' legs could adhere to any surface it seemed, even upside down.

"Anyway," he continued, casually, "Windar's my family now and this is my home. He's all I know, except now I also have you guys. Just look us, we're all the same!"

Spikez and PIG30N glanced at one another from head to claw, noting each other's obvious differences. Then the three of them looked over at Windar, who had begun scanning his draft designs onto a computer; 3D models of microchips were also laid out on a trolley, as was an array of electrical and hydraulic components.

11:57am - Windar had been working non-stop. His largest sketches, the best ones, were packed away in his satchel, along with a large memory stick, a cheese sandwich, an apple and three fig rolls. The team had been placed back in their respective cages as he prepared to leave the laboratory.

Before he departed, Windar made a phone call. "Good day to you, my name is Professor Windar ... Windar ... no, not Darwin, Win-dar . . . Well, I was hoping you could do me a favour, I'm looking for . . . No, I'm not trying to sell you anything . . . well, we're practically neighbours . . . No, I'm not ringing about the noise ... Professor Win-dar ..." Eventually, he proceeded to read out an extensive list of requirements. He sounded pleased at the response, replaced the handset and exited the lab.

Windar's feet galumphed against the cold, concrete floor of brightly lit corridors, his satchel fixed tightly over his right shoulder.

The boardroom door was made of solid oak and had the MoD emblem stamped at eye-level. The professor knocked, and three and a half seconds later it opened. Walking in, he recognised Flattery, Goodwill and Grievance, but a total of nine other men sat around a large conference table, Knights of the British realm.

The outcome of this meeting would be Windar's legacy.

14: Mag's Aftermath

It had been a severe winter. Food was scarce; only the
weather continued to bite. Most of the younger, more able
animals and birds had taken the bold step of migrating to
pastures new. But this exodus only strengthened the might of
the magpies.

The animals left behind were either very old or very young,
and few attempted to stand up to the mob that terrorised Greenacres. Some families remained hopeful for the future, believing
that spring would arrive and yield enough food for them all
to grow strong again. Such was the belief of Arim and Mira,
the Redwings. Many native birds could not understand why
they chose to settle at Greenacres when they could have gone
anywhere. Some bitterly chirped that they should 'go back to
where they came from', that there wasn't enough food for them
and that they were 'sponging off the eco-system'. But Mira and

Arim were resolute, they had made it this far and would wait for their chick to hatch before deciding whether to move on or not.

Most magpies had tried and failed to secure the Redwing's egg; most, but not all. Big Mag was perched high in a pine tree, shrouded from the sun's light by its sharp spines. He had watched, as he always did, the other magpies' failed attempts to capture the egg. Instead, he studied Arim's behaviour, learning his defence strategy. Mag also examined Mira's function from the nest, noting how she screeched orders and chirped warnings about where the next offensive would come from.

Mag waited. An opportunity would come.

"Let's see you stop this one!" Ringpull tried an audacious swoop on the nest; his wings were tucked tightly against his chest as he dived at speed towards the target. His aim was to dislodge the nest from the tree so that his squirrel allies on the ground could secure their prize egg.

Arim saw Ringpull dive and immediately went to intercept. Mira chirped anxiously at the edge of her nest. "Arim, he's going to destroy our home!" On hearing these words, Arim decided that a collision with Ringpull was the only way to stop him. With a surge of inner strength, the brave bird directed all his force at the magpie. Ringpull tried to evade Arim and plough past him, but the redwing was indignant, countering his move, striking Ringpull just below his beak. The force of the impact sent Arim tumbling.

"Curses!" cried Ringpull, careering off course. He crashed through the branches like a feathered comet, leaving a trail of leaves and feathers in his wake. The magpie managed to land. He turned and caught sight of Arim hobbling along the ground for cover and began angrily flicking his tail. "I'm gonna wipe that stripe off your filthy, little foreign face!" he chattered, hopping after him.

Mira perched at the edge of her nest and screamed for Arim to find shelter, sensing Ringpull's wild discontent.

Big Mag saw his chance. Demonically he broke cover and swooped silently to the opposite side of the nest. Mira, caught off guard, turned in horror - the enormity of Mag's shadow eclipsed her. "Chatak-chatak! What have we got 'ere then?" he cackled, plucking the egg up in his beak. Mira chirped wildly with terror; their unhatched chick gripped in the beak of their oppressor. "I don't think I've tried foreign food before." With a sinister laugh, Mag launched himself back in the direction of the East Field. Mira cried out.

Arim, still evading Ringpull's wrath, looked above him to see Big Mag's silhouette, the shape of an egg clearly visible in his mouth. His heart shrivelled up and he felt his legs crumple: his fight had been in vain.

Soaring above the woods, a blanket of azure sky resting upon it, Mag marvelled at his future – great things lay ahead of him. Secured in his beak, the egg was still warm from Mira's love. He sensed the movement of tiny limbs, shuffling about inside. This would be a delectable snack for later to cele -

BANG!

Mag felt his life explode from within. A flurry of black and white feathers erupted furiously into the sky. A trail of blood spurted out like fuel from a burning aircraft; the magpie's belly singed and numbness quickly enveloped his wings to the point where they could not move anymore. Mag's fading vision focused only on the sandy green of the field below. And as he tumbled back to earth, he let go of the egg, which flew away from his tangled, bloody mass.

Farmer Cullem's aim was as accurate as it had always been. He cradled the shotgun and ejected the shells. The smoking barrels reminded him of his wife's flaring nostrils when she had told him to 'fix that magpie before he steals again'.

Big Mag hit the ground dead. There his scorched body remained, cooled by the westerly winds. As for the egg, it was nowhere to be seen.

Ringpull and Arim had watched the drama unfold. They daren't move nor make a sound. Arim still believed that his heir was dead. Ringpull was in shock. The magpie's instinct was to hastily return back to the pack and tell the awful news. But what about Mag? Who would lead the pack now? Maybe this was his chance to become leader? Ringpull bounded forward without hesitation. He daren't fly, but hopped along the ground with such fervour that occasionally he had to flap his wings to steady himself. Farmer Cullem noticed him approach as he also marched towards Mag's carcass. 'Scavengers,' he said to himself, repulsed.

The young magpie hovered next to Mag's carcass. He glanced into his eyes to see if there were any signs of life, but only caught sight of his own reflection. Ringpull heard the farmer approach, he had to act quickly. He saw Mag's cherished emblem – the polished outline of an eagle. Without hesitation he swiftly gathered the twine and teased the object loose, clamped it in his beak and shot back to the forest.

Farmer Cullem stood above Big Mag's empty shell. He reached over his other shoulder and brought down a padded cool bag, opening it. Inside was a mass of crushed ice. Reaching down, the farmer collected the magpie and placed the remains in the bag before beginning his triumphant walk back to the farmhouse.

Arim arrived minutes later, apprehensive about what he might find. He scoured the area where Big Mag's body had lain, for signs of his egg, but found nothing. 'Perhaps Ringpull has taken it?' he thought, despairingly.

As he rummaged through limp strands of grass, he could hear Mira weeping in the tree above. Arim looked over at his wife and went to call when he heard a noise: a faint twitter, an echo of hope from the bleakness of the field. Mira's crying ceased at the sound of high pitched, muffled chirping. Arim scanned the grassy plain once more, listening. The tweeting started up again, louder this time, as though a tiny set of lungs were sampling their first gulps of free air.

Mira flew down to join Arim in his search. "Can you hear that?"

The chirps grew stronger, calling to them both. Arim flew over a patch of weeds, and there - a tiny jewel in a barren wasteland - shook the fractured remains of their one, solitary egg. Protruding from it was a tiny yellow beak and slicked black feathers. Seeing this image undid all the months of torment they had faced.

Miraculously, their young chick had survived the clutches of the most feared tyrant across the land. She would become a symbol of hope for all the creatures of Greenacres - spring had arrived.

They called her Joy.

15: Shadows

Spikez and the rest of the team were watching a video of natural habitats; grassy fields blowing gently in the wind, hills lush with hedgerows and fruit trees, and cool blue seas with stunning white sands. Occasionally the screen would dissolve into a montage of suburban streets and private back gardens.

PIG30N wept as she saw other pigeons happily scratching around looking for food or flying in clear blue skies; Spikez didn't really pay much attention, he was in deeper thought, desperately trying to attach names to the faces that circled within his mind; Trakz gave a running commentary as he munched on some lactose sticks.

The hedgehog watched the inquisitive rodent's teeth grind together and noted how his glasses seemed to bob up and down, floating on a sea of blue and grey fur.

"What's on your mind?" asked Trakz.

"Oh, nothing much," replied Spikez, "just that small, niggling thing about trying to remember who I am."

"Relax," Trakz spun round and faced him. "Stop trying to think and let it come naturally."

Spikez rested his head on his hands and tried to. "I can't. I keep seeing shapes which turn into faces, then they fade to shadows, then there are bright lights followed by darkness - that's all I see over and over again! What does it mean? Nothing makes any sense. I don't even know how I got here, yet you remember so clearly. Why can't I remember?"

"Firstly, you should try breathing a bit more often. Secondly, maybe the mind doesn't want to remember," he replied, biting off a large chunk of his snack. "I only remember because I didn't die instantly, I only lost my legs. Whatever happened to you, it must have occurred real quick!"

Spikez guessed he was right. He was very learned for a young mouse; Trakz had boasted how his dad had been a great explorer and revealed many of man's secrets to him – except the one about mouse traps!

"How come you remember everything, not just the accident: where you come from, names, and places."

"Well, I guess it's because I've always had the connection with Windar. You've never seen him before, so your mind is probably still taking it all in. It will come in time, probably when you see a familiar face or object."

"Trakz is an unusual name," Spikez said.

"It's not the name I was born with - it's the name Windar gave me."

"So what's your real name?"

"It doesn't matter. I never liked my real name anyway."

"Go on, tell me."

"What's the point, you'll probably forget."

"I won't forget. Go on, tell me," pleaded Spikez.

"I just did!" he replied.

"Did you?"

"See, you forgot!" Spikez looked embarrassed, and confused. Trakz wheeled in closer. "Only kidding."

"Don't mess with my head. Why won't you tell me?"

"Because that mouse is gone!" Trakz threw the rest of his snack to the ground and turned to watch the images, which were now of the canal. "I have accepted that things can never go back to how they were," continued Trakz, "it was hard to at first, but the crux of it is this - I'll never see my old home or family again, so why kid myself thinking it's going to happen? I've accepted life here, in this lab – eventually you'll have to do the same."

Spikez walked to the edge of the table and stared at the floor below him, at the arteries of cables and wires nestled along the walls which connected to large machines and flashing boxes. He turned his thoughts back to Windar, his maker; minutes after returning from his meeting with the generals, the professor filled a large case with syringes, gloves and a silver canister.

16: Ringpull's Revolt

A fleet of magpies gathered alongside several platoons of squirrels. They waited impatiently for their leader's return. Big Mag was late - he was never late. Hood patrolled the border of the protective circle they had created, where Mag would land and address them all.

Ringpull burst through the leafy canopy above and landed inside the circle, creating hostility amongst other magpies.

"Chatak! What are you doing?" they squawked. "Don't let him catch you behaving like this."

"Ringpull, stop being such a fool – that's where the boss stands," warned Hood.

"Well, what if I's told you that Big Mag ain't in charge no-more?" Ringpull brandished Mag's emblem in his mouth. The other magpies stared at him with envy.

"What 'ave you done to 'im, fam?" cawed Hood.

"Me . . . I's done nuffin! The farmer got him wiv 'is thunder stick."

The pack kissed their beaks in disbelief. "So, who appointed you leader?" spat another Magpie, swaggering forward.

"Big Mag did!" retorted Ringpull, about to deliver his decree. "As I tried to help him, he turns to me and says that I is d'only one strong enough to lead da pack."

"I smell cow-pat!" scowled Hood. "He told me that I was the only one he could trust to run fings in his absence. The medal belongs to me."

"He told me you'd be like this!" hissed Ringpull.

Hood hopped forward, looking for a fight. "Like what?"

"Chatak! A sore loser! Where were you when Mag was dying in the field, huh?" Ringpull addressed the whole pack. "I watched our great leader die, and I tried to save him before the farmer took him. Mag looked at me and told me how brave I was, and that I should return as leader so that we can conquer Greenacres."

"What else did he propose?" another magpie asked.

"That we take control of the skies from the raptors immediately."

"But we're not ready. With Hercules still in play, it's a suicide mission!"

"But if we don't, a message will eventually get through to 'em," cautioned Ringpull. "We can't let the other creatures know that Big Mag is dead - we stand on the edge of victory. . .

It was Mag's dying wish that we cleanse the land of raptors

completely before they do the same to us. You're either with me or against us?"

There was an uncomfortably long silence amongst the pack. The magpies were envious of Ringpull's claims. Their gut instinct was to reject him as leader and fight amongst themselves to see who was worthiest, that's how Hood would have liked it, but Ringpull's revelations had sown enough doubt and wonder within the group for them to agree to his leadership.

"We must act tonight," declared Ringpull. "We must show them that we are united and stronger than ever before! Rally the other corvids, our cousins must prove their allegiance. Tonight, Greenacres belongs to the magpies!"

Chatak-chatak-chatak! The mob erupted into a wild fit of laughing and howling, each of them working one another up into a wild frenzy; an aggressive war chant seeking revenge and retribution.

17: Rabbit Mail

Most native residents of Greenacres were settling down to rest for the evening. It would be another chilly night, but they knew that spring was nearly upon them and that food supplies would soon be replenished.

Arim, Mira and baby Joy sought refuge in Baldwin's sett, unable to return to their nest. They had recounted the full, graphic story of Big Mag's demise to the wise badger, who was inspired by the news, but Baldwin knew too well that the threat would not cease. He had called on one of his fastest young rabbit allies to deliver a message to the raptors.

"I need to find food," chirped Mira.

"Of course, but you must be careful," warned Baldwin. "We are not free from the clutches of magpies yet. Head towards the great iron perimeter and there you will find food, but be cautious – many never return."

"I will go," said Arim, his wing in a sling after his tumble with Ringpull.

"No, darling, this is something that I need to do - you are injured and must rest."

Arim knew his wife was right. "You be careful, those magpies are everywhere."

Mira gave Arim a peck on the cheek and then headed out.

Queen Eliza and Hercules came under much scrutiny from the creatures of Greenacres. It was claimed that they had not enforced the ruling of the council soon enough to subdue the corvids; that magpies were still in violation of the sacred code: pilfering foods outside of their normal diet, murdering the young and attacking other species for fun. But the reality of the situation was that no messages could get through to them, high up in the Pine Forest. The buzzards, who often patrolled the skies, were heckled by large mobs of crows and jackdaws. And all evidence of wrong doing on the ground, including massacres and public animal executions, were swiftly covered up. Many land animals were too scared to give evidence - the squirrels had seen to that.

Overlooking the valley, a fiery orange mass of feathers and chiselled features was perched alongside Eliza. Hercules had been hoping for an opportunity to settle the score with Big Mag for months; he had even planned an attack that would have unsettled the magpies and caused a coup amongst the corvids. But without Eliza able to make a decision based on hard evidence, that moment never came.

A voice called out to them. "My Queen, I bring you urgent news . . ."

Eliza looked down below to see a small rabbit at the foot of the pine tree, tufts of fur had been removed from his head and hind legs. Hercules also glared at him; a tempting morsel of food in such harsh times, but the rabbit bore Baldwin's paw print – he was a messenger and would not be considered as prey for either of them.

"Speak, rabbit."

"Big Mag has expired!"

The raptor's eyes remained motionless, blazing at the rabbit. "Who sent you?" Eliza asked.

"Baldwin sent me himself, ma'am. He also instructed me to tell you that the magpies are continuing to steal the songbirds' young and control the food supplies of all land animals."

"You are brave, young rabbit. Wait for my word." Eliza turned to Hercules, who had a sense of urgency flickering in his eyes.

"My Queen, with Big Mag out of the equation we must strike now while they have no leader. I can gather allies, but if we are to end this revolt by the magpies then it must be done tonight and by us!"

"I agree. If Big Mag has indeed perished, then it will not be long before they appoint a leader more ruthless and tyrannical than him."

Hercules gazed out across the valley. "I fear that the animals have lost faith in our ability to regulate the skies. The rabbit has confirmed our worst fears, there will be a shortage of songbirds this year, which will have a direct impact on our kind unless we take action and disperse the magpies."

"I hate to say it, but Baldwin was right, he always is." Eliza was reflective. "I've failed the creatures of Greenacres, Hercules."

"No, my Queen, you did what any great leader would have done – you strived for peace. We were deceived. It's the corvids who have failed the creatures of Greenacres, they have lied to us all like Morag did, and tonight they will pay!"

Eliza saw the fury burn in his eyes. "I will fight with you, Hercules." She looked out above the forest. "Send word to the kestrels, buzzards and hawks - tonight we make a stand."

"My Queen, it will be an honour to fight with you." Hercules stretched his wings and called to the rabbit below. "Send word to Baldwin that we will require immediate support from the ground."

The young rabbit nodded, turned and then quickly darted back to the Eastern Forest.

"Godspeed, Hercules." Eliza turned to the skies and let out an almighty cry.

Hercules beat his mighty wings, propelling him high into the sky and pushing the clouds apart. He soared towards the edge of Greenacres where the valley met the pine forest boundary: home to restless birds of prey.

Spikez and Trakz were engaged in discussion about whether they would ever be freed from the laboratory.

"You may not realise it now, but we've never had it so good," asserted Trakz. "Outside of these four walls lies a dangerous world. Do you know how many animals tried to eat me before I moved here?"

"But don't you miss it, the freedom of open space and fresh food?" replied Spikez.

"Well, if the world was one big flat surface then sure, I'd love to be outside," he said, wheeling himself forward. "As for the food situation, you've obviously never lived through a famine."

"I guess you're right," sighed Spikez. "It's just that I feel there should be more to life than just eating and sleeping."

"Well, if I'm not mistaken, I believe I watched you kick some Russian buttski the other day, if that's not enough excitement for you then I don't know what is!"

"You're right, again! Then I'm not sure what I want - I just feel that part of me is missing."

The door slid open and Windar hurried through. Two assistants dressed in white surgical robes pushed an operating table after him. The cyborgs clambered to the edge of their cages to view what was on the trolley, but Windar's team quickly disappeared behind frosted glass and lowered large lights and apparatus from the ceiling.

Spikez watched their silhouettes against the white light and listened to the sound of their voices, to machines grinding and sucking. Occasionally, Windar's assistants re-emerged in to view. They collected sharp mechanical tools from locked cabinets and vacuum packed liquids from a scientific freezer; he noted that one of the assistants, a Chinese man, seemed more nervous than the other, wavering around each object before gathering it; something electrical was embedded in his overalls.

"Hurry up!" Windar shouted, "We're wasting precious time."

The professor came out to retrieve something from a locked safe. A neon yellow sign was plastered across the door. He opened it, mechanically extending his arm inside to carefully remove an item. Spikez, Trakz and PIG3ON stared in awe at its beauty, a dazzling white light shone from within a diamond shaped box. The energy signature was off the scale.

Windar's favourite piece of classical music, Mozart's Requiem, came on minutes later as the lights dimmed. The team looked on.

"Looks like we're going to have another amnesiac team member joining us soon," Trakz said excitedly. PIG3ON was also optimistic; she was adamant she saw a feather.

Spikez retreated to the back of his cell – something wasn't right.

18: Mira's Pledge

ood led three other magpies towards a rookery, coercing their cousins to join their fight or face tough sanctions. Scuffles broke out and heated exchanges were made, but the magpies were assured and wild with rage. The rooks succumbed, for Mag had previously promised them the right to hunt freely if they declared loyalty to the magpies. Hood told them of the plan to mount an attack that night; they were all unified in their response.

Mira made good time. She was an agile songbird, swooping beneath the hedgerows and through trees towards the military perimeter where the best sources of food remained. She hoped to find mealworms and bugs, enough to fill her beak and return to Joy. But her efforts did not go undetected.

"The cheeky little bird!" one magpie remarked.

"Don't you understand English!" mocked the other. "No flyski, no huntski." The magpies fired off their watch-posts to intercept.

Her assailants came from all angles, diving from above and volleying at her from the side, but Mira was resilient – Joy needed food. One of the magpies clipped Mira across the back, sending her crashing to the ground. She was dazed but managed to fly for cover before the other magpie could pin her down and perform brutal acts of avian cruelty.

Back at Baldwin's centre of command, the young rabbit returned with the Queen's response, but not without injury. His back was littered with scabs from where magpies had pierced his flesh; he had also taken a good beating from the squirrels and lost a lot of blood.

"My dear rabbit, you have done a great deed. What news?" enquired Baldwin.

"The Queen says to prepare for an uprising - help from the skies is on its way."

"Good work, young buck. Now rest – seek shelter here whilst I call for reinforcements."

Mira hid in the brambles whilst the magpies hopped menacingly about, searching for a way in. "I'm gonna pluck your pretty little feathers out!" one cawed.

"And once we're through with you," sneered the other, "we're gonna find that young chick of yours and peck her eyes out!"

As the onset of night drew nearer, Mira grew more distressed thinking about Joy, hungry and cold in Baldwin's den. She could not return home empty beaked, neither could she hold out in dead bushes for long – more magpies would come. Mira needed to make a dash for it.

Three hardened squirrels had been keeping Baldwin's sett under surveillance. They were gaunt looking with emaciated faces, poised, and waiting to attack the badger. When Baldwin emerged they did not shy away, even though he was still as strong as ten squirrels and had thick skin beneath his wiry fur. They watched him begin clawing the trunk of a tree.

"Get back inside, Baldy," one of them shouted. "Just because you're old enough for a freedom pass, doesn't mean you can go wandering round these woods as you please."

"Don't try and stop me." Baldwin turned round and watched them drop from the trees and flex their muscles, whipping their tails from side to side.

"Listen granddad," they said, "get back in your hole before we put you down!"

"Bring it on, bushy!" Baldwin stamped his paws into the earth and charged at them with all his might, smashing into their brittle bodies. Two of the squirrels crashed into the base of the nearest tree. The third was prepared and leapt upwards. He landed on Baldwin's back and bit into him with his sharp incisors. The pain caused the smallest of grimaces for the badger as he rallied through a gap in the hedges, swiftly dislodging his attacker against the branch of a rose bush.

Nothing would stop him from travelling to Speaker's Warren

- it would be here that Baldwin intended to rally support from the rest of the wildlife population.

Magpie rule needed to end that night!

19: Night Owls

Sparks of light ignited the laboratory. Even from the safety and comfort of his cage, Spikez could not settle. The electronic whiteboard which had been projecting a montage of tranquil woodland scenes and serene landscapes was now broadcasting frantic images of a live, surgical operation.

A red and white x-ray of a creature appeared. The image had countless fine bones; Windar used it as a map to navigate his fibre-optic laser through the arteries and veins of the organism's remains, injecting liquid metals and nanobots, fusing them together with processors and microscopic semi-conductors.

At one point, Spikez watched with dread as the professor fixed two shielded lenses over dimly lit, red eyes. He did not like that feeling, he had felt it from somewhere before.

"Chataka-chataka! Come here my lovely," beckoned one of the

magpies, "I promise I won't peck too hard." The corvids cackled wildly at their own wickedness. Mira knew that time was running out. She watched them turn their heads for a second and saw an opportunity to escape.

Mira fired out of the bush like a cannonball, keeping low to the ground, the icy chill of night blasting her in the face. The two magpies were oblivious as they loitered at the opposite end of the bush, cawing obscenities. Success, she thought; a narrow escape and a story to tell Joy on a fine starry night. But as thoughts of freedom filled her head, two other magpies dropped from the sky like anvils, knocking her to the ground.

The startled redwing flapped her wings helplessly against the muddy grass. Mira's face was pressed hard into the damp earth whilst a magpie hen's claw choked her. "Don't fight it," she whispered, "it'll all be over soon."

All Mira could do was close her eyes and think of Joy, at least she was safe with Arim in Baldwin's den and would not have to watch her die. It gave her comfort as she hoped for a quick end.

Suddenly the magpies began to caw, something was wrong. Mira opened her eyes and looked skyward to see a volley of sharp, defined shadows pass overhead. The magpies about turned, confused. The defenceless redwing then watched as silhouettes hammered in to the black and white plumage of her attackers.

The claw released its grip from Mira's neck. She swiftly shot to her feet to see two kestrels, each of them pinning down one of the magpies as they tumbled about on the floor, cawing for mercy.

"We'll take it from here," they called, giving Mira a reassuring wink.

Mira chirped in gratitude. She flew at speed to the perimeter fence where she landed and frantically gathered as many bugs as possible in her tiny little beak. Joy needs me, she thought.

"Friends, rodents, country-beasts, lend me your ears!" Baldwin stood in the circle at Speaker's Warren, a protected clearing hidden deep within the forest. Mounds of rich, brown clay and heavy, green moss cloaked the roots of ancient trees and made good seats for the elderly. Creatures of all types sat wearily and listened to Baldwin's rhetoric. "Tonight, we have an opportunity to defeat our enemy . . . Big Mag is dead!"

There was a disbelieving murmur amongst the hares, rats and mice. They, like all creatures, were tired and hungry and most of them wanted to be back underground, conserving energy and praying for spring to arrive.

"And just how can you be sure of this?" questioned a cynical stoat.

"It has been witnessed, by the redwings," answered Baldwin.

Some of the creatures scoffed when they heard this. Baldwin grew disheartened.

The stoat climbed to the highest mound of clay he could find. "How do you know this isn't one of their tricks?"

"I believe the redwings," retorted Badger. "You doubt them?"

"Well, they're not exactly native to our land. I mean, look what happened with the grey squirrels. All I'm saying is that foreigners can't be trusted. How do we know that they haven't conspired with the magpies? They might have brokered a deal for their kind to mass emigrate over here. They might be leading us all into a trap!"

Baldwin was taken aback, and judging from the reaction of fur scratching and hind shuffling, the other animals considered Stoatey's words with less doubt than his own. "They are in my den, nurturing their fledgling whilst we speak. I have two separate accounts and I do not for one moment disbelieve them."

"But don't you find it strange that the only two witnesses to Big Mag's alleged demise are both immigrants? I don't trust 'em."

There were a few emphatic jeers amongst the older, patriotic members of the crowd. Baldwin grew suspicious of Stoatey's tone. "Is this how we've all become?" he remarked. "Have our souls already been diminished that we should treat good news with such scepticism? Perhaps you are right, maybe Big Mag is not dead - for I believe he is very much alive in your minds and that you have let him destroy your spirits." Baldwin struck his paws into the ground. "No one has undergone worse treatment than the redwings. In fact, we could learn a lot from their courage and perseverance. They both nearly died protecting their young from the magpies whilst others turned a blind eye. And yet, you would still have us believe that they are traitors?"

Some animals lowered their heads in shame, others remained indifferent; Baldwin realised that things were worse than he had first thought.

A sudden chill blew through the clearing. A group of mice

ducked for cover. The rats squealed in terror and also dived into rabbit holes, fearing the angel of death. A gallant tawny owl silently swooped to a branch in clear sight of the group. He shone his eyes, two glowing discs, at the crowd as he neatly folded in his wings and twisted his head.

"Deacon!" Baldwin exclaimed.

"My friend, it's been too long."

"I wish it could be under better circumstances."

"Perhaps that time is nearly upon us. I bring news - the birds of prey are commencing their attack as we speak."

The ears and tails of the doubtful animals pricked up at Deacon's words. "You see, my friends?" remarked Baldwin. "A new dawn approaches, we must act now to see this revolution through."

"There are other reasons to strike now," continued Deacon. "The jackdaws, rooks and crows have pledged their allegiance to the magpies in return for guaranteed food supplies and a license to hunt freely. The squirrels are also busy trying to recruit new allies. We simply cannot let this happen!"

"If Hercules is leading the fight in the air, then we must support him on the ground," affirmed Baldwin. "And not just for us oldies, but for the generations that will follow." He looked round the group, it was starting to work. The hares were empowered, standing tall on their hind legs. The other animals were apologetic in their slow show of support, snuffling each other and rubbing their heads. The rats re-emerged; they had never succumbed to anyone before, not even man. Baldwin glanced up towards Deacon, who gave him an affirming nod. They were united once more.

"My fellow animals, what say you?"

The response was unanimous: fight!

"And what say ye now, Stoatey?" Baldwin asked, searching the crowd of fur. There was silence. The animals waited for Stoatey's snide response, but as the badger had suspected, the stoat was no longer present. He had slithered away at the first sight of Deacon, through one of the rabbit burrows.

"Stoatey is no longer to be trusted," declared Deacon. "I saw him last night, with the leader of the squirrels."

"The squirrels have a leader?" questioned Baldwin.

"Self-appointed," added Deacon. "Or should I say, appointed by Big Mag."

Baldwin knew that there was only one squirrel capable of leading such a pack of fierce fighters. Deacon continued. "He has been brainwashing all the other squirrels and now, it seems, he's branched out to other small mammals, too."

"Then we haven't much time." Baldwin rallied the resistance. "Our fight for freedom will not be easy. There will be bloodshed. But we must stand together, not for ourselves, or for the soil we sit upon, but for justice and liberty. We must support the raptors and reclaim the Eastern edge of the forest." Baldwin raised his mighty paws into the air and cried out: "For the sake of our young!"

"For the future of Greenacres!" they bellowed.

Baldwin shook himself fiercely; a cloud of dust shrouded him in the radiance of moonlight before he launched himself into battle, his thick, grey fur glowing like armour.

The other mammals followed, guided in the air by Deacon who shimmered through the woods like a spectre.

20: Squirrel Nutcase

"**I** need to speak to Nutcase!" Stoatey hissed. He was surrounded by four squirrels, who flicked their tales from side to side like spiked clubs - they didn't trust him.

A coarse voice grumbled from behind one of the squirrels. "It's 'coz you don't 'ave the sign."

They squirrels shifted apart, revealing the brutish bulk of Squirrel Nutcase. "Back so soon, Stoatey?" he said, slinking into a blade of moonlight.

Stoatey could not help but shiver. The scar from Nutcase's past encounter with Hercules seemed to glisten; a straight white line ran from the top of his right ear, across his eye and down to his rotting yellow teeth. His arm, which had healed badly, showed strands of muscle and vein beneath a thin layer of raw skin; other tufts of grey hair also seemed to be amiss, but whether these were from his fight with Hercules or other encounters, Stoatey dared not ask.

"There's a problem," said Stoatey, curling back on himself.

"Problem, Stoatey? My offer was final."

"No, it's not about that. It's the animals, they're revolting!"

"Well, it's not their fault. That's how Muvva Nature intended them to look." The squirrels chuckled.

"Baldwin is leading a revolt!" Stoatey quickly countered.

"Well why didn't you just say that?" Nutcase stared at Stoatey, his good eye glimmered. "You said you'd fix it."

"I know, and I was," he explained, "But then Deacon arrived on the scene and broke the news."

"What news?"

"Hercules is leading the raptors in a surprise attack against the magpies."

At the mention of the name 'Hercules', Nutcase clenched his fist as if to punch Stoatey across his whiskers. "Well, that is upsetting news."

"We need to tell the magpies immediately."

"Forget 'em, they can handle themselves," he said, seething. "I'm upset because you didn't convert your friends like you said you would."

"But I didn't have time."

"You said it'd be easy!" snapped Nutcase.

"It should have been," replied Stoatey, peering at the stern faces of Nutcase's bodyguards. "I can still do the job."

"I'm sure you can, but you've already received payment and you ain't delivered." Nutcase moved towards him until they were nose to nose. "Now they'll all know your filthy little secret. Why would they believe you?"

Stoatey shook his head and shrunk towards the ground. "What are you going to do to me?"

"I just need to know one thing," said Nutcase, flexing his muscles and stretching his limbs. "D'you still wanna to be like one of us?"

The stoat glanced round at the squirrels, all of them hungry for violence and primed to give him a good beating on Nutcase's orders. The stoat noticed that their arms all had tufts of hair removed from the same place, like Nutcase, as if to identify rank. Nervously, he turned to Nutcase and nodded.

A nest of blackbirds were awoken by Stoatey's scalding screams. Only when the whimpering ceased did they return to an uneasy slumber.

21: The Battle of Greenacres

Hercules led a legion of raptors: hawks, buzzards and kestrels, high above the forest field. As he approached the eastern side of the woodland, he could see the shapes of corvids: magpies, jackdaws, rooks and crows on their way to intercept him.

"So," he observed, "you've invited your cousins into battle. This should make things interesting." Hercules circled above his allies. "Show them no mercy, for they will offer you none!" he cried. On that note he led the diving attack against the enemy. Keeei-oww!

Although smaller than their predatory adversaries, the corvids were undeterred. They had regularly defended their territory against birds of prey in past battles and harassed raptors who hunted near their nests. But now Hercules and his kind were in violation of their late-leader's curfew, and would therefore be severely punished.

Hood was the magpie captaining his gang of miscreants into combat. His wingman, a naive rook named Bruiser, saw Hercules descend upon them. "Raptor scum!" Hood cawed in his enraged state. But the young magpie had neglected his common sense - Hercules was not your average bird of prey. He should have taken evasive action, he should have reminded the adolescent rooks about Hercules' fearsome strength and size - he should have been more like Mag.

The red kite caught each bird around their neck with his mighty talons and dived perilously towards the forest floor. He had no intention of letting go.

Hood and Bruiser hit the ground with a thud. The impact shattered the rook's bones and sent the corvids tumbling across the mud, cawing in agony; their black, oily feathers now unkempt and blotted in blood, dust, and mud.

Hercules hailed a war cry: "For freedom!" He stood on the ground with his wings mantled, a sentinel in the field, his eyes cannons waiting to pick off magpie adversaries.

"You never told me I'd be up against him!" gurgled Bruiser, nursing a broken wing.

Hood flapped himself to his feet. "He's just a bird like the rest of us, he's not immortal."

Bruiser hobbled towards the forest to seek refuge. "You lied to us!"

"Come back!" cried Hood. "Pledge your allegiance!"

"Tell that to them," he replied, gesturing up at the skies.

Hood looked up at the starlit night. A scene of carnage was being played out before them; crows and magpies were targeting one or two birds of prey, but after watching for a couple of minutes he noticed how another raptor would appear, swiftly like a demon's shadow, picking off a magpie or rook until the ratio of corvid to raptor was equal; then he watched the rugged shape of his allies tumble to the ground into a lifeless heap.

"So, you're the new leader?" a voice whistled.

The magpie turned to see Hercules towering above him. He attempted to fly for safety, but as he launched himself skyward another silhouette swooped down, pinning him to the ground. It was Queen Eliza, and she was not amused.

"Are you responsible for this revolt?" she enquired, clamping her talons into his shoulder.

"No!" squawked Hood as he frantically flapped his wings.

"Then who do you take orders from now that Big Mag is dead?"

Hood protested as she clenched her talons tighter around his shoulder. "Ringpull, ma'am,"

Eliza nodded at Hercules, who ascended back into the night sky, leaving Hood at the mercy of Her Majesty.

Windar had been battling all night to keep his latest creation alive. The creature's heartbeat had stopped several times and the professor had to resuscitate it using specialised defibrillators. His assistants worked relentlessly, slicing away dead tissue and fusing nerve endings and internal organs with prosthetic pumps and limbs. Meanwhile, Windar's patented nanobots had been injected into the central nervous system where they had fought to control the host's cerebral functions.

The specimen lapsed in and out of consciousness throughout the ordeal, hearing frantic voices chatter whilst its body was cut open with steel blades, lasered and then soldered together again. And all this time, a violent energy blazed within its chest, as if the heart had been napalmed into a molten mass of iron.

Surveying the readings on his computer monitors, the professor stopped his assault. A pulse ticked steadily across the screen and the mechanics appeared to be in standby mode without error messages. Windar slowly removed his surgical mouthpiece and drew breath. His nimble hands shook from the efforts of his toils as he removed the bloodied latex gloves. The assistants continued to sweat beneath the powerful spotlights as they awaited instructions.

"I did it . . ." he muttered, laughing to himself. "The procedure worked." The professor stood up straight and moved the high-intensity LED lights away from the body they had been operating on. "It's alive. Oh, great God, Windar – look at what you've created."

Baldwin, Deacon and the resistance arrived at the forest perimeter, under the cover of small trees. They witnessed scenes of bloodshed: black and white bodies writhed frantically on the floor as the birds of prey performed brutal acts of retribution, ripping wing feathers and plumage from their bodies; some lay dead, their innards splattered across the fields. Many crows and rooks had retreated away from the battle, knowing when a fight was lost, but still other magpies arrived for more punishment whilst the jackdaws fearfully spat insults.

Ringpull, watching the battle from the cover of an old oak tree, chattered commands at his remaining fighters and cursed the traitors who abandoned them, one by one. "Chataka-chatak! Come back, we had a deal!"

A young rabbit, barely old enough to fight, turned to Baldwin with fearful eyes. "What do we do?"

"We support on the ground," he replied, thinking of ways to aid the raptors. He turned to Deacon. "We must find Ringpull and bring him to justice."

The owl gave a deep, affirming hoot before silently catapulting himself off the branch in search of Ringpull.

As the mammals stood and watched the aerial battle escalate, a large mob of squirrels - led by Nutcase - emerged from a clearing further along, accompanied by a very distressed looking stoat. "Go to 'em and demand an end to this before we kick their 'eads in," he instructed.

"You want *me* to ask them to surrender?" Stoatey replied.

Nutcase snarled.

Reluctantly, Stoatey crawled towards the resistance; Baldwin frowned upon him as he spoke. "Er, Nutcase would like you to call off the attack . . ."

Baldwin studied Stoatey's arm. The fur had been chewed off, leaving his skin exposed and crusted over with dry blood. "So, you've decided to join them?" confirmed Baldwin. "Very well." With a swift flick of his heavy paw, the badger struck the stoat cleanly in the chest, propelling him back to where he came from.

The stoat's limp body thumped along the ground until it arrived back at Nutcase's feet. Dazed and confused, Stoatey stared up at the squirrel, who looked far from impressed by his efforts. "They refuse."

Nutcase turned to his pack of rabid warriors; they eagerly hopped around each another, ready to fight. "If you value your right to an endless supply of nuts and seeds, then you will fight with me. If, on the other hand, you'd just like to fight – then that's okay, too." The squirrels rattled angrily - they would not surrender their food stores so easily. Nutcase span round and launched an acorn in Baldwin's direction.

The badger did not flinch, letting the acorn bounce off his broad shoulders. In response to this, Nutcase led the charge with his army of foot soldiers following behind him.

"For Greenacres!" bellowed Baldwin, directing a counter-charge. The rats, rabbits and hares joined together in a flurry of rage, galloping at his side.

This would be an historic battle talked about by future generations.

22: Dark Horizons

Windar slept on his chair in the corner of the laboratory, adorned in bloody and scorched surgical robes. Spikez and Trakz hibernated in their pods whilst PIG30N roosted in her cage near the window.

Amidst this silence, something stirred within its protective cell, lapsing in and out of consciousness, dreaming of freedom – clear blue skies and something warm to eat. Occasionally the cell would shake as the creation became accustomed to its prosthetic armour and got used to the sensation of having mechanics fused to its muscles. The latest 'covert weapon' examined itself in detail, at the complex network of fibre optic cables and wires beneath the impenetrable breastplate that shielded its nuclear heart. And as the nanobots and newly constructed arteries pumped artificial life around its body, it could sense that it was not alone.

Dawn was breaking. For much of the night, the creatures had battled and fought for control of Greenacres. A small pocket of magpie resistance was now surrounded by a mighty allegiance of woodland creatures. Around them, the fields were moist with blood and littered with feathers. Fagin watched from the shadows, eager to clear up.

Ringpull knew that he was outnumbered, as most of his army had deserted him and even Nutcase, who had taken a good beating from the heavyweight hares, saw little point in resisting further. Baldwin, with patches of blood crusted across his haunch, remained assertive as ever.

"Baldwin," whispered the young rabbit, shaking uncontrollably, "you're bleeding."

"I don't have time to bleed," the badger replied, focusing his attention on the queen, who was about to publicly address Ringpull.

"You have lost this battle," asserted Eliza. "Accept defeat!"

Ringpull sheepishly looked to his right at Hercules; two squirrels were pinned face down into the mud beneath his talons, one was still breathing. He knew that if he remained defiant, Hercules would follow Eliza's orders, no matter what she asked of him. To the left of him he could see hundreds of weary faces peering out from forest fringe – their eyes were like tiny pebbles glistening in the morning sun. He had two choices: die a martyr for a lost cause or live to fight another day.

"Accepted," he said, dejectedly.

The raptors and land animals erupted into a victorious cheer.

Nutcase shook his head. "We're not finished here," he said to himself.

Hood gathered with the remaining magpies and glared hatefully at Ringpull. "Some leader he turned out to be!"

"Bow your heads!" stormed Hercules. All the remaining corvids and squirrels slowly dipped their faces to the ground before Eliza.

What followed was a true moment of peace: the clouds stopped moving and the wind ceased, allowing warm sun rays to be absorbed into the fur and feathers of a community united. There was now hope that life could get back to a degree of normality - homes could be rebuilt, food sought freely again, and order slowly restored across the land.

Eliza broke the silence. "Your actions cannot go unanswered. The council will convene at the next full moon to discuss the role of magpies in Greenacres. If you fail to attend, this will be seen as another act of defiance and you will find me less charitable, should you make that decision." The Queen turned to her subjects and gazed upon the extent of their war wounds.

Baldwin nodded his head in approval. By joining in with the fight, Eliza had not only restored everyone's faith in raptors, but in the Council's right to govern.

"Go to your homes and rest. Spring has arrived, a new dawn has begun."

23: The Future of Warfare

Windar was alone in the testing bay, staring at a reinforced steel cage. One of the many hazard labels read 'risk of electric shock'. He stood in the middle of a hanger, which felt more like a futuristic shooting alley; large, ten foot screens occupied one end of the space; behind them, projectors would fire out beams of light, modelling war scenarios. The area was used to train soldiers and special-forces agents. It was just one of the many techno-enhanced rooms on the Greenacres base. But today it wasn't been used for training. Windar's latest creation was going to be put to the test in front of a live, military audience. Everything had to work, but the pressure was beginning to take its toll on him.

The professor was about to carefully unlock the cage when Flattery powered into the testing arena. "Windar, we go live in less than an hour – show me what you've got."

Windar floundered. "Well . . . I'm just making some last minute alterations. It only fully came online this morning and I still haven't completed diagnostics. Usually-"

"Listen, Professor," stated Flattery, uninterested, "the whole future of Greenacres is now dependent on the success of your creations. There's been rumours flying around that funding for your little pet hospital project is about to be cut by the new government, unless you can deliver measurable results." Flattery leaned closer. "But, if the military generals are impressed by the performance of your latest four-legged circus act, then we will all have guaranteed jobs for the next five years. Think about that - you don't want to go back to your tiny lab in Geneva, do you?"

The professor shook his head. Flattery's wry smile quickly disappeared when he noticed the cage shaking violently behind Windar. He walked round to inspect it. The door was ajar and the colonel could hear movement from within, like the scratching of claws. He bent forward and listened carefully. The movement stopped. Silence. Crouching down, Flattery looked through a small opening. Windar made half-hearted, cautionary gestures as Flattery slowly opened the door a little more, in order to peer inside.

Stillness.

Cackling and lunging in Flattery's direction, the colonel's only saving grace was a thick chain attached to the creature's legs, yanking it back inside its container. The colonel fell backwards to the floor and gasped. "My God, Windar - what have you created?"

Windar paused for a second. "I'm not quite sure." He helped Flattery off the ground. "I just need to run a few more tests before the generals arrive."

"Just make sure you get that thing under control, there's chatter going around that they want to test it tonight."

"But it's just a prototype!" exclaimed Windar.

"Spikez was a prototype until you used him, now he's patented technology, a commodity - an expendable asset. Whatever's in that box belongs to the British Military, remember that. Your country needs you, Windar." Flattery turned and exited the arena.

The professor sighed, brought his frail hands up to his face and removed his glasses. As he cleaned them, Windar began to doubt his own ability. What he needed was sleep, and lots of it, to clear his mind.

Replacing his spectacles, Windar picked up his remote control device and prepared for a simulation.

24: One for Sorrow

Windar's original creations were placed into special display cases and loaded onto a trolley. Spikez experienced mild tingles of excitement as he caught a glimpse of the long corridors with their vivid strips of yellow and red lights.

"Something big is going to happen," Trakz said, eagerly zooming back and forth.

"Are we going on another mission?" Spikez asked.

"Maybe. If we are, you might want to tidy your prickles up a bit - it looks like you've been thinking too much again."

"Prickles?"

Trakz watched Spikez' face go completely blank. "What did I say?"

"Hmm, I'm not sure. Where are we going again?"

Windar looked a little more relaxed as his creations were

wheeled into the hangar. He had five minutes to position them appropriately before the arrival of his military audience. There was a row of cylindrical pillars, each illuminated by rich, blue beams of light. He carefully opened each hatch to their cases, removed the cyborgs and placed them on their own plinth like trophies. Windar instructed the workers to give him a moment alone.

"Hey, Spikez, perhaps they want us to do some new tricks?" smirked Trakz. "Watch this!" Trakz span round and performed a wheelie across his podium.

Spikez watched his friend lose control and fall off the edge, tumbling to the floor. "Hey, that's pretty cool – you'll have to teach me that one!"

"Trakz!" exclaimed Windar, rushing to the rodent's aid. He collected the shaking bundle of fur up off the floor and carefully examined him, stroking the mouse's head and whispering reassuring words of comfort.

The hedgehog watched this unusual display of affection, secretly wishing it was him. Spikez grew frustrated; feelings of excitement were now mixed with those of anxiety and his body struggled to supress these emotions, shaking and breathing irregularly - it was difficult learning to feel again. But something else troubled him. He sensed a presence; something in the room watching them, and he could tell that it was angry. "Hey," Spikez called out. "There are four podiums."

The doors to the arena slid open and twelve men, including Flattery, Grievance and Goodwill, marched in. Before they took their seats, the group circled the three animal cyborgs, inspecting them in detail.

Several faces peered closely at Spikez, removing their glasses to inspect the seamless fusion of living tissue with robotics. He listened to their scoffs: I used to have one of these in my back garden until we had a bonfire, one remarked; what an amazing accomplishment, all that technology and they still can't cross the road properly, muttered another; you know times are hard when you see roadkill back on the menu!

Trakz wheeled excitedly around his podium, pulling off some wheelies to the delight of Grievance. PIG30N remained relatively still, blinking regularly at each face that peered at her; unbeknown to the generals, she was creating biometric profiles of their faces and uploading them to a secret database. She identified representatives from Europe, Russia, China, South East Asia and the Middle-East.

"Gentlemen, the demonstration is about to begin," Windar announced, beckoning the seniority to their front row seats. Flattery remained tense and gave Windar a questioning look. He replied with a reassuring nod.

"I'm so very honoured that you could all make it here today," gushed Windar. Flattery rolled his eyes. "Recent field tests have shown that models SPIK-3Z and PIG30N can operate successfully within live reconnaissance operations. Their greatest success, as I'm sure you're all aware, helped prevent a nuclear attack in London's Docklands, and it was all down to their adaptability and autonomy. Because of this, you asked me to create something more versatile and better equipped, to deal with the new challenges that face us." Windar directed his attention at Grievance. "An aggressor, able to act independently with stealth and the intelligence of the most advanced warfare systems."

There was a buzz within the room. The professor signalled to his assistants to prepare for the simulation. "So, it gives me great pleasure to reveal to you my latest prototype – model SPYM-A9." Windar took a few steps back and the central podium lit up. The steel cage containing his latest innovation slowly rotated and opened up.

Spikez and Trakz were transfixed – a new member of the team. General Grievance nervously stroked his moustache, for the future of his base now rested on the marketability of Windar's talents.

The main lights dimmed and a series of projector screens brought the background to life, emitting a ghostly grey hue.

There was silence.

A minute passed. The cage lid was now fully open but nothing stirred within it. They could only see blackness, as if it were hollow or even worse: empty. Flattery shuffled nervously in his seat, shaking his head and shooting torrid looks at Windar.

Windar's new creation was fully aware and had been carefully assessing its environment; it had counted the number of humans, calculated the dimensions of the room, considered threats and identified probable exit points. It was ready.

A shape, razor-sharp with flashes of white and a gleaming black beak, burst out into the arena, flying up to the highest ledge within the customised hangar. Spikez and PIG30N tracked the creation; its energy signatures were off the scale – it was as if Windar had created a living ball of energy. Some of the military chiefs removed their hats to get a better look. There was a distinct menace about the creature. It had a long, oily blue tail which it swayed rhythmically from side to side as it studied its audience's reaction.

"Sequence bravo-alpha zero," commanded Windar. The creature turned and swooped down towards the fourth podium, where it landed next to Spikez and into the light, coating it in an iridescent haze. It was now clear to everyone that Windar had used the carcass of a magpie to house his latest bundle of military technology. But this was no ordinary magpie shell; this was the reconstructed remains of Big Mag!

There was an uncomfortable silence. The military chiefs didn't speak. Even Spikez and PIG30N didn't know how to react.

Trakz decided to give it a go. "Welcome," he said, his arms extended.

SPYM-A9 turned towards them. They all jumped as they caught sight of his crimson eyes, shrouded beneath a tinted visor. He gauged them all, his head ticking back and forth as he did so.

In the audience, a heavy man with a round face and thin strips of hair - which looked like they had been glued to his pink scalp – raised his hand. "Excuse me, Professor Windar, sir - General Commodore, US army, sir - can I ask you how many units of each you've created, sir?"

"Well, for the time being all my creations are unique prototypes."

"Yes, but when America invested interest into the scheme, we were under the impression that a whole fleet of these drones could be readily assembled, sir."

"My creations have complex neural networks that continue to learn and develop. Add to this that all their mission data and artificial intelligence patterns can be synchronised and stored into a computer system, you will – in time - have the potential to create a whole swarm of cyborgs with preloaded software ready to be deployed."

"But surely you need them to go on missions to retrieve this type of data?" the general asked.

Colonel Flattery interjected. "If I may, General, we intend on testing the prototype this evening. Hopefully you'll all witness how much you can achieve with just one of these advanced drones."

Windar looked apprehensive, 'testing this evening?'.

The arm came back down but then shot back up again. "Oh, just one more thing Professor Windar, sir - can you do something about the name, sir?"

The professor was taken aback by the question, but General Commodore's comments were seconded by other snuffs and snorts from the elite audience. SPYM-A9, or spymag, wasn't as catchy as Spikez. Flattery nodded in agreement; when it came to designing the creations, Windar was a genius, but when it came to naming them his creativity ceased. "Er, are there any suggestions for an alternative?" the professor asked.

A flurry of well decorated arms shot up. "What about Magattack!" joked one of the generals, unimpressed by what he'd seen. A couple of jeers erupted from behind; another general called out, "Spending millions of pounds reviving dead animals is madness!"

Russia's General Punchemin calmly waited for the murmurs to cease. "Professor, in my country we have invested billions of roubles in state of the art drones. Why, then, should we look at your designs if we already have an army of deadly machines? Perhaps you are offering an incentive, like free pet insurance?"

The generals roared with laughter.

Grievance stood up, dwarfing all of the other generals. They quickly calmed themselves and looked attentively back towards their host. He was directly responsible for overseeing Project Carrion and keen to make sure that the invited panel of guests had faith in Windar's devices. "Perhaps if we let the professor give us a demonstration of SPY ... his latest specimen, then we can discuss names later." Grievance turned towards Windar, who acknowledged his icy stare.

"Yes, of course." Windar tapped a button on his localised remote and a battlefield scenario appeared on the four large projection screens. "Before we begin, I'd like to address some of your points. Drones will always have a place in modern warfare and surveillance, but they are still detectable by the enemy and often require human intervention. My inventions are smaller, adaptable and can think autonomously. They can access inhospitable terrains and survive independently for months, if not years, without the need for refuelling – there is even the possibility of these cyborgs interacting with and controlling similar types of species, thanks to advancements in technology. Now, will you all please fasten your seatbelts."

The generals clipped themselves into their seats and put on their 3D glasses. Two large fans started up at either end of the hangar and currents of air rippled through the auditorium. The seats elevated from the ground and the lights dimmed even more. SPYM-A9 flew towards the centre of a large spherical platform, lit by harsh white spotlights, and awaited instructions.

"This facility is where we train some of our best soldiers, a 4-D war simulator. Using satellite imagery and existing data, we can generate war scenarios and identify potential hazards before troops are deployed to some of the most inhospitable terrains in the world." As Windar spoke these words, two of his technical assistants attached targeting devices to each of SPYM-A9's wings. "This prototype has a range of weaponised add-ons that can be used against enemies on the ground or in the air. He also has the ability to penetrate areas that existing spy drones or men on the ground cannot get to, using the latest stealth technology. These are truly remarkable advancements."

A 3D image of SPYM-A9 appeared on the screens – all the generals raised their eyebrows. "The primary weapon is state of the art, the collaboration between UK and US scientists – a particle accelerator capable of firing controlled energy blasts, heat and electro-lasers. But best of all, he doesn't need to return to base to be rearmed, as you're about to see in this little simulation we have prepared for you."

The auditorium lights switched off and the training sequence began. A combat scene appeared on the screen and SPYM-A9 activated into attack mode. He spread his wings and used the upthrust created by the hangar's fans to levitate. The images showed the beginnings of an air assault, SPYM-A9 approaching an enemy base somewhere in a rugged, woodland environment. He was quick, hovering like a Harrier jet, lunging sideways and picking off enemy targets that would appear on screen: watch towers, mobile satellites, and armoured jeeps. He accelerated towards the base, swift to move and angle his body to avoid any cross-fire.

The generals sat with their glasses on, ducking and smiling as they became immersed in the simulation, watching an ordinary magpie converted into the latest advancement in the war on ter- ror. Expressions of doubt slowly transformed into those of awe as they watched the bird tactically race through the simulated environment, killing hostiles. It was a very proud moment for Grievance, his moustache saluted Windar.

The fans continued to blast cold air throughout the hangar, giving the impression of speed, and the sounds of explosions and soldiers screaming shot out from several speakers. Spikez remained fixed to his podium, watching the magpie fire with deadly accuracy, always finding his target.

The display finished with a fantastic finale - SPYM-A9 pen- etrating a fortified clearing and destroying a Russian KV-1 tank. General Punchemin sneered whilst the other generals clapped. "Splendid!" they exclaimed.

General Commodore's voice thundered: "What an awesome display of power!"

SPYM-A9 was disconnected from the simulation and returned back to the podium, where he perched motionless.

"Well, I hope that has cleared up any doubts you may have had about..." Windar looked towards the audience, anticipating a volley of questions and comments. They were silent. "Did you have any more thoughts about the name?"

A torrent of stiff arms shot into the air: "I like Magitech," was one general's response, which was quickly dismissed; "How about MAG-nesium?" the Swedish General suggested, met with a wall of silence; Commander Jobs, from the Canadian Army, spoke next, "What about the iMag?"

There were frowns, fallouts and laughs, followed by pained silences as the generals bickered amongst themselves. Windar looked bemused and General Grievance shook his head.

"Oh, I got a great one," chortled General Commodore, "what about Magatron?"

The hands all went down. Even Flattery, who was an infectious pessimist, nodded at the name, for it retained some identity about the creature it once was, but also had a marketable chill to sell at weapons exhibitions.

"Magatron it is!" affirmed General Grievance. "We will conduct a live field test tonight, followed by drinks in The Officer's Mess." A cheer erupted from the excitable crowd. Grievance nodded at Windar in appreciation. "Now, shall we break for tea and biscuits and discuss ways to take Project Carrion forward?"

Flattery unbelted himself and led the military commanders

out of the training hangar. Windar watched as the last of the generals, a stout Chinese man with wispy grey eyebrows, was ushered out by the colonel, who turned and also gave the professor a rare nod of approval.

The hangar was a dark and silent place once more. Spikez and Trakz watched Windar humming to himself as he paced around in circles like some caged animal.

"I worry about him, sometimes," said Trakz.

"The last time he looked like that, we all went out on an assignment," said Spikez.

"Great, that will give us a chance to get to know the new member of our team." Trakz successfully made a wheelie across his podium towards Magatron. "Hey, nice display back there. So, how's it going?"

Magatron remained motionless, not even acknowledging the mouse's fervent gestures.

"I'll be your rodent host here at the Windar laboratory, you let me know if I can get you anything?" Trakz waited but received no response, not even the flick of a feather. He looked back over at Spikez and shrugged his tiny shoulders. "Having memory problems, huh?" Still, Magatron didn't react. "Well, don't worry, it'll all come back in time." Trakz said, zipping back to his plinth.

"What did he say?" Spikez whispered.

"Oh, nothing much, I think he's a bit shy. Don't worry, he'll come round eventually."

"Eventually . . ." replied Magatron, motionless.

25: Morag's Whispers

It was a fine spring day. Animals and birds had been celebrating their new found freedom, singing and foraging for food in the forest. Collectively they had gathered much needed supplies, no longer restricted by the curfew imposed under magpie rule – some even reclaimed their homes.

As temperatures rose, insects and flies began to emerge and Mira was quick to gather as many as possible to feed Joy, who grew strong. Baldwin spent the day visiting the creatures who had fought in the great battle, lifting morale and ensuring that the injured were well tended to. The badger also offered his condolences to those who had lost loved ones.

Deep in the darkest depths of the forest, Ringpull was perched in a state of aggravation. He had two moons left until he would be brought before the Animal Council. His body was still littered with wounds from two battles, the most painful were those inflicted by his own kind.   Hood had conveniently stepped into his place as leader, forcefully ripping the war emblem from around his neck and banishing him from the group, but not before a good pecking. All the magpies had abandoned Ringpull.

The magpie had few cousins to turn to; the crows, rooks and jackdaws had segregated themselves away from his kind, and the Jays had remained conscientious objectors, distancing themselves from the corvids completely. But there was one that he believed he could turn to . . . maybe?

Greenacres Forest was divided by the River Charon, which coiled its way out to the cold waters of the North Sea. Across the river, the Black Woods had a ghostly and mysterious feel to them; rocks glistened with purple and red moss, toadstools and Jurassic looking varieties of fungi attached themselves to the bases of ancient trees, and there were numerous tiny caverns buried beneath the soggy undergrowth.

It was to here that Ringpull pledged to make his long and painful journey. The magpie's wing was badly damaged, and he had to hop most of his way there. He stood by the water's edge, staring at the ripples of his reflection, knowing there was a chance that he might not make it across.

'What do I have to lose?' he said to himself. Ringpull stepped backwards and took a run up, launching himself into the air. He thrashed his wings purposefully, wincing as he felt the sinews of his muscles tearing. The young magpie had travelled nearly halfway across the river when he felt the air chill, stifling his breath. He suddenly began to plummet. The sounds of a forest in bloom ceased, replaced by those of raging waters, crashing beneath him. Jagged rocks pointed angrily at Ringpull as he approached the other side of the river bank, narrowly missing them as he flapped with all his might to stay airborne.

Ringpull hit the ground, tumbling into a bed of old leaves. There was an eerie silence. He quickly got to his feet and looked around. A gentle mist infused the damp air as Ringpull bobbed nervously across the ground, regaining his breath. Tiny rays of sunshine fell upon old wood engravings at the base of a dead tree stump; it showed winged creatures with sharp and ominous shapes, but they were mostly enveloped in slime and hard to make out; patches of bark were also torn away completely from the tree and laid out in a Z shape.

The magpie stopped at the foot of an ancient willow tree and surveyed the surroundings. He had heard about this place from his ancestors as a fledgling, the Crying Willow Tree. Supposedly it was the dwelling place of Morag, the ancient raven witch who could foretell the future. Ringpull sidestepped around the base of the tree, looking for evidence of her presence, for any indication of life. There was nothing except the whispers of the leaves. 'Perhaps it's just a myth after all,' he said to himself.

Moments later, he turned to leave when a haggard voice cawed out to him. "The fall-en Ring-pull seeketh a friend?"

Ringpull flapped anxiously. "Who's there?"

"The fall-en Ring-pull desires knowledge?" continued the voice, now a murmur in the trees.

Ringpull grew angry and chattered brazenly. "Chatak-atak-atak! Speak more and identify yourself . . . Morag?"

"Yeeeeessssss . . ." A sudden shift of wind rustled the branches of the mighty tree. Ringpull plumped up what was left of his neck feathers and cracked his tail like a whip. From deep within the shadows he witnessed a black shape slowly emerge from the rotting vegetation, pushing upwards like a bulb starved of light, shaking away the brittle hummus. The outline of the figure was not sharp and defined like that of a raven; it was disfigured and bushy, with badly ruffled feathers and crumbling skin.

Morag shuffled into the open, shaking off splinters of bark. Magnetic tape from an old audio cassette was tangled tightly in a bundle on her head, whilst small plastic beads and rubber bands had been wrapped around her neck and wings, as if someone had deliberately prevented her from flying.

She hobbled in Ringpull's direction, her crackly lungs exhaling stale air. The magpie's limbs began to shiver and shake with each step closer she took.

"The fall-en Ring-pull doth seek Morrrr-ag?"

Ringpull could not respond. Only his eyeballs moved, watching her circle him as she inspected his war wounds. He could smell her, the scent of decay and rotting stench of death.

Satisfied that Ringpull posed no danger, Morag tapped him with her good wing and he stumbled forward. "The fallen Ringpull hath found Morag. Speak, what doth he require?"

The magpie remained wary, surveying his surroundings. "I don't know, my Dark Queen, I . . . I 'ave lost everything."

"Cahhh! Ringpull seeketh guidance . . ."

"In two moons I must perch before the Animal Council."

Morag hissed at the word 'council' and her eyes blazed yellow. "There is no real council anymore without Morag!" She pitched forward and stroked his beak. "You need not fear, me nor them, for a new leader cometh."

"No, there's nobody else. My fellow magpies 'ave deserted me, and Hood does not have the guts to mount another attack against the raptors – he just wants to lead. Big Mag was the only one who could 'ave propelled us to glory."

"Big Mag, you say?" Morag scratched for worms amongst the dead leaves with her good claw. "Big-Mag-not-dead."

"Morag, I was there! I saw him fall to the ground by the farmer's thunder stick. I looks into his eyes, and I sees it for myself."

"Yes, yes he is gone the way you remember him, but he still lives," Morag hobbled over to a clearing and looked up at the darkening sky. "The spirit of Big Mag has not passed over. You must seek him."

"This is madness!" Ringpull bounded past her, towards the edge of the River. "I don't know why I 'as come here."

"How dare Ringpull defy the power of Morag!" She clapped her good wing against the ground and a gust of icy wind snapped through the clearing, turning forest debris into a violent eddy. Ringpull turned to face her, fearful. "There is nothing across that river . . . nothing . . . except death!" she cursed. "You must stay here and wait for his return - he will need you to help him remember. He will give you back your inner strength. Ssstayyyy!" Morag pointed at a shallow clay ledge by the river bank.

Ringpull wanted to flee, but Morag's mystic words were compelling enough. He knew he would drown if he tried to leave, he also knew that Greenacres held no future for him. In the darkest pit of his soul, Ringpull longed for power again, for the feeling of unchallenged authority.

She had promised him that it would return.

26: The Fearful Four

Windar wheeled his cyborgs back into the laboratory. Waiting for the professor, face up on his desk, was a brown manila envelope with the words 'top secret' stamped in red ink. His wiry hands carefully opened it and pulled out a series of official documents and a DVD.

The professor scoured through the pack and anxiously checked his watch; it seemed some of the military chiefs still remained sceptical and wanted to 'watch' a live field test of Magatron in action that very evening – no computerised, gimmicky simulations would suffice.

After unloading his creations onto their customised workbench, Windar calibrated his electronic whiteboard.

"Time to wire up!" said Trakz, attaching cables into the respective slots on Spikez, PIG30N and – nervously - to Magatron, who didn't flinch when he was connected to Windar's interface system.

The screen flashed white and a series of military protocols appeared. Windar began. "Tonight the military chiefs will be watching as you are put into action once more. The target is this man." A 3D image of a stocky, middle-aged man with a knuckled nose appeared. "This is Michael Ryan, an international arms dealer. He has been trading in stolen British weapons with terrorists throughout Asia. Intelligence reports confirm that he has returned to England to conclude business dealings with European mafia bosses and secure more stolen arms." Windar clicked his remote to reveal maps and more images of suspects. "You will be assisting MI6 in this operation. Your primary objective is to record the outcome of the meeting and disable his communications and transport options, allowing human operatives to apprehend the main suspect. There is an undercover MI6 agent working within Ryan's team."

A picture of a woman flashed up on the screen. Windar was struck by her beauty; Spikez and the team just saw a female version of Windar with more hair and fatter lips. "I'm uploading the maps and data to your memory now." He clicked a switch and motioned over to the kitchenette, preparing himself a triple espresso.

Spikez looked over at Trakz as the data was uploaded. "What did he say?"

"Beats me, he always talks at me as if I understand him. The download will make more sense.

"I think there's something wrong with him."

Trakz spun round. "He's worried."

"About what?"

The mouse flashed his eyes at Magatron. The magpie remained static as light bounced off his blue plumage, creating the impression that he was glowing from within. "Hey Magatron, how are you feeling about the mission tonight?" Magatron did not respond. "See what I mean?"

Spikez also felt uneasy about the new member of the team; he studied him as the mission protocols were copied onto his memory - in the back of his mind, the hedgehog felt that they were somehow interconnected.

27: Baldwin's Unrest

The night was a menace, stealing the crisp blue skies of a promised spring and switching them with black thunder clouds. Animals that had been enjoying warmth and freedom only hours earlier found shelter and prepared for the great storm. Queen Eliza and the raptors sat high in the protection of rich pine needles as the tepid breeze was replaced by a biting easterly chill.

Baldwin rested his head on his paws near the opening of his den. Behind him a gathering of friends, old and new, settled down to rest. "Come, Baldwin, join us", they beckoned. "Tell us one of the many stories about your journeys into the man cities and crusades beyond the black rivers."

The badger resisted, he was troubled.

"You must rejoice, dear Baldwin," called the young rabbit messenger. "Come and feast with us, our hero of the hour."

"I'm no hero," he replied, solemnly. "The battle was fought by all who sought peace for the future of our lands and that of our young. I'm a patriot, nothing more, nothing less."

Deacon dipped over towards him. "Baldwin, old friend, don't suppress your value amongst fellow creatures. You inspire them, like you have so many others."

"Forgive me, Deacon, but I feel that this rainstorm will bring pain and misery upon the land."

"'Tis but a storm, Baldwin. Greenacres has many each year without incident. Come, rest and celebrate with us."

"I'm sorry, it's a habit of mine. My instincts have been good to me over the years and I have learnt to trust them like a good friend."

"And I, too, am a good friend. Sit with us, life at Greenacres will prevail as it always does."

Baldwin turned to him, his grey whiskers faintly shimmering in the twilight. With a smile he nodded and joined the group, who were gathered in a circle ready to listen to one of his anecdotes.

"Now, did I ever tell you about the time I came face to face with a wolf?"

Ringpull awoke in a daze. The trees and shrubs moved vigorously back and forth as a tumultuous wind ripped through the clearing. He had slept for most of the day, nurtured by Morag on a diet of nutritious bugs and wild mushrooms. She had promised him strength; he stretched out his wings and examined them, feeling less discomfort than before.

Cautiously, the magpie ventured out in to the open where he saw Morag chanting to the skies. Giant black clouds blotted out the moon and the flow of the river increased in speed. He marvelled as she recited spells over and over again, summoning a greater power.

Windar oversaw the loading of his team into their customised van. Flattery stood beside him, monitoring how Windar managed the creatures.

"You say that these puppets can be controlled from anywhere in the country with a valid GPS signal?" Flattery asked.

"That's right," Windar replied.

"Good, then you will run the operation from here."

"But-"

"No buts, Windar. General Grievance's orders, he's hosting the military chiefs with a special dinner. You'll be there to provide the entertainment with a live video feed of the operation."

"But what if something were to go wrong?"
"That's the whole point of the test, Windar. If something does go wrong on the ground, they want to know that it can be fixed remotely without danger to human life. You claim that they're completely self-sufficient – they want to test this claim." Flattery moved closer. "But nothing's going to go wrong, is it? Remember, professor, you're as much an asset to the operation as those toys in that van, and until we've secured a large enough order for a whole army of cyborgs, then you will remain at Greenacres as

the salesman with all the answers."

Windar found it hard to express his dissatisfaction at the decision; he found it hard to express anything to Flattery. But he had worked too hard to risk losing a lifetime's work, decades of research wiped out because of refusal to follow orders, and Grievance was not a man to upset.

The driver of the van signalled at Windar that he was ready to leave. Flattery gave the thumbs up to the driver and led Windar back towards the dining hall, where a team of technicians were preparing his mobile control room.

Inside the van, Spikez' senses were heightened, he could feel the storm brewing outside and his natural body was producing adrenaline. Trakz also buzzed with excitement - two outings in one day!

Magatron remained still. Pensive.

PIG30N slept.

28: Operation Fat Goose

The town of Grayford had few restaurants: a tame looking Indian called the Weeping Tiger, and a well-hidden Chinese restaurant called the Peeking Duck. So when three Michelin-starred chef Gaston Blumenstuhl bought an old, grade II listed pub, it was only fitting that he kept the animal theme going. The Fat Goose was a posh eatery with a three month waiting list and it was always packed with celebrity diners, chubby food critics or people with money to burn.

Michael Ryan arrived with his business associates Tamara Dahab and Rose Cheng, his Chinese girlfriend who also doubled as his bodyguard. He had reserved the private dining room where his three guests waited patiently: a chipper Englishman and two tall, fair haired European men with large teeth. Both parties carried silver attaché cases and were in radio contact with armed drivers, who were parked in their respective getaway vehicles outside the restaurant, eating burgers.

The van pulled into a side alley, one hundred and twenty-three yards behind The Fat Goose. The cyborgs listened as the driver switched off the engine and exited towards the rear.

"I'll be in contact, just like last time," assured Trakz, as the doors were pulled open to reveal orange streetlights whimpering against black storm clouds. There was a grumble of thunder in the distance. "Nice night!"

Windar radioed in for the birds to be removed from the van first and released from their cages. As the driver did so, PIG30N and Magatron burst into life, rapidly ascending to the highest phone masts they could find, synchronising with base and transmitting data.

The military chiefs looked up from their sautéd foie-gras as Windar's monitor flickered on. The live images were being projected onto a larger screen for all to see in the officer's dining hall. The professor had not touched his red wine, or his melon starter; the whole situation made him nauseous, and angry that his work was seen as nothing more than in-meal entertainment as he ran some system diagnostics whilst cutlery tapped against the porcelain plates.

In another van close to the restaurant, a team of MI6 special agents were also receiving the images. The lead agent, Woods, had been briefed that the latest spy-drone technology was being trialled in the operation, but did not know that they were using cyborgs – it was part of the test.

Spikez began his second mission, leaping from his cage and

cannon-balling towards the rear courtyard of the restaurant. Using maps of the area and footage from PIG30N and Magatron, he timed his ascent up the wall so that no-one could see him.

"We need to get audio and visual inside that restaurant," instructed agent Woods.

"You heard the man," relayed Trakz on the intercom. "Your directives are to infiltrate the restaurant so that they can make some arrests. No snacking!" he added, chomping on a protein stick.

Spikez landed effortlessly in the courtyard, just outside the kitchen door where he could hear the chef barking orders at his staff. He directed his attention at the first floor of the building to identify a suitable entry point. PIG30N landed on the guttering of the building opposite. From here she was able to highlight a section of window linked to the brasserie's lavatory. This was where Spikez would break in.

Meanwhile, a young waitress brought Ryan and his associates their main course: stuffed wood pigeon. He would not discuss business or exchange information and money until he had eaten a good meal, and until then the only thing traded at the table were compliments about the food.

The military chiefs brushed the crumbs off their thick, grey moustaches, focusing their conversation from the round of golf they had enjoyed earlier to the operation in hand. Flattery wiped his brow; as Windar's manager, his job was as much on the line as the professor's, despite his cordial relationship with Grievance.

Windar's screen displayed the vital signs of all his creations

– he could monitor stress levels, heart rate, chemical imbalances and power consumption; and most importantly whether or not they were in AI mode – full autonomy.

"Get up that wall and use your laser to cut a hole in the toilet window," commanded Trakz. Spikez accessed his utility belt and fired a grapple hook, piercing the wooden window frame. The cable then acted as a pulley between the ground and the target as he wound himself upwards.

PIG30N flew to the window ledge outside the dining room and covertly watched. Even though the curtains were partly drawn, her unique vision and thermograph allowed her to capture images with exceptional clarity.

Agent Woods sat up in his seat, studying the visuals and sound in their control van. "Okay, we're in business." The rest of his team checked their screens and listened. "Audio's a little muffled, we need to get a microphone inside."

Spikez pushed his snout against the window pane and saw that the toilet was empty. He removed a laser cutting device, no bigger than a cigarette lighter, and held it steady between his claws as a fine green beam cut a perfect hole, big enough for him to fit through.

"Congratulations, your first circle," commented Trakz.

"Do you ever stop talking?" asked Spikez, gently removing the glass and placing it aside.

"Only when I'm nervous. Aren't you nervous?"

Spikez squeezed his spiky bulk through the opening and shimmied along the window sill. "Quiet a second, I think someone's coming." Spikez dropped down to the base of the toilet pan and froze.

Windar watched the whole thing, his eyes darting back and forth between two screens. The mood was sombre amongst the generals as they waited. Barely a fork was raised. Then the dessert trolleys arrived.

The tallest of the European men entered the lavatory. Spikez had few places to hide, quickly retracting into a ball next to the toilet brush. What followed was broadcast via Spikez' live audio feed to the team of crack operatives seated only hundreds of metres away. Agent Woods grimaced as Ryan's client merrily hummed Prokofiev's Romeo and Juliet to himself, accompanied by an orchestra of plops. "Okay, the audio's pretty clear now – can we turn it down a little?"

The man stood and flushed the pan. Washing his hands, he noticed the perfectly cut hole in the window. He peered through it, into the courtyard below, but saw nothing out of the ordinary. He was just glad it was there to provide some ventilation. Satisfied, he returned to the table.

"That was close," remarked Trakz.

Spikez uncoiled himself and crept towards the door leading to the hallway. He heard the waiters below, walking upstairs to clear the table of bones and top up glasses with expensive wine. "Okay, I'm in – giving you visuals now."

The generals whispered to one another, some of the sceptics were warming to the idea of using cyborgs to replace military drones. There was a general anticipation of excitement as Spikez moved closer to the target.

Michael Ryan cleared his throat and turned to his business associates. Years of living in Asia did little to taint his coarse Irish accent. "Gentlemen, let's talk business."

Klaus, the sternest looking European, sat forward and threw his napkin to the floor. "Two million pounds. That was the agreed figure."

Ryan scoffed, curling his face up into a ball. "Get real, gents. My client in China's never paid more than one-point-eight million pounds for a shipment of this kind – can ya explain to me where this extra two hundred grand is coming from?"

As the parties became engrossed in discussion, Spikez spun himself neatly towards the dining table, covering several feet within seconds, and uncoiled himself at the base of a wooden leg. He removed a small microphone from his belt and secured it to the table. Ryan now had a wider audience for confession.

"Weapons are getting harder to come by, what with budgets being cut. People ask more questions if weapons are . . . misplaced," Klaus said.

Ryan shot an irritable look at the undercover agent, Dahab. "We had a deal, the same as every other deal we've ever made for the past three years: you get me my weapons, stick 'em on a boat in Liverpool and ship 'em to Egypt where my little Pharaoh fellas take care of the rest. All for the fantastic price of just one point eight million pounds – VAT free, hassle free, deal done, nothin' more ta say."

"Mr Ryan, you forget so easily what your client requested in his last order. The two prototype missile launchers were very difficult to come by. People got hurt."

"Collateral damage!" snapped Ryan.

"Well, that's how it was and there is only one price that we are looking for: two million pounds."

Ryan looked down at the empty place mat whilst one of his hairy hands twiddled a silver spoon across the tablecloth. A burst of air erupted from his nose. "One-point-nine million!"

"It seems we are wasting our time," Klaus said, looking at his straight faced acquaintances. He stood to leave the table and picked up his suitcase. "Thank you for a wonderful meal, the scallops were exceptional."

"Sit-down!" he demanded, visibly agitated. "Negotiations haven't finished."

"The price is two million, there's nothing to negotiate."

"Fine," Ryan flicked a look at Cheng and instructed her to load the laptop. "We'll wire the money direct to your account. I trust your offshore bank details remain the same?"

Woods' team had enough evidence to take up positions and launch an assault. He signalled his men: "We need to neutralise the getaway cars without causing disruption."

Windar responded via his radio. "Leave that to me." With some quick typing on his keyboard and negotiations with his joystick, Windar took control of Magatron. Using the satellite data available to him, Windar identified the two targets: a large black Ford saloon car and a red BMW. "Generals, you're about to see your new weapon in action."

Magatron, who had remained idle until now, was perched on top of a disused street lamp, cloaked in darkness. He rapidly responded to the professor's commands, gliding over The Fat Goose towards the two cars.

Both drivers sat with their windows down; one was texting friends whilst the other listened to Jazz. Magatron swooped, targeted his electro-laser, and fired at both vehicles. The cars shook momentarily, hit by an invisible force; the electrics died, silently and without warning; smooth saxophone melodies were hushed as the radio crackled, and both drivers were plunged into darkness. They reacted instinctively by turning the key, trying to start the engine, but it was to no avail. Even their phones were frazzled.

Then it dawned on them - they were under attack.

Ryan's driver emerged from his car first and raced towards the restaurant, only to be rugby tackled by two armed officers who held him to the floor. Klaus' driver saw this, hastily exited his vehicle and tried to hi-jack the first car he saw, waving his gun around threateningly. As a car skidded to a halt he was clipped across his back by more officers, gagged and speedily loaded into the back of an unmarked van.

"So far so good," exclaimed Grievance, chomping on his last morsels of walnut and grapes. Windar watched the generals' faces reflected in his monitor, moving closer to study him operating the devices.

Codes and passwords were being busily exchanged in the restaurant, along with fingerprint and retinal scans. PIG30N recorded everything. Satisfied that the money had been safely transferred, Klaus gave Ryan the password for an encrypted USB file. "This will give you the freight container details and mobile numbers of the contacts carrying the goods." He stood up and extended his hand.

Ryan poured himself some wine instead.

Klaus shrugged his shoulders and exited the room, the two other Europeans trailing behind him. They left a very disgruntled Ryan to reflect on the deal as he drank some Muscat. "Well that wasn't great!" he fumed, turning on Dahab. "Your intel has just cost me two hundred grand!"

"I'm sorry Mr Ryan, I don't know why-"

Ryan swung his arm forcefully, smashing her across the face with the back of his hand. She yelped and fell off her chair to the floor. He then ordered Rose to pack the hardware away. "It's time we got to the airport."

Dahab looked up from the floor towards Ryan, but was distracted by what she saw under the table. There, poised on its hind legs like a gunslinger, was a hedgehog.

Spikez took a biometric scan of her face.

```
Confirm id - Agent Dahab . . .
Directive: 'protect at all costs.'
```

Before Dahab could react she was hoisted from the floor by Ryan and shoved against a wall. He held her close to his face; his breath was saturated by blackcurrant tones of heavy wine and the odour of gamey flesh. "If you let me down again," he said,

"I'll bury you with all my other ex-employees."

Klaus and his men reached the main entrance of the restaurant. They were about to step into the heavy rain but stopped. Their driver, who they could always rely upon, was not in his vehicle. "Where has he got to?" Klaus muttered. He nervously scanned the road and pulled out his phone to call his driver. No signal. Magatron had scrambled all communications. Then, in the corner of his eye, the European mafia boss noticed an agent duck his head behind a car. "We've been set up!" he cried. "Head back upstairs, we'll find another way out."

The agents commenced their raid on the restaurant. Four burly, armed MI6 operatives burst through the front door and followed Klaus and his men up the stairway. A waitress screamed out.

Ryan heard the commotion and was surprised to see Klaus and his men return. "Come to give me some change, gents?"

"You set us up!" Klaus yelled. "The place is surrounded by cops."

Cheng pulled out her phone. It was dead, just like all other comms devices. "Signals are all jammed," she said, opening the window. PIG30N flew for cover, she had recorded enough evidence to win them all lengthy jail sentences.

Ryan looked suspiciously at Dahab, reading her facial expression. "This is this your doing, isn't it?" He reached into his jacket and removed a gun, pointing it at Dahab's head.

Spikez did not hesitate to react. He rolled out from under the table and, with a lightning flick of his spines, fired a tranquilising dart at Ryan's bottom. Before he could even acknowledge being stung in the rear, his body slumped to the floor in an instant.

Cheng looked over in disbelief; she hadn't seen Spikez strike but she cared not to hang around and ask questions. Cradling the laptop, she leapt through the window down to the courtyard below.

Trakz radioed in. "Nice work, buddy, but before you start wooing your new lady friend, I think you should focus on retrieving that laptop!"

Klaus and his men went to follow Cheng out of the window, but as they weighed up the possibility of making it safely without snapping their legs in two, agents charged through the door and restrained them all. Dahab, still undercover, was also forced to the floor. Amidst the commotion she searched for traces of the hedgehog on the carpet, but Spikez was already gone.

PIG30N followed Cheng as she sprinted down a back alley, away from the chaos. The pigeon was recording the events for the generals back at base, who watched events unfold on the big screen. An agent managed to intercept Cheng but was aggressively countered by her martial arts skills. The generals winced as the agent writhed from a sharp kick in the groin. The target had a clear run again.

Having abseiled down the restaurant walls, Spikez joined the pursuit on foot "Where's she heading?"

"She's already two hundred metres due south, and moving fast. Better hurry it up a little."

Cheng emerged onto a dimly lit back road. She saw her car,

raced towards it and quickly got in, tossing the laptop onto the passenger seat.

Seconds later, Spikez emerged from the path to see the vehicle start and accelerate away from him. Unable to disable the vehicle, he flicked forward, firing a tracking spike from his shoulders, which embedded itself neatly into the boot of the car as it roared into the night. He looked up to see PIG30N in pursuit, only to be overtaken by the distinctive shape of Magatron.

"Good effort Spikez, but it's time to let the rookie have a shot." Trakz watched his screen as Magatron gathered speed.

Windar could smell his audience. Having eaten, the generals all sat around the professor and studied him, an orchestral conductor flicking his wrists from side to side and jerking his shoulders forward and backwards as he reacted to the events on his screen. Some were studying the equipment and assessing its ease of use, wondering if real soldiers could be controlled in the same way.

Cheng's car thundered through country lanes, hitting eighty miles an hour at times as it weaved in and out of sharp bends. She was two miles from joining a busy network of roads where she could escape detection amongst the evening masses. Magatron flew directly above her, silently aided by a dynamic thrust system. PIG30N followed behind him, her objective was now to document Magatron's ability to operate effectively in the field.

"Get that car!" ordered a voice. Windar looked nervously at Grievance who stood over him. "At whatever cost, Professor, it's time to see what Magatron can do." Windar fulfilled the general's wish with a single strike of a key.

Magatron's eyes flashed red.

```
Hostile AI mode: activated . . .
Target acquired - Objective: immobilise.
```

He accelerated ahead and charged his primary weapon.

"What's he doing?" one of the generals asked. "He's moving away from the target."

Grievance was also confused. "Windar, shouldn't he be turning around to immobilise the car?"

"General," Windar replied, wiping the condensation away from his glasses. "This is what you all wanted to see - I'm not in control anymore."

"Then who is?" a voice heckled.

"Magatron."

The wind blew wild and icy shards of rain peppered the land. Magatron hovered just a few meters above the ground on a long stretch of straight road, cloaked behind the cover of branches, waiting for Cheng's car to peer over the brow of the hill.

Cheng clicked the wipers on max as she eased out of the bend. The car's lights antagonised the blackness of the night, but even they could not spot Magatron fire. The headlights were the first part of the car to explode. Then the vehicle shook as the engine rattled to a halt, killing all the power. The dashboard blackened and the steering wheel locked. She struggled to keep control of the car as it hit the verge at seventy, desperately pumping the brake, but the vehicle had already begun its tumultuous spin into the unknown, toppling over an oily black ditch. Its metal shell was battered repeatedly by the unforgiving terrain until it lay stripped of life, consumed by its surroundings and tipped upside down against some bushes of bordering fields.

The rain cascaded down. Magatron perched on a tree branch as the crackle of thunder and lightning echoed in the background. He streamed the footage, as did PIG30N, to all parties involved in the operation.

Agent Woods, who had been debriefing Agent Dahab, gave a sigh of relief at the news. Dahab guessed that the hedgehog had been involved in some way to help neutralise the target.

Windar was given a rapturous applause by all of the generals, even Flattery gave a short clap in recognition of his success, although it was out of relief more than anything. Grievance stood beside the professor and addressed the audience. "I think we've just witnessed the evolution of warfare and a glimpse of Magatron's amazing potential. Professor, you've done another remarkable job." Grievance raised what was left of his port. "To Windar!"

The generals all raised their glasses. "To Windar!" they cried.

"Gentlemen, the next generation of drone warfare is here, in England – at the bar!" The generals applauded once more. Grievance tapped Windar's shoulder. "This is a good night to toast the success of Project Carrion. Windar, please join us in the Officers' Club."

"I'd love to - I just need to ensure the safe return of my team."

"Come, Windar, you said these machines can think independently."

"Yes, they can."

"So, surely they are able to make their way back to base unaided?"

"Well, yes – they are all programmed to know where home is."

"Then wrap up the operation here and now. That will fully complete the demonstration. Your other robots are already in the process of being loaded into transit as we speak. You can play with them in the morning when we have an official debrief."

Windar looked at all the eyes watching him. To refuse their offer would upset Grievance and Flattery and show a lack of confidence in the autonomy of his drones. The meal and demonstration was still very much a sales pitch – now the generals had questions and Windar was the man to close the deal. Someone handed him a gin and tonic and got him to his feet. "Cheers," Windar said, sheepishly.

29: The Prophecy unfolds

The storm was at its wildest. Sheet lighting ignited the sky in a kaleidoscope of yellow, red and white. Magatron watched as the police cars arrived, each one skidding to a halt. Rain sliced across the bonnets as officers leapt from their vehicle toward Cheng's battered car chassis.

Cheng was pulled out by two officers. Cuts and grazes covered her forearms and face where she had absorbed most of the impact. She was laid to the ground and covered with a foil blanket whilst they waited for the ambulance to arrive. Another officer withdrew the laptop from the wreckage. The operation was officially over.

Magatron received his instructions to return directly to base. For a moment, he had a flicker of a distant memory as he cross referenced an image of the base, with its wire fences and glowing lights, against GPS co-ordinates. The interference was momentary. Silently he pushed himself off the branch and dissolved into the night sky.

Spikez was secured in the van alongside PIG30N. Trakz hooked them both up to a computer where their data from that evening would be processed and archived. "Where's Magatron?" Spikez asked.

"He's making his way directly back to base, Windar will debrief us in the morning. It's a shame really, I was really looking forward to catching up with him – I felt we were really starting to connect."

The doors to the van closed and the engine started.

As he traversed his cage, Spikez felt symptoms of tiredness. He was achy, perhaps he was still growing? He studied his muscles, beneath the finely brushed hair of his arms; they continued to fuse to his robotic components and the neural networks of his brain adjusted and adapted to his behaviour. Spikez believed he was learning to feel again. Comforted by this thought, and the gentle hum of the engine, he drifted off into a deep slumber.

Magatron owned the night sky. No other birds challenged him as he glided towards Base. With perfect night vision he mapped the ground below him; the River Charon meandered through the valley, a slow and steady trail towards unchartered seas. Magatron's sensors detected increased electrical activity ahead of him. He adjusted his flight vectors and tilted to the left, but as he did so lightning struck him from above.

The force of the energy bolt disabled Magatron's electronics. He saw a wall of light followed by a blanket of static noise. For a nanosecond he was fully conscious - then blackness. Every part of him crackled with energy as he plunged out of the sky like a fallen star, hurtling towards the forest below in a ball of flickering electricity.

Ringpull awoke. A large clap of thunder shook the forest floor; even mighty oak trees trembled in the wake of such natural force. The magpie hopped in to the open and saw a meteor shooting over the woods. Curious, Ringpull hopped across to the river until he saw Morag's coarse outline, chanting by the water's edge as the storm continued to rage.

"The great leader has returned," she whispered. Her crooked body turned and she glared at Ringpull with burning yellow eyes. Ringpull flapped backwards, he could smell her breath: rotting wood and putrid carrion mixed with the earthy damp. "Go!" she strained, raising her good wing, "You must find him before they dooooo."

30: Reflection

Morning light pushed hard against the heavy black clouds that had stifled the night. Baldwin was seated by the edge of the forest. He watched the sunrise stain the sky red and listened to the birds communicating by song to see if everyone's nest had remained intact.

In the laboratory, Windar lay heavily sedated in his armchair. Around him lay a number of empty port glasses and plates littered with cheese crumbs. Trakz watched from his cage, his nose gyrating, salivating at the prospect of tasting such riches once more. The mouse also noted that Magatron had not returned. Despite his reservations about the magpie, Trakz activated the alert signal which started Windar's computer and woke the rest of the team.

Windar shuffled. His head bobbed, causing a break in his snoring. Then he sat upright, and fell out of his chair. His hands gripped the table as he pulled himself up, where he proceeded to fumble around for his spectacles.

"Is he sick?" Spikez asked.

"He will be when he realises what's happened," commented Trakz.

Windar swayed to one side as he focused on the screen and studied the alarm message in double vision – never in his life had he drunk so much. An exclamation mark buzzed inside a flashing red triangle next to an icon of Magatron.

The professor did a double take between his screen and Magatron's cage; despite his genius, the neurons of his brain were misfiring and he couldn't seem to make the connection, and then he checked his watch and a stark realisation of what had happened hit him, immediately sobering him up - one of his cyborgs was missing!

In the thick of the forest, by a pool of stagnant water, a wing flapped and then froze. It attracted the attention of a young deer that had been drinking a few metres ahead where the river water ran clear. At the same time, a blanket of grey mist stopped floating, as if it also wanted to identify this strange phenomenon.

Silently, the fawn crept towards the bed of reeds where rustling systematically started and stopped. She kept checking over her shoulder, just in case someone was watching. Foolishly she ignored any of her father's wisdom as she peered over the reeds.

One more step. She could hear buzzing, like that of a small motor. Another. The fawn paused, she could now smell burning. A step more. The fawn saw a body, tangled in reeds. Is it dead? A burst of white light and compressed gas exploded from it, causing the fawn to leap so high in the air, that when her legs finally found the ground again they were galloping at full speed. As she raced to safety, the young deer considered that whatever lay there, breathing fire, was not of the forest.

The creature was Magatron, or what remained of him. Inside his shell, the computer was desperately trying to signal for help but the transmitter had been permanently damaged. At the same time, unaware of its environment, Magatron's core processor was trying to reboot the jet propulsion system – but the result of this process did nothing but repeatedly singe a small patch of reeds and generate plumes of steam and smoke. But eventually, a neural path connected and Magatron was able to turn his face away from the damp weed and look up at the leafy canopy above.

```
System online . . .
Host.carrion . . . unable to connect
Initiate local reboot
Weapons . . . temporarily offline
Fission regulator . . . stable
Comms . . . disabled
Please contact your system administrator.
Running spym-a9.exe . . .
```

The mist, which had acted as a blanket, quickly dispersed as Magatron emerged from the reeds. His visor was missing; two piercing red eyes burnt like embers as he stomped across the river bank, trying to get his bearings. His legs felt different. Every time he walked he had the urge to hop. His tail ticked back and forth and sometimes patted the ground as he stopped to listen to the sound of the forest. His throat was parched, as though he hadn't drunk for weeks, and the sound of cool, trickling water was too tempting. He hopped towards the river's edge and took a sip, it was cool and refreshing, the elixir of life. As the water settled, Magatron saw his reflection.

Ringpull stopped in his tracks as he heard an unearthly wail, like that of a corvid being brutalised. He was close now. Part of him wanted to turn back, the whole experience with Morag and her dark magic had unnerved him, and now he stood within squawking distance of his prophesied redeemer. As he stood, listening to the rabid chattering, he noticed two shiny strips of metal on the ground.

Magatron studied his reflection in more detail. His face was sharp and heavier than before. His eyes flickered as he focused on two discreet tubes curling away from his neck towards his spine. He snapped his wings open to reveal scorched feathers and patches of shiny metal mesh beneath. His head tilted, staring back at his reflection, at two red eyes – windows into a troubled soul. But the one attribute that Magatron noticed more than anything was the gaping hole in his chest, a circular chamber that led straight to his heart. It began to glow. He felt it with his wings, sensing the raw energy raging within. 'How is this possible?' he whispered to himself, warming to his new guise.

```
Weapons . . . online
Thermograph . . . online
Some local data files may be damaged or corrupt.
Please restart spym-a9.exe in safe mode and con-
sult your manual.
```

Magatron searched deep within his memory to locate his last thoughts: being airborne, clear azure skies and then a crash of thunder. He grimaced in anger, triggering him to fire an uncontrolled blast of energy at the water. A plume of steam mushroomed into the air and dissolved his reflection.

Branches snapped behind him. Magatron turned and scoured the area. He could distinguish a heat signature shaking behind the cover of an evergreen shrub. Mag studied its shape and behaviour, assessing its threat potential. He recognised the bird's mannerisms; flicks of a long tail, fretful hopping and ticking of the head which had something tiny and metallic resting upon it. He motioned slowly and mechanically towards the shape without sound.

Ringpull was rooted in fear. Morag was right, Big Mag had returned - although as a fire breathing, mechanical demon, not the handsome, charming thinker he idolised. Before the magpie could plot an escape, his protective branches were snapped aside by a pair of broad wings.

Mag stepped forward, dwarfing the cowering Ringpull. "What happened to me?"

31: A Flattering Wake-up Call

indar had been babbling incomprehensibly to himself for the past hour. He was completely baffled. Why didn't Magatron's emergency transponder activate? Spikez, Trakz and PIG30N looked on from their cages, saddened to see their creator in such turmoil.

"What a mess," Trakz remarked.

"What do you think happened to him?" asked Spikez.

"Too much gin."

"I meant to Magatron."

"Well, a sociable bird like that probably stopped to have a chat and lost track of time."

"Very funny. We should help Windar find him."

Windar ingested another shot of coffee as he deliberated over possible explanations for Magatron's disappearance. He tried to ignore the sounds of clinking wine glasses, echoing in the temporal lobes of his cortex; the kind words of the generals, all of whom had invited him to visit their bases across the globe; and then came the memories of raucous singing of the national anthem at The Lamb & Flag Inn, before being carried across the car park by Flattery. Then he remembered the storm.

Spikez, PIG30N and Trakz gathered around one of Windar's electronic tablets and began formulating a rescue mission. "Look, I've studied the weather data from last night, he must have ran into some trouble on his way back to base," deduced Spikez.

"So, you think he's just out there, lying in a field waiting to be collected?"

"Where else could he be?"

"He might have landed in the river. If that's the case then there's no way we'll be able to find him," assured Trakz, "those currents are strong enough to wash anybody out to sea."

Windar picked up the phone and dialled, it was not a call he wanted to make - he knew that the person on the other end of the line wouldn't react so well to bad news.

When the animals declared liberation from Magpie rule, Rosie made a conscious decision to leave Greenacres for pastures new. She continued to blame herself for her brother's death and regularly thought about him and the happy times they had spent together, especially when her mum and dad argued with each other. The memories of her brother refused to die, and he kept appearing to her in dreams. In the latest vision he looked older and stronger, floating along the river against a raging current, telling her to cross the bridge.

Mr and Mrs Hog rarely talked about Prickles' death with Rosie, because they got too upset, and partly because Rosie's lies had led to his untimely demise - that's what Rosie believed. Neither mum nor dad caught wind of her intentions to run away. It was whilst her parents dozed after a liberation feast of worms and bugs that she slipped away from the coldness of the nest, consumed by her own grief.

In two days, Rosie had continued upriver towards the town of Grayford, where she planned to seek adrenaline filled adventures in her self-destructive state of mind. She thought that being alone would ease the pain, but it only made the feelings of emptiness stronger and she felt colder. Continuing beside the clear waters, Rosie would often stop, drink and stare at her reflection - seeing her brother's face.

The phone rang. Its unearthly racket resonated from the bedside table as Colonel Flattery rolled over and huffed to himself, trying to focus on the clock. Who would call at this hour on his day off? The walls twirled as he reached for his phone. He snarled when he read the caller display. "Windar!"

Windar's voice retreated back inside his throat. He tried

again. "I'm very sorry to call you, Colonel, it's just . . ."

"This better be important, Professor, a colonel still needs sleep like everyone else. I'm not like one of your machines."

"No, of course," he hesitated. "There's a problem."

"With what?"

"Magatron."

Stony silence followed. Windar could hear Flattery breathing heavily. "It's killed someone, hasn't it?"

"No! Well . . . I'm not sure."

"How can you not be sure?" Flattery flipped out of bed and lunged towards the curtains. "Talk to me Windar, where is Magatron?"

"Well, that's the problem," the professor replied. "I can't find him. He never made it back to base."

"See you at O-eight-hundred hours." With that, the colonel hung up. Flattery opened his drawers and took out freshly ironed underpants, socks and a handkerchief – he might need one.

Windar exhaled to the point where his ribs snapped inwards. He turned to his creations on the console table who stared back at him with pity. He had until Flattery burst through his door to manufacture a rescue plan.

Ringpull stood at the edge of the river, behind Big Mag. He had been recounting the moments leading up to Mag's death and describing, in graphic detail, the revolution that had ensued.

Big Mag said nothing. He did nothing. It was if he was in a

state of meditation. He did not even react when Ringpull begged for forgiveness, confessing his greed and the lies he had told to secure support from the other magpies - although he mused that he would have done the same. Instead, Mag focused on the sensors in his body processing information, reacting to sounds and light in a heightened way. Every time he replayed fractured memories of terrible pain and falling - or heard the names Eliza, Hercules or Baldwin mentioned - he felt a burning physical reaction in his chest where his main weapon was fixed; but overall, Mag felt pleased with these new powers he had inherited from somewhere, someone.

"Say something!" cawed Ringpull.

"Something," Mag replied, his wit sharp as ever.

"What are you thinking?"

"I'm thinking it's time we revisited old friends. What say you, Ringpull?"

"Because of me, magpies no longer have any allies. Tonight I must attend the Animal Council hearing to learn of my fate. I will face death at the hands of the raptors if I do not attend."

"Perhaps I can fix it so that won't have to happen."

"Big Mag, things are different. Don't you understand?"

"Oh I understand perfectly." Mag pivoted to Ringpull, malice simmering deep within his crimson eyes. "Things are very different now. Stay loyal to me, Ringpull, and all will be forgiven."

The doors to the laboratory broke open and a furious Flattery bounded in. Windar jumped up from his desk where he was busy highlighting Magatron's most likely locations.

"This whole project is a mess," yelled Flattery, grabbing hold of Windar by the collar. "You better have some good news for me before Grievance pulls the plug on this pet freak show of yours."

"You've told General Grievance?"

"Of course I haven't, you fool! He's busy closing deals with the generals over a game of golf before they depart. They've all bought into the idea that these furry soldiers of yours are the future of modern warfare. They cannot know anything different – find Magatron!"

"Well, that's what I was doing." Flattery let go of Windar and beckoned him to continue. "I've narrowed down a two mile grid radius of where I think Magatron may have crashed. I'm about to upload the directives to the rest of the team."

"You want to mobilise more machines to find a machine that's missing?" he shook his head. "You're madder than I thought, you mumbling, melon-headed moron!" He stood and mulled it over for a moment. "If I didn't want to keep a lid on this operation I'd send in real soldiers, but that requires authorisation." He took a breath and paced across the lab, rubbing his temples. "Okay, talk me through your stupid plan."

"Well, Spikez will be our eyes on the ground, whilst PIG30N will conduct aerial surveillance. It'll be quicker that way - they know what to look out for. That way, nothing should look out of the ordinary – no soldiers at all."

"Windar, we can't afford any mistakes. If Grievance finds out about this, you and Project Carrion will be terminated."

"I understand."

"And I will deny any knowledge of this operation ever taking place."

Windar wavered uneasily at Flattery's readiness to distance himself. "I don't understand what you're saying, Colonel."

"What I'm saying, Professor, is that you've created these electronic abominations, therefore, you take full responsibility for whatever happens to them out in the field."

"But-"

"No buts, Windar, except yours. You're on your own – I'm not officially authorising this clean up. If Grievance catches any wind of what's happened, it'll be bad news for all of us."

Flattery turned and exited the lab.

Trakz looked up from the plate of cheese crumbs, his eyes glazed. "What did he say?"

"It looks like we're going hunting," Spikez replied.

32: King of the Skies

The raptors celebrated another day of victory on the western edge of the pine forest. Buzzards glided on warm currents of air, kestrels hovered freely over wheat fields on the hunt for small prey, and Hercules perched proudly on his favourite branch. He overlooked the whole of Greenacres Farm, enjoying the invigorating westerly wind. The red kite watched birds traversing freely between trees and bushes, rabbits and deer wandering across overgrown plains without the threat of harassment, and in the east field he could see Farmer Cullem rounding up his last remaining flock of sheep, prepping them for market. Things were back to normal.

A series of thin branches snapped behind him. Hercules' eye muscles snapped tight as he turned and scoured the depths of the forest. He saw nothing but felt a presence nonetheless. He leapt forward onto another bough, balancing with his powerful terracotta wings. There was a smell of sulphur in the air and he heard a faint sound, like that of a magpie. The very thought made him angry, who would dare invade his private space?

"Who's there?" he called.

Ringpull surreptitiously darted between the branches in an attempt to antagonise Hercules.

"Magpie," yelled Hercules. "Identify yourself!"

Ringpull landed a wingspan away on a branch behind Hercules. "Morning. Glorious day, isn't it?"

"If you've come to test my patience, Ringpull, then you have succeeded," stormed Hercules. "What do you want?"

"Oh, nothing much," he replied. "Just the opportunity to settle an old score."

Hercules laughed out loud. "Why Ringpull, that would make my day. In fact, it would save us all the trouble of attending your hearing tonight."

Ringpull looked back at him with a glassy expression. "You're going to pay dearly, Hercules. An eye for an eye."

Hercules thought about Ringpull's odd choice of words – not a response he had expected from a corvid half his size, about to feel his wrath. As the raptor pondered, an acorn flew in from the right and struck him across the back of his head. Hercules flicked his shoulders round and focused his vision on a young squirrel sniggering on the trunk of a tree. Ringpull laughed. Hercules turned back to the magpie and scowled: "So be it!" The red kite propelled himself at Ringpull, who in turn quickly dropped to the forest floor, weaving between the branches. Hercules read

Ringpull's tactic and stopped.

Moments later, Ringpull checked over his shoulder to see if the mighty bird was in pursuit. Confused, he stopped and scanned the branches for any trace of him. There was none. He continued down to the forest bed, to a peaceful and calm arena of fragrant pine needles. But the silence was shattered by crashing and yelling. Ringpull glanced up to see Hercules' mass hurtle downwards, a shower of pine cones and a vortex of twigs following behind him.

The mighty red kite smashed into the ground and stood opposite Ringpull, the body of the miscreant squirrel gripped in his talons, writhing and screaming for help. "I'm going to enjoy this." Hercules effortlessly flicked the squirrel to the side, its brittle body slamming into a tree trunk where it lay to rest.

Ringpull laughed nervously as Hercules motioned towards him. "You can't hurt me," the magpie said, standing firm. "There's nothing more you can do to me."

"We'll see about that!"

A voice called from the shadows. "Not so fast, my dear Hercules."

The bird of prey froze. He recognised the coarseness of the bird's call and turned. Emerging from the cover of trees, the sharp and menacing outline of Big Mag came to light. Aggravated by this sight, Hercules looked back at Ringpull and struck him with his wing, sending him flapping over to the unconscious squirrel. "Big Mag," Hercules confirmed, sizing up his new opponent. "You look good for a dead bird."

"Oh, Hercules, I'm very much alive."

"For now," he replied. But something troubled Hercules about Mag's new thickset appearance; the eyes showed no flicker of emotion, or fear. "Still, I guess we can look at changing that."

Mag laughed. "I see some things have not changed," he remarked. "Let's see if your actions can speak louder than words this time."

Hercules angled his head forward. "I've been looking forward to this day."

"Oh, Hercules, so have I!" Mag extended his wings. "So have I!"

33: Unauthorised Actions

Without official consent from his ruling superiors, Windar was about to break every code in the Green-acres Military Research Facility Staff Handbook. He pondered the consequences as he covertly wheeled PIG30N and Spikez in a supplies trolley towards the loading bay.

Windar's moped was far from hi-tech. It was painted in duck egg blue and held a battered, enamel case that was barely big enough to carry a packed lunch and some paper documents, let alone a robotically enhanced pigeon and a hedgehog cyborg. He parked himself beside it and looked up at the rotating CCTV camera, which flashed its all-seeing eye at him every thirty seconds.

In the security office, watching on their monitor, two guards chuckled to themselves as they watched Windar potter around with tools. They knew him by rumour and reputation: a nutty eccentric who enjoyed meddling with robotics and mixing up chemical potions in his customised lab; not the demigod of animal prosthetics, cybernetics and neuroscience. "Maybe he's installing upgrades?" one of the guards joked as they watched him kick the back wheel of his scooter.

The camera looked away, time for Windar to move. He flipped down the back lid of the carry case and, with sleight of hand, placed PIG30N and Spikez neatly inside. By the time the camera looked back at him, Windar had stacked his tools back on the trolley and strapped on his white bike helmet. He swiftly mounted the scooter and started the engine, which coughed out a plume of smoke, before riding towards the main gates.

Two soldiers stood guarding the exit. One of the men, a portly, flat-nosed fellow, stopped Windar at the barrier. "Good morning, Professor Windar. Would you mind turning off the engine for me?"

"Is there a problem?" Windar asked, watching the guard pull out some latex gloves.

"It's just standard stop and search procedure, sir." The guard rapped his fingers on top of the enamel lid. "Open the case, please."

Windar stalled, fiddling with his keys nervously. "Well, they really are trying to tighten things up around here."

"I'm just following my orders, Professor. It's nothing personal."

"Quite! Yes, right, now, you'll, er . . . need one of these keys to open it." He dismounted the scooter and nervously walked round to the box and placed the key in the lid, twisting and turning for several seconds. "My my, it's a bit stiff as always."

"What's happened to your car?" the guard asked.

"Oh, it's being repaired."

The guard smiled and gestured towards the lid. "May I?"

Windar clicked the lid open and stood back. With a numbed expression, the guard peered at the contents: a few loose note-pads, over-ripened bananas, and some apples. The guard closed the lid and stood back, examining the moped once more. "This is a nineteen eighty-four model, right?"

Windar nodded.

"I wanted one of these when I was a cadet." He ran his hand along the top of the moped and looked back at Windar. "I'm glad I didn't waste my money, for some reason they've put the fuel tank near the front and the carry case is exceptionally shallow. How bizarre!"

"Oh, well," Windar replied, "I guess that's why they don't make them anymore. But it does its job quite well, I've never complained."

"Have a nice day, Professor." The guard stood back and buzzed the gate open. Windar hopped back on, restarted the engine and whizzed off.

PIG30N was pressed tightly against Spikez, much to her discomfort. The ceiling above them slid across and they were raised back inside the box where a small LCD screen was glow-ing at the rear. Behind them another secret compartment slid open and Trakz wheeled himself in.

"That was a close call," the mouse remarked.

"Where have you been?"

"Windar carried me in his jacket. I used to ride with him loads before he got tired of the rain and bought himself a car."

"Are we going to Windar's house?"

"No," Trakz raised his hands to reveal two data cables, one for each of them. "It's stunt hedgehog time." Trakz wired them both up to the screen.

Windar, heading along a country road towards Grayford, spoke through his helmet which was linked to a computer integrated into the moped. "Drop off point will be in about five minutes. I've uploaded coordinates for probable crash spots. PIG30N will collect images from the air, Spikez will search the undergrowth on foot. We have a small window of opportunity."

In his wing mirror, the professor noticed a car trailing him in the distance. "I'll monitor the progress from home since I fear that my actions may not have gone unnoticed. This means we will have to initiate active deployment."

Trakz had been relaying the professor's instructions, which were decoded through an AI translator, to Spikez and PIG30N.

"What's active deployment?" Spikez asked.

"It means you get to eject whilst the bike is still moving. It'll be fun!"

"Oh . . ." Spikez looked over at his winged teammate. "I still don't see how we're going to find Magatron if he doesn't have a transponder reading. We could be searching all day, why can't Windar help us find him on the ground?"

"It's complicated," replied Trakz.

The moped hummed along the winding roads, nearing drop off point. Spikez attached his utility wire to a clasp on PIG30N's foot.

"When Windar gives the signal, PIG30N will fire out from the box, creating a slingshot effect for you to propel deep into the undergrowth," said Trakz, pointing to a simulation on the screen. "Are there any questions?"

Spikez rubbed the fur beneath his chin. "No."

"Really?"

"We'll see you back at base," he replied, bracing himself.

Windar accelerated out of a bend, getting as far out of sight from the car as possible. "Prepare to disengage," he called, the speedometer creeping upwards.

Trakz raised his arms to prepare PIG30N and Spikez for lift off. Windar flicked a switch above the ignition key and the rear lid flipped open. The wind caught the bird's wings, pulling PIG30N skywards. Spikez held the wire tight until it went taut, then pushed with his legs. PIG30N dived towards a clearing between two large trees, creating the desired arc that gave Spikez the momentum he needed to reach the hedgerows.

Spikez held his breath as he detached the wire. Seconds felt like minutes as he flew through the air. The micro-processors in his brain calculated his velocity and angle, mapping probable landing spots; they commanded him to coil into a ball, so that when he hit the ground the force of impact could be distributed more evenly. Spikez rolled to a stop, surrounded by the sights and smell of dense vegetation.

The pursuing vehicle reappeared in Windar's wing-mirror, but his team were safely out of sight. His focus was to return home and monitor their progress from there.

The hedgehog uncurled himself and stood, listening. The hum of traffic noises was replaced by the buzz of a forest in spring. His vision flickered momentarily. PIG30N landed next to him and awaited his lead. "This place is beautiful," remarked Spikez, watching butterflies dancing between nettles and hollyhocks. He looked at PIG30N, and for a moment he imagined her perched on a rafter in a dimly lit barn. Interference flickered across his visor again.

PIG30N angled her head and cooed at him.

Spikez shook his head. "Sorry, Pidge, all that tumbling's made me dizzy." He completed a thermal imaging sweep of the immediate area. "Let's head towards the river."

PIG30N lurched forward and beat her wings, flying upwards until she was gliding high above the woods. She transmitted the images directly to Spikez so that he could navigate his way to the first probable crash site.

Their mission protocols flashed within their minds:

```
Locate: SPYM-A9 to HQ - priority 1.
```

34: An Invitation

Nutcase was joined by several other hardened squirrels at the twisted roots of a large oak tree. In their boredom they had chewed and scratched off the bark from its base, leaving coarse outlines of birds and mammals which depicted scenes from the Battle of Greenacres. Following their defeat, some squirrels had abandoned Nutcase, retreating to pastures new; this did little to appease his temper. Being identified as enemy leaders in the great fight, Nutcase and his toughest soldiers were to appear before Queen Eliza and the rest of the Animal Council to learn of their fate. The mood was solemn at the possibility of being banished from their home, pushed out to suburban areas to join other magpies and scavengers, and the many new challenges that would bring.

Ringpull burst through the canopy and landed on a low hanging branch directly above them. "Morning rodents."

Nutcase looked up and scowled. "You've got some nerve turning up here, Ringpull!"

"Calm down a second, Nutley."

The squirrel volleyed an acorn in Ringpull's direction. "That's what my father used to call me. It's Nutcase to you!"

The magpie didn't flinch as the projectile narrowly missed his beak. He was filled with a new confidence, empowered by a new hope. Ringpull flew down to the ground, beating his wings firmly to show that he was strong again. "I needs to talk to you about tonight's hearing."

"I'm not going," replied Nutcase. "None of us are. What's the point? They're going to banish us anyway, we might as well go down fighting."

"Quite right," replied Ringpull, hopping closer to Nutcase. "But what if I were to tell you that the outcome could be different?"

"I'm not a very patient squirrel, Ringpull. Get to the point."

"All in good time, Nutcase. I need you to attend - I've a little present for you."

"There's nothing you can give me that would persuade me to go. You're starting to annoy me." The other squirrels began encircling Ringpull.

"I'm a magpie of my word, tonight you will receive everything you've ever wanted," proclaimed Ringpull.

Nutcase pondered for a moment, scratching his head and twitching his tail; he contemplated leaping on Ringpull and tearing all his feathers out with his teeth and claws, then hanging the cocky magpie by its tail and using him as a punch bag. But there was something about Ringpull that was different - he had the poise of a magpie that did not fear. "If you're lying to me," Nutcase snarled, "I'm going to rip your beak right off!"

"Be there tonight, you won't be disappointed." Ringpull turned and flew back into the thickness of the forest canopy, leaving the gang to quarrel over their reasons to attend or not.

35: Searching For Clues

S pikez had climbed a tree at the first probable crash site, scanning the area for any evidence that Magatron had been there; PIG30N landed beside him, conducting an electronic sweep of the clearing with her enhanced vision: they found nothing.

A young deer, the same one that had stumbled upon Magatron earlier, emerged from the bushes. Spikez watched it rummage for shoots and seeds on the forest floor before the fawn abruptly raised her head, ears pricked, searching the undergrowth. She then caught sight of the hedgehog and pigeon up in the tree canopy, staring back in her direction.

Spikez raised his hand and called down, "Hey, how's it going?"

The fawn did not respond. She didn't know what to do, was this a bad dream or were all the forest creatures being transformed into shiny woodland demons? Her tan and beige hind quarters began to shuffle.

"It's okay, we mean you no harm. We're looking for a friend," he continued.

Cautiously, she crept towards them, peering into the shadows of the forest - just in case that water monster she had encountered earlier was following her. "I didn't think hedgehogs could climb trees," said the fawn, studying them both.

"It's a special talent of mine," replied Spikez. "I'm using it to find our friend, a magpie."

The young deer frowned at the word and stepped back. "My father says that magpies have no friends, and that should anyone tell you different then they are traitors like them. Are you traitors?"

Spikez and PIG30N turned to one another, they did not understand. "No, we're not from this neck of the woods. We're more of a team and we think he's lost - he's probably very different to all the other magpies you've known."

"My father says that all animals are equal, what makes him better than all of us?"

"Well, I never said he was better, just different. He had an accident - in fact, we've all had accidents." Spikez dropped to the branch below, revealing his robotic underbelly. "We think our friend's injured and urgently needs our help."

The young fawn thought for a moment. "A magpie, you say?"

"Yes, a big magpie."

"Well . . . I was drinking by the river earlier when I heard something making a lot of noise. It was the same colour as a magpie, but it was very misty, so it was hard to tell."

"Can you lead us there?"

"Sure," the fawn crept forward, glancing at either side of her. "Will I be safe?"

"I give you my word, we just want to find him and take him home."

"Okay," she said, "I can give you a lift if you want - it'll be quicker?"

"Oh, I doubt that," replied Spikez.

"Would you like to bet on it?"

"I don't think your father's the type of deer who'd want you making rash decisions."

"Actually, he says it's good to be competitive. Now, let's see how different you think you really are." The fawn turned and bounded through the forest.

Spikez instructed PIG30N to track the deer's movements in the air. He opened his utility belt and fired out a wire which attached itself to a thick branch ahead of him. Using his momentum, he swung himself through a large clearing in the trees, released the wire and volleyed back up towards the tree canopy. Spikez found it much easier to leap and bound between branches than to navigate the uneven terrain below.

PIG30N circled up above, watching the fawn snaking in and out of the bracken, predicting her route and sending Spikez coordinates towards the most likely stretch of water.

The fawn broke through the brush into a clearing where the water trickled gently. She slowed, raised her head and peered back into the forest depths with excitement, panting wildly. She had enjoyed the race and could see no trace of the hedgehog. "I said I was fast!" she boasted.

"Not fast enough," said Spikez, casually.

The fawn turned back in disbelief to see him standing near the stream. "How did you do that?"

"I took a shortcut." Spikez turned away from the puzzled young deer and surveyed the clearing. "Where did you say you found him?"

The fawn tentatively stepped forward. "Over there, by the reeds."

PIG30N, who had already surveyed the area, landed beside Spikez and shook her head. The fawn looked surprised. "I'm not lying to you."

Spikez ran over and analysed the spot; there were scorch marks and heavy indentations to suggest that something big had landed in the immediate area. A particle scan of the canopy floor didn't yield much, but his visor highlighted an energy trail leading away along the river bed. "Thank you, you've been very helpful."

"You're welcome," she turned to walk away but stopped. "My name's Flora, by the way."

"That's nice," commented Spikez.

The fawn frowned. "My name's Flora, and . . ."

" . . . You're a deer?"

"You really are different, you should get out more," she laughed. "My name's Flora, and you are?"

Spikez paused. No one had asked him that in a long time. "I'm model number . . ." he stopped himself for a second. Trakz and Windar called him Spikez, but the name suddenly felt very alien to him in this strange environment. The hedgehog stared at the ground. "I'm not sure."

The fawn wriggled her hind. "Okay, well, it was nice to meet you, whoever you are." She turned and bolted into the trees.

Her fun and inquisitive nature reminded Spikez of someone. As he tried to remember her name, Trakz called in on the internal comms. "Hey, buddy, how's it going in the field?"

"We've located the crash site but there's no visual on Magatron. I've picked up an energy trail, we're going to follow it on foot and track him down. Spikez out."

"Hold up a second, I'm picking up some unusual readings – you feeling okay?"

"I'm fine, just taking everything in. It's beautiful out here, Trakz."

"That's right, rub it in," Trakz said. "Take some nice pictures for me, I'll be monitoring you. Trakz out."

PIG30N launched herself into the air as Spikez began his steady jog upriver.

Rosie took a well-deserved break from all the walking. It was a clear day and she felt liberated; free from her parents' control, free from the boredom of living in Greenacres, and free from the constant reminders of places where she and Prickles had once played happily together. However, she was not free from the memories of that awful night. The sun's shimmering reflection on the water's surface reminded her of the flashing beacons. Rosie felt cold - she had never spent so long out in the day before.

Lurking in the undergrowth, unbeknown to Rosie, the eyes of a hungry predator studied her. He had been tracking her fateful trail and, as time progressed, the desire to kill grew stronger. Fagin cautiously slid out between the coarse grasses, his face contorted by murderous thoughts. He had timed it well, there were no hiding places for Rosie to bury herself away in this time. Fagin slavered as he approached, wondering whether he should drown her in the river first, then feast upon her cleansed carcass.

Persuing Magatron's electron trail, Spikez raced along the riverside when his senses suddenly flared. Something was wrong. Spikez had felt this sensation before, he knew it, and he knew it was bad.

Windar tapped his video monitor as strong interference infected the computer screen.

Sensing Spikez' unease, PIG30N circled overhead, and identified two heat signatures across the river. Spikez looked over and saw the faint outline of a hedgehog and a menacing orange bulk creeping up behind it.

"Spikez," radioed Trakz, "what's happening out there, your vitals are starting to go through the roof!"

Rosie stirred as a branch snapped behind her. She turned, peering directly into Fagin's soulless eyes as he leered over her. His muzzle pushed aside the final few blades of grass that separated them. She could see his fangs, yellow and dripping.

"Hello again, my lovely," he whispered. "All alone?"

Rosie could not breathe. She recognised the same chilling voice from that fateful night. Maybe this was her destiny; perhaps the woodland spirits had meant her life to end on that dreadful night. Rosie's eyes closed as she brought her trembling paws to her face and stifled a scream.

Her cry did not go unheard. Even at a distance, Spikez recognised the voice. He signalled PIG30N to pitch low and readied himself with his utility wire, casting it around her foot as she passed above him.

The fox laughed to himself, at his luck; it was not often that he was granted such an easy meal. He angled himself to snap his hard jaws across Rosie's neck when a figure flew at him from the side. Fagin glanced, only to feel a ball of sharp spikes bury into his muzzle. His whole body flinched, the force of the impact tearing a strip of fur away from his cheek, leaving him bleeding and howling with pain.

Hearing the commotion, Rosie opened her eyes. She watched Fagin writhing in agony on the muddy bank. And stood between her and the fox was the familiar shape of a hedgehog, guarding her protectively.

"I'm not leaving here without a meal!" scowled Fagin, blood glistening along his jawline. He slowly rose from the ground, sizing up his opponent.

Spikez stood upright on his hind legs, his front claws extended, ready to fight the beast.

Fagin studied the hedgehog's face. "Wait a minute, I know

you. But . . ." he ducked his head, inspecting the mechanics beneath Spikez' mass of erect spines. "You're dead! I watched you die!"

Spikez did not respond. He had taken a wire-frame analysis of Fagin's face and processed it against all his past and present memory files, and it had triggered something.

The words echoed in Spikez' head: 'You're dead! I watched you die!'

It matched the same menacing tone that had been locked away, buried in the deepest, darkest sectors of his brain - until now.

'I know you.' Fagin's sneering voice replayed again, again and again. 'You're dead!'

Spikez was frozen to the spot, wavering like a sheriff too drunk to draw as the outlaw prepared to attack.

'I watched you die!'

```
F:404 [SYSTEM ERROR] SPIK-3Z offline . . .
. . .
SPIK-3Z.exe has encountered a problem and needs
to close.
Would you like Carrion.sys to search the inter-
net for a solution to the problem?
```

Windar yelled and struck the monitor. "No!"

Rosie looked on in disbelief, was this really happening? She stood and cowered behind her brother.

Fagin seethed, saliva bubbling across the wound on his snout.

"So, still trying to protect your little sister, huh? Well don't you worry - I'll take care of her." His fangs seemed to lengthen. "But not until I've finished you off for good."

Rosie screamed: "Prickles, look out!"

Spikez' spines flinched. His sister's cry travelled along his quills and buried into his skin, where it was absorbed into his bloodstream amidst the ions and plasma, pulsing through his veins, past the hydraulics and pumps, mixing with the nanobots, which in turn generated an electrical signal - retreating through his neurons to the central core of Spikez' brain. It did enough to reboot his memory and primary functions, giving Spikez the narrowest of margins to react to the set of rabid jaws about to maul him.

Fagin's mouth snapped powerfully across Spikez' face, but the hedgehog's claws reacted and held the fox's chops ajar. Fagin withdrew, hoping to strike again but he had not banked on the hedgehog's grip to remain so firm.

Rosie watched in horror as her brother clung to Fagin's face. As the fox desperately tried to shake him off, the rest of Spikez' defence mechanism slowly came back online. He twisted his own body, which in turn flipped Fagin's lower jaw upwards, causing the fox to slump sideways. Fagin's front foot desperately tried to scrape Spikez away from his mouth, but he could not reach beyond the artillery of sharp spikes.

PIG30N angled her body for a dive, her feet primed with a high voltage charge. She hit directly against Fagin's neck, delivering a sharp bolt of electricity. Fagin wailed and convulsed over on to his back as the current burned along his skin. His breathing became erratic and his eyes rolled upwards as he lapsed out of consciousness.

Spikez released his grip and rolled clear of Fagin's limp body. PIG30N landed beside the fox and looked at Spikez for reassurance that her partner was unhurt. He raised a weary hand at the pigeon in appreciation. "Thank you, bird."

Windar fervently attacked his keyboard, trying to regain control of his most prized asset, but it was to no avail. The circuitry in Spikez' brain had fused to the synaptic threads of Prickles' past life, causing his memories to defragment; directories and information had been reorganised into an organic compound of intelligence, a neurological labyrinth.

Spikez was now fully self-aware.

PIG30N pitched forward, sensing a change in the hedgehog's behaviour. Spikez watched the pigeon beating her wings and rapidly dipping her head in an attempt to get some kind of response, but he shied away. "Nice birdy."

A gentle voice whimpered behind him "Prickles . . ." Spikez turned to see the quivering shape of a young, female hog looking directly at him, tears streaming down her speckled brown muzzle. "Prickles, is that you?"

Spikez remained transfixed, replaying her voice again and again in his head. 'Prickles'. He studied her, watching as she hesitantly shuffled towards him. A tear fell from her eye and he calculated its velocity, watching as it fell to the ground. 'Prickles, is that you?' Spikez held out his paw and studied it - it looked different to what he remembered, and it felt firm. Rosie took it and cupped it against her face as she wept; feelings of joy conflicted with memories of sadness.

"Rosie . . ." The words came from his lips without him thinking. The image captured within his visor now matched to a name. He knew her name. "Rosie. Rosie. Rosie . . ."

"Yes," she said, weeping uncontrollably. "Yes, yes. It's me. You're alive!"

Prickles studied his paws again, they were not his. "Sis', what's happened to me?"

Rosie could not speak. She gripped his hand tightly, pulling it close to her heart. Prickles turned to see the Pigeon still staring at him, gazing into his vacant expression. He looked across at the unconscious body of Fagin, whose tongue slithered along the ground with each deep breath he took. He remembered. Disjointed memories slowly repaired themselves, pasting together what had happened: the worms, the chase, and the bright lights.

"How long have I been away?" he asked.

Rosie's face remaining bundled with emotion, but he could still detect her smile. "Too long, Prickles. Too long . . ."

"I don't remember. What about mum and dad, are they safe?"

Rosie nodded. "Mum and dad will be happy to see you." She took a step back - studying her brother's enhanced physique. It was only then that she began noting the little differences; Prickles' feet were slightly bigger, wider than she remembered, and his hands had felt so cold, heavy and hard. She paced back some more, focusing on the pigeon and looking at her eyes; her left socket protruded slightly, and it was fixed clearly on her with an artificial glare. Rosie glanced back at her brother, who gauged her reaction.

"What's that covering your eyes?" she asked, seeing her wary face in the reflection. Prickles brought his claws back up to his face. "And your stomach, all your fur – it's missing!" Her smile quickly disappeared. Rosie was unsure if this was really happening or another one of her terrible dreams. "Prickles, what's happened to you?"

Prickles shook his head, unable to answer. "I'm not sure, but I feel fine." He looked at the pigeon, perhaps she knew. PIG30N flapped her wings and cooed lightly. She made no sense. He looked back to his sister and then down at his two heavy hands. "I don't know what's happened to me, sis. I don't remember anything."

Rosie gawped as she watched Prickles walk over to the river on two legs, sit and stare at his reflection in the water. He was bigger, stronger than she remembered and the flecks of white had all but disappeared from the tips of his spikes.

Prickles desperately tried to remember what had happened after the car accident and found himself cycling through memory files; but they were not memories he understood: images of buildings, people, faces, flashing lights – none of it made any sense.

"I don't remember anything."

Windar placed an anxious looking Trakz into his pocket and picked up his car keys. His moped would not be able to transport the Kraken-200 away from base. As he opened the front door, the professor checked his watch - he didn't have long before the onset of nightfall.

Chapters

Part Two: **Evolution**

The driver had no intention of slowing down; she had a dry, straight road and good visibility. Ringpull remained perfectly still, staring at the oncoming vehicle, now less than fifty metres away. The driver pulled up into fifth gear, cruising comfortably. Ringpull looked up at the birds in the trees. He was unafraid. The jackdaws chattered frantically for Ringpull to get out of the way, that he was crazy, that he didn't need to do this. He ignored them, watching as the vehicle raced towards him.

The radio was blaring out fine classical music, one of Elgar's finest works, until the car juddered and the dashboard fizzed violently, catching fire. The power-steering locked. There was little the driver could do except thump the brakes, but this only caused the vehicle to veer sharply towards the verge, and the ditch. The corvids listened to her screams as the machine struck the bank and began its perilous roll into the forest depths, slamming into the trunk of a mighty oak, where it came to rest. The wheels of the upturned vehicle slowly clicked to a halt as steam hissed from the car radiator.

An eerie silence followed.

Inches from death, Ringpull's faith in his leader had paid off. Mag had been watching from the depths of the forest, studying the behaviour of the other bird, eliminating any doubt when he fired at the car. He watched as the crow flew back down to the carcass where Ringpull was gleefully ripping fine shreds of meat off the bones.

The magpie stared with wild eyes back at the crow. "What would you choose?"

The jackdaws flew down and flanked the crow on either side. "Show us how there's another way," they said.

Ringpull smiled. "Support me at my trial tonight and you will see."

Prickles was flanked by PIG30N. They were being led by Rosie along the River Charon towards Greenacres. She recounted the story of how the magpies nearly took over Greenacres, describing the mighty battle that took place and how the community united to overthrow the corvids and restore order across the land.

"What was his name again?" Prickles asked.

"Ringpull, he was a nasty piece of work. It's his trial tonight - everyone will be there, including mum and dad."

"I can't wait to see them again," he said, happy to be at his sister's side. "Who were the others you mentioned?"

"Hercules, he's the raptor no-one wants to mess with – all he has to do is look at you with his fiery yellow eyes and you're paralysed with fear!"

"He sounds pretty cool!"

"And then there's Baldwin - for an oldie, he taught Nutcase and his gang of thugs a few lessons in manners. I used to think he was all talk, but that badger's got some serious moves on him ..."

Prickles was fascinated by her account of events. Her passion, enthusiasm and energetic mannerisms reminded him of a character he knew from somewhere, a small and blue looking rodent whose name he had forgotten. He kept looking at the

Pigeon, trying to figure out their connection. PIG30N cooed and dipped her head; Prickles shrugged and shook his head blankly in return.

"Why does that pigeon keep following us?" Rosie asked.

"I don't know," he replied. "I'm having problems remembering lots of things right now. Where are we going again?"

"To the barn, it's where the hearing is taking place. If we're lucky we can be make it before nightfall."

Prickles felt his heart flutter; he'd longed for a nice snuggle with his mum and had glimpses of her gentle face in his mind, nuzzling his cheeks. The thought kept him warm as they trekked along the river bank. "Do you think it'll be a problem, me just turning up out of the blue?"

"Why do you keep asking that?"

"Well, look at me!" he stopped and removed his visor. His eyes were round and fretful. "You even said it yourself, I look totally different."

"Okay, as your sister I'll be honest with you – I was a little freaked at first, but now we're talking again it doesn't really bother me. Sure, it'll take some getting used to, but you're still my brother and that's all that counts."

"I just wish I didn't have to wear this glass strip over my eyes, but if I take it off I'm practically blind."

"No, I like it. You look pretty cool!" she remarked.

37: Release the Kraken!

"**B**ack so soon, Professor? You really should have a day off, sir," the guard commented, wearing the same pained smile.

"Yes, unfortunately it's the nature of my work," replied Windar, retrieving his ID card.

"I see you've got your car back. Made some secret modifications have we?" The guard was straight faced. A second soldier appeared behind him, inspecting the vehicle's underneath with a bomb detection mirror.

Windar looked at the guards sheepishly. "M-m-modifications, officer?"

"I'm sorry, Professor. Just having fun. Enjoy the rest of your day, sir." The guard waved the car through.

Windar logged on to his computer and called up some mili-

Part Two: **Evolution**

36: Fearless Ringpull

A rook, two jackdaws and a crow were hungrily eyeing up some carrion; a pheasant had forgotten that black rivers were not the best place to go looking for food and, as a result, had recently come to a dead end.

After several cars rocketed past, the crow landed beside the bird's remains and pecked the flies away. The carcass was still moist. Hopping on top of broken feathers and bone, the crow stabbed his coarse beak into the flesh and pulled at some stringy innards. The jackdaws watched with envy before swooping down to dine with their cousin. The crow cawed at them both to stay away, but the jackdaws reacted with fury, throwing themselves at him to make him peck from the other side.

Another corvid chattered from the trees, not a rook, jackdaw or a crow. They turned to see its shape, sharp and elongated, slicing through the undergrowth towards them. Ringpull landed beside the three birds and cracked his tail against the ground.

"What do you want?!" they snapped, blocking him from their meal.

"I've come to tell you that it doesn't have to be like this."

The birds beat their wings angrily. "You're a failure, Ringpull. Why should we listen to you? You led us into a battle with false hopes. We have all paid the price because of you."

"There is a way," assured Ringpull. "We were unlucky. Unfortunate, you could say, but we are not permanently beaten."

"Cahh! Then where are the other magpies? I hear that Hood now makes the decisions for your pack."

Ringpull flicked his tail-feathers. "Hood is not a leader - he would rather be ruled by the raptors. But we, cousins, can still make this forest our own."

"If I had a choice," the crow continued, "between putting my faith in a nice juicy carcass or you, which d'you think I'd choose?"

The corvids all laughed together at Ringpull. As they cackled, an engine roared across the horizon. "Kaw! Kaw! On your left," cautioned the rook from up in the trees. The birds turned their heads and then greedily pecked away at the carcass before the oncoming car crushed the flesh deeper into the tarmac.

"Let me show you," said Ringpull.

The car continued to accelerate. The crow and jackdaws swiftly flew back up to their branches. Ringpull bobbed out further into the middle of the road, standing alongside the pheasant's remains.

tary databases. He sent an email request to a team of men in the tech-warehouse, explaining that he needed some electrical equipment taken off site 'for a field test ahead of a new experiment - part of Project Carrion.'

Trakz circled about on the console table, concerned about the fate of his friends. He became distracted by Windar's reaction to the laboratory doors opening, watching the professor's face turn white. The mouse saw a full bodied military officer with a thick moustache enter, his massive hands neatly tucked behind his round waist.

"Professor Windar," boomed Grievance.

"Good afternoon, General."

"I've just had a request to authorise some communication equipment be taken off site, is this correct?"

Windar's heart skipped a beat. "Yes, General."

"What are you planning this time, eh old boy? Not up to mischief, hunting animals in the dark are we?"

Windar held himself up against the table, had Flattery told him? "I, er, only use dead animals in my experiments, General."

Grievance erupted into a hearty fit of laughter. "Yes, yes, of course you do – ethics and all that. I was only joking." The general's attention focused on Trakz, who was staring back at him. "Ah, I see you have company." He marched over and inspected the mouse. Trakz stretched up as high as he could, sniffing Grievance's musty breath. "Yes, I like this little fella a lot. Where are the others?"

"Others?"

Grievance scoured the empty cages in the lab. "Yes, if my calculations are right then there should be three more of these magnificent little blighters."

Windar picked up a clipboard, rustling the pages. "I'm . . . having them cleaned."

"Really?" Grievance raised an eyebrow. "Well, they do say that a good workman always looks after his tools." The general clapped his heels together and brought his hands to his side. "I shall leave you to carry on with your research, or whatever it is you do in here. You have my authorisation. Keep up the good work, Professor." Grievance took one last glance at Trakz and giggled affectionately at him before exiting the lab.

Windar eventually regained control of his breathing. Having lied to the head of the entire operation, his job and the whole of Project Carrion was now in jeopardy if he didn't bring back his bots.

38: The Trial

The sun was sinking into the horizon, dissolving into a pool of red cloud. The animals of Greenacres began their final approach towards the farmer's decrepit dairy barn.

Chaffinches and blackbirds arrived first, securing prime perches; rats and other rodents emerged from different corners of the barn, as though they had secretly buried their way in. Eliza was accompanied by representatives from the kestrels and hawks. She had hoped to find Hercules already waiting for her, but he was absent. The sparrowhawk made enquiries with the other raptors, but they had heard nothing from their battle commander about his intention not to attend.

There were no sheep, they had been driven away and sold at auction that afternoon. Instead, Baldwin and the eldest of the hares converged by the main entrance, ushering animals in.

Harold and Henrietta Hog were making their final steps

towards the barn, hoping to arrive on time for once. Both had lost a great deal of weight since the last meeting. Mrs Hog was apprehensive about her daughter's whereabouts; she wanted to make enquiries with council members.

Voices chattered and grumbled as the creatures waited for the trial to begin. There was a buzz of excitement from the small birds and rodents; rumours were spreading that Hercules had already killed the magpie leader and Nutcase, which explained their absence.

Amidst the steady gossiping, a black and white figure shot through a gap in the wall and landed on the central gate. Ring-pull stood with his beak raised high, flicking his tail to repel the jibes thrown at him. Another pack of birds: jackdaws, rooks and crows followed behind, perching themselves neatly around him, eyes on the crowd.

At the main entrance there was commotion; the geese honked and the rabbits and hares were pushed aside to form a walkway for Squirrel Nutcase and his hardened gang. Nutcase drew back his lips, bearing his teeth at all the small birds and mammals he had so cruelly victimised over the cold, winter months.

All parties were now present, except for Hercules. Eliza nodded reluctantly at the woodpecker to begin. He hammered furiously against the iron roof to start proceedings.

Prickles and PIG30N both heard the din rattling in the distance. They could also detect movement up ahead. Prickles stopped.

"What is it?" Rosie asked.

"I'm not sure." He looked at PIG30N, who turned and flew towards the barn. "Something's not quite right," said Prickles. Static blurred across his visor momentarily, he saw a bright energy trail, and a feeling in his stomach made him stumble backwards. "I keep seeing things flashing across my eyes – I don't know what it means."

"Look, you're probably apprehensive about seeing mum and dad – I'd feel the same," Rosie explained. "They'll be so excited to see you. Everything's going to be fine for all of us, just like it used to be." She held his hand tightly and smiled.

Prickles trusted his sister. He looked back at the barn and noticed that the energy fluctuations had ceased. "Okay," he said.

Tensions between the birds in the barn had increased. There were now more than a dozen jackdaws, crows and rooks sur-rounding Ringpull, and several more tough looking grey squir-rels; all exchanging angry chirps and grunts with the maddening crowd.

"Enough!" cried Eliza. "You will not bring this council hearing into disrepute." The creatures slowly composed themselves. "Ringpull, you are charged with bringing disorder and chaos across the land of Greenacres, inciting murder, and preaching hatred. How do you plead?"

"Oh, I'm very guilty of that, Eliza," Ringpull sneered.

"You shall address me as Queen Eliza!"

"On what authority?"

"I beg your pardon!"

The magpie was calculated in his response. "Who gave you

the authority to be Queen? Was it Morag?"

"How dare you!" Eliza mantled her wings. "You speak of Morag - Morag was a threat to the whole forest, to every creature that lived and breathed within its free lands. If you've made a deal with that witch, then this shall be added to your crimes, for you will have jeopardised every living soul within this forest – including your own!"

Ringpull chuckled brazenly. "I don't think it's her you should be worried about."

"Your insubordination is testing my patience, Ringpull." She flashed her eyes towards the hawks. Where was her loyal friend?

"What are you going to do, set Hercules upon me?" The corvids chuckled to themselves.

Eliza was livid, but grew fearful of their new found confidence. She looked at Baldwin, who was equally concerned at their behaviour. The badger shook his head.

"Oh wait," continued Ringpull, "I think I can hear him coming."

The animals and birds looked up at the gaping hole in the roof. They could hear the sound of mighty claws bouncing across it, heavy and firm, the type a fierce red kite would make. The creatures winked at one another, reassured that Hercules would teach the magpies and squirrels a much needed lesson in manners.

There was a moment's silence as all eyes, beaks and ears pointed skywards, and then they saw him. Like a fallen angel, Hercules tumbled from the sky, a twirling mass of broken wings and burnt feathers rolling downwards. His body slammed against the barn floor, mushrooming particles of dust throughout the packed space.

"Hercules!" gasped Eliza.

Her trusted commander and confidante was sprawled across the floor for all the creatures to see. The rabbits and starlings were the first to rush to Hercules' aid.

"He's still breathing," one of the finches called, "but only just." Songbirds hopped nervously about him, inspecting his horrific injuries – his wings were littered with scorch marks.

Ringpull laughed out loud, gazing back up at the sky, expectantly. The other creatures followed his stare, at the two menacing red eyes that glared in.

Animals squealed and birds shrilled as they realised that the impossible had happened. A dark figure hovered downwards, Big Mag had returned . . .

PIG3ON landed beside Prickles and Rosie as they neared the back entrance of the barn. Having conducted an aerial sweep of the barn, she now rapidly flapped her wings, bowed her head and cooed as much as she could to warn them of the dangers.

Prickles looked at the pigeon, trying to comprehend her actions.

"What's the matter?" asked Rosie.

"I'm not sure, maybe she's hungry," Prickles said.

PIG3ON shook her head and tapped him with her wing, giving Prickles an electric shock. His spikes shot out and he flinched backwards.

"Hey, you cut that out!" snapped Rosie. "Shoo! Buzz off you crazy bird!" PIG3ON back-peddled and flew off.

"Wait, Rosie, perhaps she was trying to warn us about something." Prickles could feel specks of energy ripple across his back spines and his vision blurred again.

"Prickles, what is it?" she asked.

He turned to her, feeling his muscles tighten. "I keep getting that same terrible feeling, Rosie - like something bad is about to happen."

"But Mum and Dad are inside that barn, if they're in danger then we need to tell them!" She turned and ran towards the entry hole.

Prickles grabbed his sister by the hind leg, pulled her back and held her steady. "Rosie, we can't just rush in."

"So what do you propose we do?"

Some panic-stricken animals tried to vacate the barn, only to have their exits blocked by snarling squirrels and embittered magpies.

Ringpull's team of miscreants parted for Big Mag as he landed on the moonlit stage, a ball of white energy swirling within his chest. "Good evening, Your Majesty." Mag said, his eyes burning with vigour.

Queen Eliza could not speak, terror had also infected her.

Nutcase, who until this moment was unaware of Mag's revival, turned to Ringpull. "How's this possible?"

"I have friends in dark places, Nutcase."

Big Mag studied the trembling crowd of fur and feathers. He monitored their heat signatures and stress patterns; there was no danger here, not even from Eliza and Baldwin.

"What's happened to you?" asked Nutcase, swaggering over.

"I've evolved," he replied. "I've brought you a gift," he continued, pointing at Hercules. "I hope that makes good our deal: an eye for an eye."

Nutcase snarled with delight; his good eye glazed with wrath. "Oh Big Mag, it's so good to 'ave you back. Things were getting quite boring without you."

"Our Queen," cawed Big Mag, for all to hear. "Our former-queen."

"How dare you, you . . . beast," she scowled. "On what authority do you come here and practise such barbarity."

"On my authority!" Mag thrust his chest towards the ceiling and fired a bolt of energy, shattering another hole in the roof. The sound was deafening. Thousands of tiny, red hot splinters showered down on the rodents and birds beneath.

Convinced he'd heard a loud crash, Farmer Cullem looked up from the kitchen sink, out through the window at the barn. Mrs Cullem was engrossed in an omnibus edition of *Admissions* and could not be disturbed for want of an ear bashing. The farmer didn't give it a second thought; he left the kitchen and ventured upstairs to fetch his dressing gown and work slippers so that he could investigate.

Rosie held Prickles' hand tightly. "What was that sound?"

Prickles shook his head. He noted a tiny entrance between two crumbling breeze blocks. "We'll go in there," he said, dashing forward.

Eliza had been shoved from her perch and was made to stand with the more common birds. She was flanked by two severe looking rooks whilst other pawns loyal to Mag continued to enter the building, securing all the exits.

Big Mag began. "Tonight we rewrite the rules of the Animal Council, and put an end to the years of so-called royalty dictating how we must live our lives. Tonight," he bellowed, "the future of Greenacres rests once more in the wings of the Magpies." There was a chorus of rabid chants and caws from his followers. "We will revolutionise the way that the forest is run. No longer will you have to answer to the raptors, who have distanced themselves from all the other birds and animals. You will never have to succumb to their demands, or to that of the phoney council. Instead, you will all answer to one voice – a voice that will lead you all, showing you how we can reclaim the land from all authority - even man!"

Rosie and Prickles shuffled through the hole into the barn when they heard a voice caw: "Where do you think you're going?" They turned to see a magpie and a squirrel approach them. "As from tonight, all animals must stay in their respective homes under curfew."

Rosie trembled, grabbing Prickles' prosthetic arm. The magpie strutted up to them, as if to peck them both across the face. "Youngsters, huh? I think you need teaching a lesson or two." The squirrel walked around Rosie and examined her. "I'll start with this one."

"I wouldn't do that if I were you," warned Prickles.

The magpie and squirrel laughed in unison, focusing their attention on Prickles. "Or what?"

"Gather all the creatures together, but keep the raptors separate," Mag ordered. He had dissolved the Animal Council's right to govern - the magpie was now in control. His lead henchmen, Nutcase and Ringpull, circled the helpless Hercules. "It's time to provide my new subjects with some evening entertainment!"

Nutcase sneered at Hercules, ready to exact some bloody vengeance. "I've been dreaming about this moment for a long time," he said, lifting a sharpened piece of rusted wire, twisting it in his hands. Ringpull watched, thirsty for blood.

A scuffle erupted from behind a stack of tyre treads in the far corner of the barn. Seconds later the body of a screaming squirrel hurtled through the air, crashing against a metal gate post where it fell to the ground, twitching.

Everyone, including Mag, turned to see what the commotion was about. They listened to a magpie's final plea for help, replaced by a muffled silence. All eyes, ears and noses twitched in anticipation.

Enormous shadows of spikes were cast against the barn floor. A prickly silhouette appeared from the darkness, walking into the moonlight on thick hind feet.

Big Mag exercised caution, angling forward and capturing a range of data on this new assailant. He processed the hedgehog: foe or ally? Prickles subconsciously did the same, mapping Mag's energy signatures and completing a threat assessment against a database, but the link was damaged:

'Unable to connect. . .'

They stood, motionless, waiting for each other to act.

Ringpull hopped over to Big Mag. "What is it?" he whispered.

"I'm not sure." The magpie elevated himself into the air and glided over to the centre of the barn. Prickles marched forward to meet him. "What is the meaning of this?" demanded Mag.

"I've come to see my mum and dad," Prickles replied.

The magpies and squirrels burst into laughter. "Well, if they are here then you will join them along with the others."

"I haven't come to join anything. I just want to see my parents and make sure they're safe."

"Is it possible that you don't know who I am?"

"You're a magpie, what else is there to know."

All the creatures fell deathly silent as the two adversaries squared up to one another. Mag had the advantage of size and aerial ability, but Prickles had already demonstrated resilience. Only their eyes flinched as seconds ticked away.

Ringpull called out to the crowd of animals. "Who claims this hedgehog?"

A bewildered looking Mr and Mrs Hog were rolled into the open to identify the stranger. "Is this your hog?"

Prickles looked over at them, instantly recognised the spiky bulk of his father. He watched them both uncurl themselves, seeing their glistening black snouts and the gentle face of his mother. Prickles raised his hand and smiled, calling over at them. "Mum, dad . . . it's me."

Harold Hog looked on in disbelief; Henrietta studied Prickles' shape and wept, this was not their Prickles, parts of him were shiny - and what had happened to his eyes, hands and feet?

"No," snuffled the hedgehogs, clearly in shock. "Our son is dead." Harold turned and comforted his wife. "Our son died a long time ago."

Prickles was stunned.

"Wait!" shouted Rosie, running to join her brother, "Mum, dad, it is . . ." A pair of squirrels leapt upon her and gagged her mouth with some old hay. Prickles twisted around and his feelings of utter disappointment quickly switched to anger. "Let her go!"

"That decision lies with me," replied Mag, his energy levels accelerating. "Surrender yourself to me and she will come to no harm?"

"Don't do it!" cried Baldwin, realising Prickles' potential. "He'll kill us all."

A swift punch across the chin from a brutish squirrel silenced Baldwin.

"Never!" said Prickles, defiantly. His stomach muscles slid across and the grapple hook ejected into his hands. He then fired it at the roof. Magatron rapidly discharged a pulse of energy, narrowly missing Prickles as he recoiled upwards to the safety of the rafters. Mag turned and fired another blast at him, but his targeting was off. It blew another hole through the roof and set the supporting beams alight. The barn was now a melting pot of fear, noise and despair again.

Farmer Cullem froze in his tracks, halfway between the house and the barn. Unable to find his own dressing gown, he was adorned in his wife's pink housecoat and slippers, the torch shaking in his hand. "Bloomin' 'eck!" he cried, turning and running back to the house. "Call the police, the fire brigade, the air ambulance – I want the whole bloomin' lot!"

Inside the barn, squirrels wrestled and boxed with hares; hawks and blackbirds gave it their all against their despotic captors, and Prickles fought with Mag. The hedgehog swung down from the rafter, looping and propelling himself towards the magpie; he did not question where these defensive instincts came from as he rocketed through the air, his feet extended. But at the last second, Prickles felt his weight adjust and he skimmed past Mag, slamming into the squirrels that held Rosie captive instead. Both rodents were pounded against the walls.

"Thanks," said Rosie.

Prickles turned, seeing Mag was powering up his weapon again. "Get to safety!" he yelled, rolling to the corner of the barn. A powerful jet of light and heat flared in the hedgehog's direction, but Magatron had missed again. He couldn't figure out why his targeting didn't lock on – he was programmed never to miss.

The blast destroyed a core section of the barns infrastructure. The whole hangar shook. Flames whipped across the walls like slow motion bolts of lightning, splintering the wood and nails into thousands of charred fragments. The animals fled the vicinity as a section of the roof collapsed, burying Prickles beneath it. Big Mag took evasive action to avoid being hit by the debris himself.

"Fall back!" Mag called. His posse fled, even Nutcase - livid at not being able to even the score with Hercules.

"Prickles!" Rosie cried, rushing over to the smouldering rubble. There was no response.

Baldwin directed the animals out of the barn, keeping a reliable group of hares behind to help carry Hercules' body to safety. The badger could see Rosie weeping at the other end of the barn amidst the smoke. "Get out while you still can, dear!"

"I'm not leaving without my brother," she bawled.

At that moment, a fist burst through a brittle section of the collapsed roofing. Rosie watched as another hand punched through and gripped the jagged sides before Prickles pulled the rest of his body into sight. "I thought I told you to get to safety?" he said, the flames reflecting off his visor. He looked past Rosie at Baldwin and two hares, who were struggling to pull Hercules clear of danger. "Rosie, find mum and dad, I'll be out in a minute."

As Prickles ran over to assist Baldwin, Rosie fled outside. The hares looked warily at the young hedgehog, backing away. Baldwin shot them a disapproving glance. "Help us, please."

Prickles deftly removed a small hook from his utility belt, tying it around Hercules' talons. "We need to be quick," he said, nodding towards the central rafter which was engulfed in fire. "We've got 28 seconds before the whole barn collapses." Thick black smoke from burning tyres began to cloak them all. Prickles ran outside and over to the heaviest, solid looking object he could clamp his body around. Using all his available strength, he held tight and reeled the wire in with Hercules attached to it.

Mrs Cullem was in a state of panic as she spoke to the emergency services (Mandy was about to reveal the identity of her new born baby's father!). Farmer Cullem watched the inferno from his kitchen window – something wasn't right. The sheer number of birds and animals leaving the barn baffled him. Suddenly, a large bird landed on the window ledge and pecked aggressively at the pane of glass. Farmer Cullem jumped backwards at the bird's audacity, and then froze as he took a closer look.

Big Mag's eyes blazed. He had remembered everything from his past life, right up to his last conscious moments. Mag hammered at the windowpane again, cracking the glass. Farmer Cullem stammered in horror, "M-m-magpie!" He quickly turned and hurried upstairs to fetch his camera – he needed photographic evidence of the bird's futuristic features to prove that he wasn't going insane.

From his bedroom window, Farmer Cullem saw that the magpie had flown to the roof of another outbuilding. He began taking pictures, zooming in as far as he could to pick out the magpie's marked differences. Mag's eyes flickered like the flames, aiming them at an object parked in the yard. Farmer Cullem followed the bird's gaze down towards his vintage sports car: nineteen sixties, limited edition Aston Martin, which he had bought from the proceeds of the land sale two years prior.

"Don't you bloomin' dare!" he cried.

Big Mag monitored the farmer's stress levels; it seemed he'd found a suitable object for revenge. As the animals and birds continued to retreat back into the forest, Mag's primary weapon surged once more. His chest tumbled wildly as the power raged and pulsated within. The target locked in sight, Mag fired - this time he did not miss. In one spectacular blast the car disintegrated, exploding into a ball of magnificent orange and red flames which erupted from the fuel tank; the fire danced with strips of hand finished leather trim and walnut veneer, spiralling outwards like a giant Catherine wheel.

His thumb pressed tightly, Farmer Cullem bawled obscenities as he took pictures until the camera beeped: memory full. He stood aghast, blubbering to himself; dreams of a happy, peaceful retirement shattered, watching as the remains of his car choked in the smoke and fire. Farmer Cullem tossed the camera aside and ran back downstairs.

Mrs Cullem was left howling in horror as her husband grabbed his shotgun and burst out into the open. Through the window, she watched him aim it at the roofs of the outbuildings, for any trace of the feathered fiend, but Mag had vanished.

39: Rumours

Prickles stood beside the body of Hercules, as the barn began slowly collapsing behind him. Baldwin, the hares and several other birds and animals did nothing but stare at the young hedgehog.

"What's your name, hog?" asked Baldwin, diplomatically.

"My name is Prickles."

"Prickles, huh? I heard a rumour that you died on the *black river*."

"You're not the first animal to tell me that today, badger."

"Please, call me Baldwin."

Prickles looked up at the badger, recognising the name. Despite the looks and whispers that surrounded him, he sensed no animosity between himself and the gallant mammal.

Baldwin looked over his shoulder, at a pile of unevenly

stacked logs where Prickles' family were huddled together. "Come and rejoice at this miracle," he called, beckoning them over, "come and see your son!"

Prickles looked on, hopeful. A pain inside his chest twisted and pulled at every remaining nerve ending that was left in his body. Mrs Hog looked over at him; Prickles could see the flecks of emerald buried deep within her glistening brown eyes. He remembered the many happy moons they'd spent together in their log pile house when he was a hoglet, recounting stories about great hog explorers and mythical monsters that lay beyond Greenacres' seemingly tranquil setting. In many ways she had been right, a dangerous world did exist outside the comfort of the woods; and like an explorer, he had departed and returned, retaining some of those mythical attributes.

He could hear the animals, muttering between themselves that he was 'the work of woodland demons'.

"I promise you, it's him!" implored Rosie, trying to settle her parent's doubts. "Go and see for yourself."

Henrietta walked forward, leaving her husband behind with Rosie. "Prickles?"

"Yes, it's me." The eager hedgehog stepped towards his mum, but she backed away. "Do you not recognise me?"

"My dear boy, what have they done to you?" said Harold, keeping his distance.

Prickles looked down at his hands and lifted them up towards his visor. If they could see his eyes, he thought,

233

perhaps they would finally be assured that it was *him*. Carefully, he ran his claws along the silver rim, dug them into the fine mocha hairs of his face and unclicked the visor, pulling it away slowly.

Recognising the glimmer in her son's eyes, Henrietta stepped forward to embrace him when a sudden cry from the hares startled everyone.

Farmer Cullem burst round the corner of an outbuilding, his shotgun raised. He was muttering to himself repeatedly: *going to kill that pesky bird, gonna kill it once and for all!* Shuffling over to a small clearing, he turned to see a badger and some hares sat beside four hedgehogs and the body of a red kite. "What's this!?" he shouted, even more confused. "More creatures plotting to destroy my property?" He raised his shotgun and took aim, desperate for retribution.

Without his visor, Prickles was slow to react. All he could do was listen to the farmer's unsteady breathing and the sound of his chubby fingers tapping against the gun's barrel.

All the creatures froze. Then, without warning, a blast of light flooded the area. Sand and debris spun wildly around them like a dust cloud, funnelling in smoke from the barn, as the sound of high speed rotor blades disorientated everyone with their menacing whisper.

Farmer Cullem yelled, bringing his hands up to his eyes to protect them from the dust and burning bright light. In front of him, a chrome, rectangular vessel appeared, hovering silently above the hedgerow.

"It's another demon!" cried a young rabbit, bolting for cover. "The hedgehog is possessed, it's all a trap!" yelled another, disappearing into the haze.

The farmer staggered back, watching as a series of bright green, neon eyes sprouted out from a metallic hull, gauging its surroundings. Farmer Cullem dropped his gun and ran, crying out to his wife, "An alien UFO!"

Prickles also ran to protect his family, but before he could get close, two silver appendages sprung from the menace's bulk and caught him with hydraulic claws.

"No!" screamed Rosie, watching as the mechanical arms pulled her brother away.

"Rosie!" Prickles tried to struggle free, but it was useless against the device's strength.

The machine hastily ascended and its searchlights died, plunging the animals back into darkness and despair.

Rosie wept into her father's chest, her brother cruelly taken from her once again. Henrietta remained in shock. Cautiously, the rest of the animals bundled together in small packs, staring at the grieving hedgehogs.

Baldwin was the first to offer his sympathies. Then he turned and addressed the crowd. "His brave efforts must not be in vain. The council must reconvene immediately - send word for all creatures to meet in my sett at once!"

Unable to move a muscle from the contraption's hold, Prickles watched Greenacres fade into the distance, until all he could see was an orange bubble. Ahead of him, he saw two bright headlights and the shape of a man holding a remote control device stood beside them.

The hands controlling the gadget were thin and nimble, steering it with great care. Windar was relieved to see that Spikez had been secured. Trakz was parked on the roof of the car directing a small searchlight, also thankful for the safe return of his friend.

The Kraken-200 hovered down to a large cage, extended its arm deep into the back of the enclosure, let go of Prickles and swiftly withdrew. The door snapped up, too fast for the hedgehog to escape. Instead, Prickles grabbed the bars of his confine and pulled with all his might.

Windar shook his head. "My my, we best get you back to the lab and find out what went wrong." He kicked open a silver attaché case and switched off the remote for the Kraken-200. The device automatically responded, retracting its thin limbs and packing itself away neatly in its box.

Windar bent down and looked sympathetically at Prickles. As he did so, PIG30N landed on the professor's shoulder and cooed.

Prickles grew animated, snorting and barking at the pigeon he recognised. "You betrayed me!"

PIG30N shook her head vigorously. Windar caught sight of this and sighed. "Don't tell me you're coming down with bird flu."

As Windar secured them all into the back of his car, Trakz

rocked back and forth in his cage. He tapped nervously against the rail of his friend's cage. "Hey, Spikez - what happened out there?"

There was no response. Prickles did not stir, even as the car engine started and the vehicle began to move. He just sat, staring into the corner of his container.

"Hey, Spikez - it's me, Trakz. What's going on?"

Prickles turned, irritated by the noise the mouse was making. "Are you talking to someone?"

"Whoa, steady on Spikez, I'm just worried about you, that's all."

"What did you call me?" Prickles walked over and studied Trakz. "Oh my gosh, what happened to your legs?"

Trakz rolled his eyes. "This is why my parents warned me never to roam the woods late at night. First Magatron, now you." Trakz turned his attention to PIG30N in the opposite cage. "What next, I guess you'll learn to speak!"

PIG30N gave a glazed look in return, bobbing her head from side to side.

Prickles thought about the name 'Magatron'. Some of the spikes on his back tingled at the thought. "Who are you? Why am I here? What's going on?" he asked the mouse frantically.

Trakz twirled round, reacting to his friend's amnesia. "Your questions always come in threes! Listen, Spikez, we've had this conversation before. Let's wait until we get back to the lab and the professor can fix you up."

"It's Prickles," he replied.

"What is?"

"My name – it's not Spikez. It's Prickles."

40: Spirits

The animals congregated in the depths of the Eastern Forest, at Baldwin's hideout. The crowd remained restless, spooked by the evening's events; every twig snap or leaf rustle caused alarm. Hares and rodents shuffled close to one another, away from the hedgehogs.

Baldwin had moved Hercules to safety in one of his most secretive underground dens, where he was being nurtured by Mira, Arim and Joy.

Deacon arrived, accompanied by Eliza and some songbirds so that the meeting could get underway.

"My Friends, I fear that we are now fighting a new enemy," Baldwin began.

"I'm not fighting anymore," whimpered one of the young rabbits. "Enough is enough. We only just managed to defeat them last time. Look at us!" His eyes, like so many others amongst the crowd, were bloodshot. "We need to leave Greenacres before Big Mag kills us all."

"Oh, I don't think he wants to kill us," assured Baldwin, trying to prevent mass panic. "He would rather lead us all in a life of misery than destroy the very fabric of his ideal society - he wants us to work for him. If we run, he will follow and bring destruction to other communities. We must try new methods and seek new allies if we are to defeat our renewed enemy."

The animals all shook their heads. "By looking for new allies, I suppose you're suggesting that we all take a trip down to the man-base to become transformed into demons!" snapped a normally quiet and timid shrew.

"Whatever are you saying?"

"You saw it! We all did - what they've done to that young hedgehog. They mutilated him, sucked up his guts and turned him into something wicked, as bad as Mag."

Eliza interjected. "No one ever said it was wicked. Without him we would all still be prisoners in that barn. The young hog was oblivious to his physical differences, sadly we were not. He is still out there, as is Mag, and unless we can find another way to defend ourselves, then we may have no choice but to find the young hedgehog and ask for help."

A blanket of silence met her comments. "You can't suggest that we put our faith in a freak?" the shrew replied.

Deacon flew into the centre of the clearing, next to Baldwin. "We're not asking you to put your faith in anyone but yourselves. If we've any spirit left, then we must work together whilst we are still free. Without faith, there is no resistance - we must make plans to prepare ourselves for a long battle."

"This is madness," scoffed one of the Kestrels, flustered by Mag's display of power. "We must pray that whatever captured the hedgehog will capture Big Mag and send it back to the spirit world where he belongs."

Whilst the creatures bickered, Mr and Mrs Hog said nothing. Rosie listened eagerly to the council, seeking answers from their dialogue about where her brother might be, but the pain was too much for her parents. As plans were formulated, the couple silently slipped away to grieve privately back at their nest.

41: Hood's Curse

U naware of the explosive outcome at Ringpull's trial,
Hood was busy preaching to his clan of magpies in a
dark region of the forest. Hood was popular amongst
the magpies, for the way that he had exiled Ringpull so swiftly
– and the fact that he wore the pendant, which hung from his
neck, swinging hypnotically as he spoke.   The eagle emblem
was still synonymous with authority.

Suddenly, out of nowhere, magpie chattering echoed through
the trees around them. Ringpull burst out of the darkness and
into the clearing, chased by two magpies loyal to Hood. They
quickly landed on top of him, pecking fiercely at his neck. A
crowd soon gathered around them and watched, eager to do
the same.

"Wait," cried Ringpull. "Hear me out just this once, and then
you may do whatever you like to me."

Hood scowled, clipping him across the beak with his wing. "You're forgetting something, Ringpull. You don't tell us what we can and can't do anymore." Hood volleyed forward and knocked the magpie hard in the face.

The other birds huddled together to form an impenetrable ring as they relished their leader's display of aggression. "Kill him!" cackled one magpie; "Peck his eyes out!" cawed another. The crowd were frantic with anger, egging Hood on as he grasped Ringpull's neck tightly with his claws. "Hood! Hood! Hood!" they chanted. Youngsters were ushered to the front of the mob, encouraged to watch the grown-ups fight.

"Any final words?" Hood asked.

Ringpull looked at the rabid eyes surrounding him, and then slowly and unexpectedly began to laugh. "Yes, as a matter of fact I have three." Ringpull fixed his eyes at Hood. "Look-behind-you!"

Seeing it as a last ditch attempt to break free, Hood ignored the comments and maintained his choke hold, but there was something sinisterly odd about Ringpull's tone. The magpies' ranting gradually ceased. Hood turned to see that their beaks had stiffened and were pointing at the forest behind him. He looked for himself - something was definitely there, lurking amongst rotting debris and the tangled limbs of dead tree branches.

A mystical orb appeared and then disappeared, as though one blazing eye had blinked at them all.

Hood pushed himself to the front of the pack, alert. The light flickered again, this time burning brighter until it suddenly extinguished. The magpies shuffled nervously as it appeared again, hovering above them like a glowing omen. Closer it came, blinding those stood on the edge of the circle; magpies flapped frantically and cowered behind their leader. Hood stood firm, ready to face the threat trespassing on *his* clearing.

Emerging into clear view, Big Mag landed and marched forward purposefully, his chest ablaze. Hood turned back at Ringpull. "What is the meaning of this?"

"The great leader returns."

Hood pivoted defiantly at Mag. "Never!" In his eyes, Mag was dead and whatever stood before him would be reminded of this.

Fine bursts of steam funnelled out from behind Mag's neck and his eyes glittered like rubies. "Hood, I commend your bravery, but I have returned to finish the job."

"You are not real. None of this is real - this is witchcraft!" He spoke so that all the magpies could hear. "He is a demon, he no longer has any authority here. He has come to try and lead us all to our deaths!"

Ringpull got to his feet and hovered dangerously behind Hood.

"It is I, Big Mag, and you will give me what is rightfully mine. Do not make me do this the hard way."

Hood's heart beat fiercely - he looked down at the crest around his neck. He wasn't ready to surrender it so quickly, not without a fight. "No! You can't have it. Get away from here – leave us!"

Mag had expected some opposition to his return, but did not

anticipate Hood to be so consumed by the emblem's power – a curse to all who wore it. Mag bowed his head and took a few paces back. "So be it."

Hood reacted triumphantly, beating his tail up and down forcefully as he watched Mag retreat further, slowly slipping into the shadows. As he turned to address the magpies, a burning sensation zapped across his face: Ringpull had savagely pecked out his eye! Hood was left flapping and cawing in agony.

The magpies erupted in a chorus of furious squawking, bouncing fretfully from side to side. Chataka-chataka! A couple of them nudged forward, as if to avenge Hood, but they were terrified of Big Mag who still lingered in view.

"Don't believe your eyes, 'ey?" cried Ringpull, Hood's eyeball grasped neatly in his beak. He laughed fanatically, flying up to the branches.

Hood spun wildly, chattering in sorrow. With his good eye, he had enough time to see the white of Mag's chest burn like phosphorous before unleashing its power directly at him.

Fumbling upwards and sideways, the magpies flew from the blast zone in a blind panic. When they turned back towards their leader, all they saw was the shape of Big Mag lifting the treasured motif up from the floor with his beak, and a cloud of scorched feathers drifting to earth around him like dead angel's wings. Hood had been completely vaporised – except for the eye, which Ringpull swiftly threw into the air and devoured.

The emblem attached itself magnetically to Mag's chest; he was now leader again, self-appointed but in charge nonetheless.

Ringpull flew down beside him.

The rest of the magpies peered nervously from the trees. Mag scanned each of their faces, mapped their heat signatures, and searched for signs of further trouble: there was none.

Eventually, a lone magpie courageously bounded out into the open and lowered his head before Mag. "What do you want from us?" he asked.

Mag slowly stepped forward. "Loyalty," he affirmed.

42: Secrets of the Mainframe

At approximately 5am, Windar was busy interfacing with his computer, preparing to run diagnostic tests on Spikez. A series of long, thin cables were lined up on the table linked to flashing circuit boxes and computer terminals. The surroundings seemed familiar to Prickles, but he still couldn't make complete sense of his situation.

"What's he doing?" the hedgehog asked, directing his attention at the blue mouse who was busy carrying wires back and forth.

"He's going to connect you to the mainframe," replied Trakz.

"What's the mainframe?"

"I'm a mouse, not a scientist – can we ease up with the questions?" Trakz looked up at Prickles' vacant expression. "Okay, think of it as something that will help fill the gaps in your memory."

The hedgehog looked on in anticipation as the professor withdrew a large, chrome sphere and connected it to two red wires which led to Prickles' docking pod. He noted how Windar kept checking his watch every few minutes, glancing at the lab door.

"Have you ever been connected to this . . . mainframe?"

"Sure, all the time - Windar uses it to train me."

"Train you to do what?"

"To look after you guys." Trakz sensed Prickles' bewilderment. "Don't worry, I'll be connected to the mainframe with you, you won't feel a thing."

PIG30N had already downloaded all her mission data. It was her GPS signal that had allowed Windar to locate Prickles with the Kraken-200, a recovery bot. Using these files, the professor planned to cycle through Prickle's short term memory, cross-referencing missing video footage to ascertain what had led to his malfunction.

Prickles' cage was lowered on to the table as the laboratory lights dimmed. PIG30N looked on as Trakz ushered the hedgehog out and over to his docking station. Prickles remained reluctant, in his mind he had a frozen image of his family staring back at him with cold, fearful eyes.

Trakz connected the first cable to Prickles' stomach. "That tickles," he said, watching the mouse connect another cable to one of his spikes. Trakz left and returned again with a thicker, sharper looking wire, wheeling himself out of sight behind the hedgehog's docking station.

"Now," muttered Trakz, "this one may tingle slightly."

Before Prickles could react, a surge of pressure shot up his spine and into his head until his mind felt ready to burst. Then he blacked out.

Prickles' mind awoke, floating somewhere between the physical world and what he imagined to be the animal spirit world. The feeling lasted for hours, or was it seconds? The concept of time and reality no longer seemed to exist, or did it? Blackness was soon interrupted by tiny flickers of green light, shooting from all around him. Insignificant neon doors gradually appeared and encircled him, they were carefully ordered and uniform like 0s and 1s, hundreds, thousands of them; dancing digits flashing on and off like fireflies in a clear night sky.

Windar watched his monitor whilst the computer accessed Spikez' hard drive.

```
synchronisation complete.
connected to host . . . SPIK-3Z
repairing bad sectors . . . please wait
```

The professor began mapping Spikez' recorded data with location grid references to access appropriate video files. Trakz also watched the monitor, seeing the pictures flash back and forth: he saw an image of a young deer, bounding along the forest floor; serene river settings and thick leafy canopies swaying gently in the breeze; there was a flicker of interference in two frames just before an image of a hedgehog appeared, resting by the river, and in the background a fox lingered; another glitch and then the video froze.

Humming to himself, Windar cross referenced the error log. "Looks like primal instincts took control," he deduced. Trakz was a little more perceptive, identifying the hedgehog as the cause of the malfunction, not the fox. He could see that there were clear similarities in the shape of her snout and pattern of her spikes.

Windar shuttled through the footage again, frantically hand-writing notes and checking his watch intermittently. The female hedgehog appeared again; Trakz could tell that she had been crying. The images continued to roll forward: river trails, paths through bracken and the gradual onset of nightfall. Eventually they came to images of Spikez motioning towards a barn, then being attacked by a magpie and a squirrel - but it was just a warm up to a marvellous spectacle.

"Good golly!" he exclaimed, refixing his glasses.

Trakz saw it, too. "I knew it!" he squeaked to himself.

The professor was distracted. He got up and paced the room as he thought about what he'd seen. Windar thought back to the work on swarm intelligence he'd conducted with researchers at Goldsmiths, University of London, years earlier. He was witnessing something totally unique. One intelligently enhanced being was controlling swarms of other creatures. He had recorded such behaviour before in small lab tests with insects and microbots, but nothing on this scale.

Trakz felt the opposite, it confirmed what he had suspected all along – that Magatron had a dark side.

Knowing that he was on the verge of one of the greatest scientific developments in animal behavioural science, Windar sat back down and watched sheepishly as Spikez and Magatron demolished the barn in their attempts to destroy each other. He was just glad that their failsafe mechanisms, designed to avoid injury through friendly fire, had not remained offline. The only way they could fairly fight each other would be if their locator chips were completely removed or if Windar reprogrammed them.

Baldwin and the other land creatures had finally agreed a plan. They would offer shelter to the weakest, young and elderly population of Greenacres in their respective dens, setts or burrows. It was also proposed that the more physically able would work together to protect these havens and gather food whilst the agile would become messengers, going beyond Greenacres to warn neighbouring woods and scrublands about possible magpie invasion.

The morning sun slowly diluted the dark hues of night. Baldwin was about to call the meeting to a close when a cold and heartless voice shouted out: "Nice plan, Baldy, but how do you expect to win the battle if you keep running away from the fight?"

"Nutley!" Baldwin replied, peering into the darkness.

"It's Nutcase to you," the squirrel retorted, pouncing into the light. He was accompanied by Stoatey.

Eliza clenched her talons, as did Deacon. They both contemplated dealing with Nutcase there and then, but they were conscious that the rodent was not alone. Surrounding the meeting, a wall of exposed teeth and rabid eyes reflected the sun's rays; Nutcase's followers were plentiful, and poised to scratch, kick and bite to the death if Nutley so desired.

"I'll make you an offer, Baldwin. Give me Hercules and you can all leave here unscathed."

"Never!"

The rabbits and mice looked nervously at the depraved looking squirrel faces. The ruthless rodent strutted over to the badger with an air of assurance. "Whether you cooperate with me or not, Baldy, you can't stop the inevitable. Hercules will never fly again. Let me put him out of his misery."

"You're a coward!" squawked Eliza.

"Shut it, Queenie! No-one care's what you think now you're the same as the rest of us."

Stoatey piped up. "Why Eliza, you are a bird of such little faith. Is it so hard for you to believe that a magpie could lead us all to greater things, more than your worthless Animal Council ever did for these lands and those that depended upon it? You arrogantly expected them all to follow your ways, your rules, and your . . . leadership, handed down from sparrowhawk to sparrowhawk without so much as a vote? And you call that a democracy? Times have changed and that's why you're all here, hiding from reality. We've evolved!"

Deacon interjected. "You sound like him."

"Like who?" snapped Stoatey, roused by his own rhetoric.

"Big Mag – everything about you oozes the same type of evil expression. You're so blinded by his ambition to rule and control, that you have no value of what it means to have complete freedom, or to make choices," proclaimed Deacon. "Eliza has always put the creatures of Greenacres first and we are all proud to have her as our elected Queen!"

"No, wise owl, it is you who is deluded. When you live on land that is owned by man, there is no freedom. The black rivers and shiny walls surrounding our homes take away that privilege. That's why Mag is different - he will take back the land from the humans and restore natural order."

Prickles continued to float in a conscious state. Many of the neon doors surrounding him were now unlocked and open. Bit by bit things made more sense – the accident, the lab, Rosie's plight and the identity of Magatron; he remembered the blue mouse's name and felt bad for calling the pigeon a traitor. And as his memory thrived, he replayed the outcome of the evening's events at the barn over again in his head. These heightened, synchronised memories brought with them a deeper apprehension about his situation, and raised questions about his future – would he see his family again, would he ever mate with another hedgehog, and what were Magatron's intentions?

```
Defragmentation complete
Please back up your files regularly to avoid
future memory loss . . .
```

Trakz peered down at Prickles' face as he awoke. "Welcome back . . . to the real world."

The hedgehog sat up, gasping for air as he grabbed Trakz' tiny arms. "Steady on, Prickles, there's no danger here."

"No, you're wrong," he countered. "The animals are in danger. Magatron's going to destroy my home unless we do something now. You need to help me."

"Buddy," Trakz said, removing a wire, "if I could, you know I would . . . but Windar is the only person who can take you back into the wild, and he's looking pretty flaky right now."

Prickles looked across to see the professor propped against the coffee machine on his fifth cup, making notes on an epad. "Then send him a message, tell him that I need to get back to Greenacres."

"Look," Trakz wheeled in closer, "I know it's hard to accept, but things are very different now. I really wish I could give you some hope that it'd be possible to go see your family again, but it's time for another reality check. Look at you!" Prickles glanced down at his claws and complex mecahnics. "You've got your full memory back, which is great, but you're not a normal hedgehog anymore. Things can never go back to how they were, however much you want them to. It's the painful truth, no matter how hard it is to admit. The lab is your home now."

Prickles watched Trakz wheel himself away. He looked up at PIG30N, who was roosting in her coop, and then at an empty enclosure . . . his cage, the one that read 'SPIK-3Z' across the top of it.

It was 6:03am when the laboratory doors crashed open and Flattery bounded in, earlier than expected. "Give me some good news, Professor."

Windar floundered. "Well, I've located Magatron."

"Is he here?"

"Er, no, not yet."

The colonel yanked Windar by the scruff of his neck and pushed him against the cages. Prickles wanted to intervene like he had with agent Dahab at the restaurant, but he quickly reasoned that it would not be good move for Windar or the rest of the team.

"I told you not to mess this up, Windar. I've a morning briefing with General Grievance in little over an hour."

"I'm sorry."

"So am I," replied Flattery, releasing Windar and straightening his own uniform. He walked over to the door, stopped and glanced back. "Have you ever considered a career in taxidermy?" He tutted to himself and then stormed out, shouting: "I'll be back!"

43: Animal Rights

General Grievance sat in the back of his chauffeur driven car, on his way to the Greenacres Military Base. A copy of the Financial Times lay at his side as he gazed out across the splendid British countryside; it was a glorious day and he was feeling rather patriotic.

As the vehicle approached the barriers to the complex, the driver slowed and called back. "Sir, I think you should see this."

Grievance sat forward and gazed through the windscreen. A mass of news reporters had blitzed the site and a very angry looking Farmer Cullem had barricaded the entrance with his tractor and trailer. He was in the process of being arrested by army police to a furore of screaming and heckling from local villagers and animal rights protestors, who continued to gather in numbers. Activists waved banners high, painted in blood red across white sheets: 'Animals Have Rights', 'Stop this Bloody Abomination' and the most damning of all, 'No to Military Animals!!!'.

Grievance pondered for a moment - did he have a mole at the base leaking secrets to the general public? 'Perhaps that bloke at Wikipeeps has been at it again?' he thought to himself. This troubled him, but it didn't explain Farmer Cullem's behaviour since he had benefited financially from the construction of the base.

The car rolled to a halt. Photographers and protesters ran towards the vehicle, peering through the tinted glass. Army guards rushed over to disperse the crowd, pushing them aside. Grievance blew heavily through his nose, ruffling his moustache to attention. He was not one to take a back seat in the face of anarchy. "Unlock the doors!"

General Grievance stepped out and stood proud. Despite his age he still had the vigour and presence of an Olympian bull. He looked over at the main guard by the base entrance, beckoning him over with his eyebrows.

"General, sir, I think you should read this," the guard said, formally handing him a copy of the Daily News, a low brow national tabloid. Grievance's eyebrows danced above his eyes as he read the headline. He lowered the paper, rolled it up, tucked it under his arm like a staff, and marched forward.

Reporters targeted their recorders and microphones at him, firing accusations and anticipating a response to the questions that ricocheted off the general's thick skin.

Farmer Cullem was being restrained by two guardsmen as

his tractor was moved away. He looked up at the approaching enormity of Grievance, recognising him by rank and stature.

"Farmer Cullem, you remember me?" Grievance asked.

"Yes, General."

"Then what is the meaning of this?"

"You're weapons nearly destroyed my farm!" he yelled, for all to hear.

"Weapons?" retorted Grievance. "I can assure you, Mr Cullem, that I run this base as tightly as any military operation. Nothing leaves this site without my knowing. Now explain yourself!"

"The magpie!" Farmer Cullem exclaimed. "That bloomin' bird, he came back."

"Magpie? Dear boy, you're not making any sense," he glanced at the reporters and whispered to him. "Are you well?"

"Don't you patronise me, Mr Grievance-"

"General Grievance!"

"Sorry, General. Your professor: Professor Windar." Farmer Cullem turned to the cameras as reporters frantically scribbled down the name: Win-dar. "He rang me and asked for some birds to experiment with. So I gave him a magpie, the biggest and peskiest one that I could find on my farm. Weeks later, the bird came back and destroyed my barn and my . . ." Farmer Cullem's voice began to break. "He killed Moneypenny."

"Your wife?"

"No, no - my car!"

Grievance thought for a moment, then he directed the guards to lead the farmer away. "Get that man a hot drink and a soft pillow."

"General Grievance ..." A young female reporter with pouting red lips pushed herself to the front of the pack. "What do you have to say about these extraordinary allegations?"

"Well, they are just that, my dear – extraordinary. There is no operation that I know of that could substantiate such wild claims. I will, of course, investigate these allegations in the interests of public safety and we will scrutinise any credible evidence passed before us."

"Does this Professor Windar work for you?"

"I'm not at liberty to give out that type of information, but rest assured we will get to the bottom of this!" Grievance looked over at his car. The driver gave him the all clear. "Now, if you'll excuse me, I have pressing matters to attend to."

The general marched back to his car, ignoring several feral accusations made against him. As he did so, an animal rights activist broke forward and blocked his path. He was a starved looking man with thick matted hair and wild eyes, his nose and ears were littered with black piercings. In his hands, dirty and laced with strands of black wool, he gripped a placard which read 'Animals will have their REVENGE!'.

Grievance snorted to get past, but the man refused to move, blocking the general's advancement. "Step aside, boy!" the general growled.

Staring him back in the eyes, the man threw his placard aside and pulled open his ragged cardigan. Beneath it was a black, skull-print t-shirt; Grievance noted that the protestor's arms were tightly wrapped with rubber bands and that the skull was actually that of a corvid's. "Caaahhhhh!" he squawked.

259

The photographers erupted with laughter; the military guards could not disguise their smirks at the absurdity of the whole situation.

Grievance deftly removed the rolled newspaper from under his arm and struck the activist across his beak-like nose, sending him flapping to the floor. Protesters jeered and camera bulbs flashed as Grievance stepped over the man, continued to his car and got in.

The protester got back to his feet and sneered. "He's coming for you. He's coming for all of you!" he shouted, before disappearing through the crowd and vanishing out of sight.

The driver accelerated through the main entrance. Grievance unrolled his baton, brushed off a black feather from his tunic and studied the front page once again. "This is not how I like to start my day."

"You know I'll find him sooner or later," Nutcase snarled, striking Baldwin across the jaw.

The badger barely winced. "Even if you do, you can never destroy his reputation amongst the creatures of Greenacres. There will be other red kites, badgers and even honourable squirrels who will replace us all - repairing this dreadful mess you've created. Nothing good ever comes from chaos."

Nutcase swiped Baldwin across the face again. "Fool, when will you stop your boring lectures about the past and the future?" Nutcase turned his attention to Eliza, guarded by two rooks. "And what say you, Eliza?"

"I have nothing to say to you," she said. "Hercules will grow strong and return to save us."

"He cannot save you!" a voice boomed.

The animals turned their heads to see Big Mag hovering under the canopy, Ringpull loitered closely behind him. Mag's chest burned brightly like the morning sun as he approached Eliza. "I've made sure that he will never fly again, yet you continue to put your faith in a bird that cannot even raise a feather for your pathetic cause. By withholding his location you are only extending his pain. Where's the humanity in that?"

"What do you know about humanity?" spat Baldwin. Nutcase ran over and kicked the badger in the stomach for his insubordination.

"You do not know Hercules like I do," Eliza retorted.

"Obviously not," Mag replied. He turned to Nutcase. "There's been a change of plan."

"What do you mean?"

"Forget about Hercules for now, let him suffer – he poses no threat to us."

"But you promised me we'd find him."

"There's a new priority, we need to find the hedgehog."

"How? My sources say that he was taken away."

"He will return," continued Big Mag. "And we need to be ready for when he does, I'm not letting anything ruin my plans this time." A burst of steam shot out from his neck leaving a ghostly trail in the canopy. "Find the hedgehog's family."

"And then what?"

"Wait and see."

44: Grievance for Windar

Unaware of the disturbances at the gates, Flattery arrived for his morning meeting with Grievance. Miriam, the general's secretary, directed him through the large oak doors to his office; a grand room filled with war memorabilia, books, antique furniture and several military filing cabinets.

Grievance was sat at his desk, casually handwriting a memo. "Take a seat, Colonel."

Flattery sat opposite. "What's on the agenda today, general?"

"Would you like some tea? Miriam's prepared a nice pot of Earl Grey for us both."

"Thank you, General." The cups were finely decorated with the MoD insignia. The gentle scent of bergamot relieved some of Flattery's tension as he poured himself a steaming hot cup.

"Have you read today's papers?" asked Grievance, sliding a copy of the Daily News across the table.

Flattery choked, spraying his tea across the table. Grievance looked on as Flattery dabbed his mouth with a hanky, before steadying his hands around the paper:

BIO BOTS BLITZ BARN!

Reporter: Harry Brown

Britain's armed forces were steeped in controversy today after experimental, military robots wreaked havoc in the peaceful village of Greenacres.

These stunning images, captured by a local farmer, suggest that the Ministry of Defence has been experimenting with British wildlife to create state of the art weaponry.

Farmer Cullem, who fell victim to the animal cyborg, alleged that the base had transformed a common magpie from a native pest into a lethal killing machine.

"I was at home when I heard a disturbance outside" Farmer Cullem said.

"When I went to investigate, I saw my barn going up in flames. As I called the fire brigade I noticed a magpie with burning red eyes!

"I rushed to get my camera and watched as the monster blew up my beloved car with a laser!"

The astonishing images, which are still being examined by experts, show the robotic bird obliterating the vehicle with high-tech weaponry in a scene reminiscent from science fiction comics.

Another villager, Verity Stiles, also claimed that a magpie was the cause of a near fatal car accident, which occurred along a serene stretch of country road. Crash scene investigators indicated that the car had suffered from 'abnormal' loss of power caused by 'external forces'.

All fingers point towards Greenacres Military Base, a site which has been steeped in controversy since its opening last August.

"I sold my land to the military believing that I was doing my bit for England," continued Farmer Cullem.

"Now I don't feel safe anymore, I feel betrayed. I thought the military were supposed to protect us from danger. Who knows what else they're hiding in there."

Police forensic teams are still investigating the scene of the fire and are working alongside military officials.

More focus is due to be directed at the military base in the coming days, and MPs have already called for an inquiry, with some critics suggesting that the base will jump to the front of the queue in light of harsh budget cuts.

Did you see anything happen in the area? Call our news-line NOW on 0800 123 4567. We pay cash for your stories!

"There's a whole mob of reporters and demonstrators outside," said Grievance. "I've also just been on the phone with the Home Secretary – he was very upset."

Flattery shook his head in disbelief, studying the image of Magatron firing at the car. "What did you say to him?"

"I denied any knowledge of the operation, of course," continued Grievance. "I've since spoken to three of the generals from France, Germany and Holland who joined us for the launch of Project Carrion. They have all distanced themselves from this venture."

"This is bad news," said Flattery, rubbing the top of his head vigorously.

"Bad news is good news," said Grievance, "if you're a reporter writing this type of nonsense. No doubt there will be more stories and further investigations. I have already given an impromptu statement to the press this morning."

"Saying what, sir?"

"Exactly what I told the home secretary - that I had no knowledge of such an operation and that we would investigate any claims made against our team of scientists." Grievance rested his pen back in its holder and sat up sharply. "Which leads me to ask you this, Colonel: did you know of any such operation?"

Flattery looked on, confused. "General?"

"Were you aware of Professor Windar conducting any live tests with robotic animals?"

The colonel stumbled; it took him a few moments to catch the shimmer in Grievances eyes. "No, General."

"Then you know what you have to do?"

"Yes, General."

"Very well, you have my authority."

Replacing his cup and saucer on the table, Flattery stood and saluted. As he walked towards the door, Grievance called out. "It's a shame really - I was rather fond of Windar and his pets."

Flattery wavered by the door for a moment, contemplating Grievance's sincerity for Windar - he felt none.

Prickles, Trakz and PIG30N were in their respective cages as Windar made final preparations to retrieve Magatron from the field. He was interrupted by the sound of doors opening and three pairs of army boots marching in. A pair of shiny black shoes followed them.

"Good morning, Colonel. Is there a problem?"

"You really should spend more time reading newspapers rather than instruction manuals. I don't suppose you've watched the morning news, have you?" enquired Flattery.

Windar, bemused, shook his head. The colonel flicked on the main projector and selected a 24 hour news channel. Prickles and his team pressed themselves against the bars to view the images. A young female reporter, with thick auburn hair and a red suit, stood outside the base entrance. Blue ticker tape flashed along the bottom of the screen 'Breaking News: Scientist Named' as she spoke.

"I'm standing outside the military base which has been at the heart of the latest scandal involving the British Ministry of Defence. Earlier, I spoke to the commander of the base who claimed he was unaware of any secret military operation involving the use of robotically enhanced wildlife. This comes after allegations from a local farmer that a militarised magpie attacked his home, destroying thousands of pounds-worth of property. There have also been fresh developments here this morning, with speculation that a man called Professor Windar is behind this operation . . ." Windar felt the colour of his cheeks drain slowly away to his feet.

"Further investigation has revealed that Professor Albert Windar is indeed a scientist who has worked extensively with animals and robotics. Researchers are claiming that Windar experimented with several types during mine clearance operations in North Africa. He later left his esteemed job at the Humanitarian De-mining Organization in Geneva to work on unconfirmed experiments for the military. More details are still trickling in, but we hope to have more for you as this truly explosive story unfolds . . ."

"What's happening?" asked Prickles.

"I think Windar's going to vomit," replied Trakz.

Flattery clicked the sound on mute and looked at Windar. "You know what this means, don't you?"

Windar pleaded. "Colonel, I can fix this."

"I'm sorry, Windar, really I am." Flattery walked over to the cages and peered in at the professor's creations. "But I did warn you that if you messed up this would happen. The operation is over - Project Carrion is terminated." He nodded towards the guards who seized Windar by the arms. "There will be an internal review and possible charges brought against you, but don't worry, the investigation will yield nothing. All of the evidence will be destroyed, including your little friends."

"No!" Windar cried, motioning towards the cages. The officers held him back and awaited Flattery's orders.

"I must hasten to remind you that you are bound by the official secrets act. Take him away. Make sure he stays far, far away from here."

Before Windar could protest further, he was dragged out of the lab and led down the corridor.

Flattery was left alone in the room with Prickles, Trakz and PIG30N. "Well, I guess we'll have to sell you on to the highest bidder. I think the Chinese liked you a lot – it's just a shame we have to dismantle you first." Flattery smirked to himself, turned then froze.

General Grievance stood at the door, surveying the lab. "Is it done?" he asked.

"Yes, General."

"Well done, Colonel. Lock this place down, no-one goes in or out without my authorisation, is that clear?"

Flattery affirmed Grievance's orders and watched him pace over to the specimens. He gave them all a hard look and glanced at the empty cage of Magatron. "We will need to send our men out into the local woods to seize the remaining . . . monstrosity. Use whatever means necessary but be careful of snooping reporters, they're easier to shoot but harder to cover up."

After scouring the lab, the colonel returned his attention to the TV news – cameras were zooming in towards the main gates where Windar was being ejected. A pack of reporters and a mob of angry activists ran towards him but he was quickly bundled into a military car and driven away.

"Have the crowds moved away from the base immediately, use force if necessary, they have their story now. If we keep our communication channels managed tightly, these sensationalist newspapers will have to start inventing their own facts and figures, making the whole operation seem unbelievable. Drip feed them every now and then, and be selective with the files you leak about our old friend, Windar."

Grievance went to leave but couldn't resist taking one more look at the little blue mouse, who had been staring at them the whole time. Trakz peered up at the general with two magnified eyes, his nose twitching. He then spun in a circle on his tracks and held the bars with his paws. The general gave a hearty laugh. "Yes, I do like this one a lot. Have him transferred to my office."

"General, are you sure? I don't recommend meddling with any of his pets."

"Flattery, he's just a mouse. What harm can he do?"

Flattery shrugged his shoulders. "I'll have him delivered to you by lunch."

45: Scapegoat

Windar was shielded in the back of a car as fists banged on the doors and windows. He was in deep thought, worried about his creations – he knew what would happen to them; a lifetime's work destroyed, the patented technology resold to other organizations and countries regardless of their ethics or intentions. The professor felt betrayed by Flattery. He could not accept this cruel injustice, yet at the same time he was humble enough to recognise that his creations had malfunctioned. But Windar knew he had the means to prevent further mishaps.

As the car reached the main road, Windar began formulating a plan to rescue Spikez, PIG30N and Trakz from destruction.

The journey to his house should have taken ten minutes; Windar was puzzled as to why the driver had taken a much longer route. He had said it was to 'shake off' pursuing paparazzi and that he was just following 'standard military protocols'. It gave Windar more time to figure out how his plan would work. He would remotely control the team from his home and release them to safety in the wild where he could then retrieve them and dismantle their locater chips. But he had to think of back-up plans - the military would come looking. It was dangerous, high risk, a massive gamble - if he got caught trying to recover them, he would be jailed for stealing military secrets! But then Windar was a man with nothing to lose - it was the only way to set things straight.

Approaching the penultimate turn towards his house, 13 Woolcroft Drive, the professor tingled at the thought of launching his own counter operation. However, as the vehicle turned the last corner, all his hopes were dashed.

The wheels ground to a halt. The driver turned to Windar and gave an apologetic look with a glint of knowing in his eyes. Windar fumbled with his belt and got out of the car.

"There he is!" A horde of reporters stampeded over to the professor amidst an ambush of camera flashes, shooting at him from all angles. Windar attempted to break through the barrier, pushing his arms forward to see what was happening outside his home. He battled his way to the front gate. Investigation Officers from the Ministry of Defence were busy removing computer monitors, hard drives and other technical paraphernalia from Windar's home.

"Stop!" Windar cried. "You can't do this!"

The TV crews had already taken up prime filming positions,

seemingly knowing what to expect, capturing Windar in an emotive close-up as he pleaded with officers to let him into his own house.

"Professor Windar, how do you respond to claims that you've manufactured weapons of mass destruction using British wildlife?"

Windar looked round, bewildered and confused. Amongst the sets of teeth and lips, chattering and pouting around him, he tried to identify where the voice had come from. It was a man's voice, stern and absolute. It belonged to Harry Brown, a reporter from the Daily News, standing at the front of the queue of journalists waiting to interrogate Windar. "Farmer Cullem claims that he gave you a dead magpie, and that you brought it back to life as a weapon which was used against him. What do you say to that?"

"I think nothing of it, this is insane."

"Then why are the military raiding your house and why, Professor, have you just been expelled from the military base at Greenacres?"

"I'm being blamed for something I haven't done." Windar wanted to tell them the truth, to tell them his version of events, but Flattery had warned of the consequences; he was gagged by red tape.

Harry Brown pointed his pen at Windar once again. "The military has just released a statement saying that you were operating outside of their knowledge and that you are to be psychologically re-assessed. How does that make you feel?"

Psychologically re-assessed? Windar had to get away. "No comment."

Another voice called out from the crowd. "Professor Windar, is it true that you were fired from your job in Geneva after experimenting with mice and machine guns?"

"No comment."

"Is it true that your wife left you because of your unhealthy passion for rabbits?"

"That's a ridiculous claim!"

A mature female reporter with tinted red glasses added to the scalding accusations. "Is it true, Professor, that you once left your own nephew and niece to play at your home – alone - with military experiments?"

"What?" Windar faltered, wondering where were they getting this information from and how they could possibly know about what happened with Josh and Emily. "I have nothing more to say on this or any other matter until I find out exactly what's going on."

Windar searched the crowds for an ally - anybody. He recognised some of the officers emptying his house, but they were stony faced and ignored the professor as he ground his teeth in frustration, counting several clear plastic bags full of tools, transponders and terabytes of sensitive data.

"Not my laptop!" he cried, amidst the continual flashing of bulbs, all of which gave Windar an intense migraine. He felt like his head was about to explode, and then it did. His right cheek splintered and his glasses became congealed with albumen. There was a chorus of cheers from the animal rights mob. "Animal butcher scum!" they shouted, happy to see that the egg they'd thrown had hit the professor in the face.

Windar dropped to the floor and began to hyper-ventilate.

A motorbike exhaust roared into life. Windar heard it above the maddening scrum of reporters. He knew his bikes and recognised the deep sound of the sports muffler rumbling at him. The professor peered through the forest of legs to identify the source. The engine revved again. A biker, dressed in black leathers with her visor lifted up, stared back at Windar. His eyes caught hers. There was a hint of familiarity, but he couldn't quite place them - not yet. The bike engine purred as she glanced down at her hands, which grasped another helmet. Windar paused for a second, processing the situation. He concluded that today was the day to be daring after all.

Harry Brown was about to inflict more sarcastic accusations upon the professor, when Windar got up and charged through him, knocking the reporters pad into a puddle on the ground.

The biker threw the helmet towards Windar as he approached and readied herself to accelerate away. She flicked her head to the side as he mounted the bike at the rear: "Hold on Professor, we're going to get you out of this mess."

The crowd looked on in disbelief as the bike roared into life.

For the press, this was as exciting as a live scoop could get; for the military officers, this was not mentioned in their clean-up debriefing.

An officer, who had been coordinating the seizure of materials from Windar's home, picked up his phone and dialled the base. "Colonel, we may have a problem," he said, watching the professor vanish into the horizon.

46: The Condemned Mouse

Trakz whizzed about in his cage as he was transported down one of the many long, underground corridors that piped life through the base. The excitement he usually felt was replaced with that of worry; his creator had been marched out of the laboratory, and he was leaving his friends behind bars. He felt particularly awful about how dismissive he'd been toward Prickles, quashing the hedgehog's hopes for a normal life outside of the lab.

Using his own inbuilt GPS system, Trakz knew that he was now on the opposite side of the compound as his cage was parked outside a large office. He could see huge windows and daylight, lots of it. Beside him, a woman in her fifties sat nervously at an office desk, glancing up at him now and then as he scuttled about the cage.

Solid oak doors, etched with the MoD emblem, began to

open. The trolley moved again, slowly. Trakz recognised a gruff voice bark instructions. His cage was lifted from the trolley and carried over to a desk, where it was spun round and laid to rest.

A big round face with puffy red cheeks stared down at Trakz, chuckling away. Grievance's breath was musty and stunk of... cheese! Trakz perked up, what a delightful smell. He searched the desk and saw, next to a large, half empty glass of port and coarse oatcakes, a selection of vintage cheeses. Lactose overload!

"Come on then, little fella," said Grievance, opening up the cage and pulling down the ramp. "Let's have a look at you."

Trakz wheeled himself out to the amusement of Grievance, who merrily tittered in delight. The mouse glanced at the cheese and then back towards the general, his tiny paws clutched towards his chest. Grievance, delighted at the mouse's manners, broke off a piece of stilton and handed it to him. Trakz cradled it in his arms and inhaled – all the memories of home came flooding back, why had Windar never given him cheese like this? He lifted the cheese up to his mouth, then quickly wheeled himself to a safe spot on Grievance's desk, behind a picture of the general's wife. Trakz' eyes were glazed in awe as he finally bit into the cheese.

Grievance licked his lips, what a delightful sight this was - even the curls on his moustache sighed in admiration for the little mouse.

Trakz was in a different dimension. His senses were over-stimulated to the point where his tracks moved uncontrollably, jigging with joy. Grievance erupted with laughter as Trakz spun and swaggered rhythmically. The general went to break off a piece of vintage cheddar when the phone rang. "Hello," he answered.

"General," replied Flattery, "we might have a problem."

Grievance cleared his throat with a mighty cough. "Problem, Flattery?"

"Well, I'm not exactly sure."

"Colonel, need I remind you that this was supposed to be a simple clean-up operation."

"One of our men on the ground just informed me that Windar was picked up by a motor cyclist and taken away."

"So, tell your men to follow them and find out what the hell he's up to."

"That's the problem. We can't find him."

Grievance smoothed his moustache; it had a tendency to flick up at bad news. "We have all his computers and you've secured his home?"

"Yes."

"Then there's nothing more we can do. Sooner or later he will resurface, keep communication channels on the look-out for anything unusual. Without his tools and data, Windar's several years behind working for another organization – just focus on bringing back that damn magpie!"

"Yes, General."

Grievance slammed the phone down, irate at the news. He was unaware that Trakz' sensory reaction to the cheese had inadvertently activated his recording chip (so that he could savour the whole experience again and again).

47: Hogs for Hostages

Nutcase led an elite team of squirrel commandos through the forest. By intimidation and brute force they had located the nest of Mr and Mrs Hog. Flanked by his two meanest looking rodents, Nutcase loomed over the hedgehogs. Harold and Henrietta Hog were curled up as tight as fists.

Rosie was more defiant. She stood rigid, her claws clenched and lips pursed tightly, as they approached. "What do you want with us?" she snapped.

"You've been summoned by Big Mag. He wants to know where your brother is hiding."

"Even if I knew, do you think I'd tell you?"

"You've got an attitude," said Nutcase. "I like that."

"You furry slug, you've betrayed us all!"

"No, princess, your brother's let you all down. And 'cos of that, you're comin' with us whether you like it or not."

"Never!"

"Rosie," her mother said, uncurling herself. "Let's do as the squirrel says – we don't want any more violence."

"But mum, if we go to Big Mag he will do terrible things to us."

She shuffled towards Rosie and whispered in her ears. "And if we don't, they will do even worse things to us here. Let's go along with them, it will give us more time to come up with a plan."

Rosie didn't like giving in. She looked at Nutcase as he bared his teeth, which were yellow like the rotting leaves that surrounded them. "He'll come for us." she said.

"We're counting on it."

MEMO

To: All staff (Strictly confidential)

From: Colonel Flattery

RE: Project Carrion S & R Operation

In light of recent events, General Grievance has made it clear that we are to find and recover Magatron using whatever means necessary.

Equipment and resources have been arriving throughout the day to assist us on the ground. A team of special ops will lead the hunt, which will commence at 20:00 hrs. Please be on guard at all times until then; several undercover reporters and animal activists have already been prevented from infiltrating the grounds.

May I also remind you that, in accordance with the official secrets act 1989, you are bound from discussing this matter with any persons outside of the operation. All internal and external communications will be strictly filtered.

There will be a finger buffet and drinks at the Lamb and Flag after the operation. Thank you for your co-operation.

48: The Loft

Prickles did nothing – it was pointless trying to escape from his reinforced cell. His only stimulation was the sound of soldiers preparing for the clean-up operation, the grating noise of test alarms, and distant hum of helicopters circling above the base. Visions of Rosie and his mum circled within his mind. He was angry that the Kraken-200 had captured him so easily before he could savour the physical contact he had craved for so long. Instead he replayed the memories of those brief moments and dwelled on the disappointment he saw within his parents' eyes.

The hedgehog desperately wanted to talk to someone, but it was a waste of time trying to make conversation with PIG30N, who roosted in her cage above him. He missed Trakz, imagining what terrible things his friend was being subjected to outside the comfort and security of the lab. Prickles kicked the bar of his cage in frustration, believing that he would never taste freedom again.

PIG30N was in a deep slumber. Her wings flapped intermittently, and her feet flicked ever so slightly, as her conscience became fully immersed in the beginning of her dream.

It was racing day. Delicate wisps of stratus clouds framed the sapphire skies as PIG30N travelled in the back of an old lorry, along with hundreds of other pigeons, towards the open foothills of South Wales.

There was a buzz of excitement amongst the birds, not just about the big race that lay ahead of them, but at the opportunity to meet new birds and mingle. PIG30N had already attracted the attention of several handsome males and blushed at their amorous calls towards her.

The truck juddered to a halt. They could hear human voices, talking and laughing aloud. She recognised the voice of her keeper, hard not to since she was the only woman there. Anne Beaumont was the keeper to beat. Many of her male colleagues would sidle up to her - just to discover tips about how she bred such good natured, successful Racing Homer pigeons.

PIG30N, known then as Echo, was one of Anne's most successful racers. She would always finish within the top ten, along with her racing partner Hammond. He shuffled excitedly in the cage next to her as they waited for final race preparations. Hammond was a fine-looking bird who attracted as much attention from the other females as she did from the males. And there was always gossip about how Echo and Hammond would make such a nice couple, but she was always too bashful to talk about the possibility.

Anne walked over to the truck and spoke to them all. PIG30N didn't understand what she said, but she sensed that it was upbeat, motivational and sincere.

In the distance, dark clouds bubbled on the horizon.

A man dressed in thick green khakis and heavy, mud stained boots paced near the truck on his phone, looking in the direction of the approaching storm. He looked agitated, as though he were being advised not to continue with the event, but eventually he gave the keepers a hand signal they'd been waiting for: go ahead.

PIG30N braced herself; Hammond was primed next to her. A harmony of excited coos followed as the rest of the flock scratched eagerly. Hammond turned to her and said his final words of comfort. "See you back home."

The cage ripped open, startling the whole pack of birds. A volley of beating wings, and the sound of hundreds of eager lungs emptying, culminated into a magnificent cloud of activity. PIG30N beat her wings as hard as she could, ascending high into the sky so that she could find her bearings and catch a thermal. Above her, she watched as Hammond thundered past several other birds, angling heavily towards the East. She did the same, swooping in an arc as she caught a wave of warm air.

Slowly the birds separated, dividing into groups, smaller and smaller until there were just a few of them heading directly at the thickening mass of dark clouds.

PIG30N thought about the many advantages to being a racing pigeon: a keeper who feeds you and looks after you, prestige amongst other birds, and a great social life; but there are also many drawbacks: a great deal of stamina is required to get you back home, you fly over unfamiliar territory, and there is always a possibility that you might not make it back.

Thirty minutes had passed and the cobalt skies had been tarnished black. Heavy droplets of rain tumbled down, switching to hail at times; icy-sharp stones peppered across PIG30N's wings as she beat them, trying to steady herself against the fierce wind. She was on her own now, following a route back home, but she could sense electrical disturbances above. The bellies of storm clouds flashed white as sparks of lightning digested within them. Thunder rumbled. Ahead, PIG30N saw the outline of dense forest – she decided to find shelter.

PIG30N landed on a sparse branch of a mighty oak, beyond the fringe of the woodland. Her attention was held by the sinking clouds. She was unaware of the watchful pairs of eyes that studied her, formulating a surprise attack.

A blinding flash of lightning ignited the sky and for a moment PIG30N thought she saw the outline of four feathered shapes perched a couple of trees away. Perhaps it was a group of other racing pigeons seeking shelter?

Thunder clapped directly above. As the rain cascaded downwards she glanced back at the trees to try and identify the other birds, but a momentary flicker of lightning revealed empty branches. Suddenly a pair of claws swiped across her back. PIG30N fell forward and dropped downwards. She did not see her attackers, only heard their menacing call.

Instinctively PIG30N tried to fly again, only to be hit a second time from the side. This time she caught a glimpse of the black and white feathers beating above her. She hit the forest floor stunned, hearing the rattling call of magpies as they rallied together, encircling her.

Chatak-chataka-chatak!

Menacingly, one by one, they struck the forest floor and heckled her, cawing that she had 'landed in the wrong part of the woods'. The most aggressive of the pack was a young female, flapping angrily at her from the side. PIG30N did her best to parry the pecks, but was clipped above her right eye. She could hear the others laughing as the physical torment escalated.

Another female landed on top of her, pinning her to the floor. It was fight or flight time. With a hard crack of her wings, PIG30N got to her feet and launched herself into the air, towards the only bleak opening she could see. The magpies fired after her like arrows, but they did not have any chance of catching one of the country's fastest racing pigeons.

Seconds turned into minutes and PIG30N knew that she had made a lucky escape as the chattering blended in with the swooshing of branches. Faster and further she flew, snapping her wings together, blue sky in the distance and the feint outline of other birds – racing pigeons! This would be a story to tell Hammond back at the loft as they snuggled up together. This would be her most infamous race yet. The thoughts buzzed frantically like the electricity in the clouds, when a shooting pain shot down her spine.

PIG30N had no time to react: talons had her firmly gripped. The tips of the raptor's claws were like pins, piercing her flesh as the clouds and fields tumbled into one, then they let go of her and PIG30N saw the blazing yellow eyes of a Peregrine Falcon watch *her hurtle back to earth.*

The patio slabs, though doused in rain water and sandy in colour, were as solid as you would expect. PIG3ON's neck cracked painfully as it struck the cold stone and she writhed momentarily. Droplets of rain smeared her view, but she did not want to watch the falcon approach. Her attacker landed beside her, mantled his wings and tightened his grasp on her.

As his beak fixed round PIG3ON's neck, all she could think of was Hammond's warming coo with a gentle twinkle in his eye as he said, over and over again, 'see you back home.'

The falcon began his meal, hastily stripping away feathers and ripping out her eye. When patio doors opened and a figure stepped out into the rain, the falcon squawked and held out his tongue, hissing at the intruder. But even his sleek wingspan could not repel the two marching brown shoes, complete with odd coloured socks.

PIG3ON awoke in the solitude of the lab. She could hear Prickles clambering about in his cage, restless. She searched the room for signs of Windar, but in her heart she knew that he would not be back – reliving the same feeling she had for Hammond and her keeper.

She stared at the small strip of glass at the top of the room and cooed in frustration.

It was fast approaching dusk.

49: Leaving Tracks

Trakz was back in his cage, watching Grievance approve final arrangements for the evening's military operation. Colonel Flattery was also present, accepting the terms of Grievance's demands.

"I don't want any more front page stories in tomorrow's papers, Flattery."

"I can assure you, General - we have our best search and recovery team ready to act."

"Good work. What about Windar?" Grievance looked affectionately towards Trakz.

"Still nothing, but he'll resurface eventually."

"Not dead I hope – we don't need any more official investigations. You remember what happened to the last fellow."

"Windar will turn up. I can't imagine him being detached from technology for longer than a day or two." Flattery followed

Grievance's eyes towards Trakz.

Trakz read their heat signatures and monitored their stress levels. He knew something big was at stake, and he recognised the name 'Win-dar' as they conversed. And despite access to cheese, the mouse had already decided that he could not spend a night in the office without the rest of his team and began formulating an escape plan, rotating in his cage and scanning the room.

Grievance laughed at his pet's quirky attributes. "What's happening with the others?"

"A team from London shall arrive tomorrow morning. They will study them before taking them away to be dismantled. The technology can then be sold."

"Hmph! I guess they'll be wanting this little fellow, too?"

"Yes, General – all traces of Project Carrion are to be removed from the base."

"Well," Grievance paused for a moment, "bring them to me before they visit the lab."

"Yes, General."

"That will be all, Colonel."

Flattery stood and saluted before leaving the room and closing the door.

Grievance leant forward and Trakz intuitively wheeled over to him, resting his paws on the bars of the cage. "Sorry old chap, looks like you'll be leaving with your friends after all."

Trakz continued to sniff the air. He watched Grievance stand and fix his military tunic before calling his secretary. "Miriam, have the driver meet me by the officer's club in half an hour."

He replaced the phone and turned back to the mouse's cage, staring at him sympathetically. "Bah," he muttered, "I can't let a condemned mouse spend his last night in a cage." He bent over the enclosure and lowered the ramp so that Trakz could have some freedom. "Enjoy your last night of liberty," said Grievance, chuckling as he exited the office door.

Trakz couldn't believe his luck - free run of the office! He descended down the ramp and mulled over his predicament: did he stay and enjoy a large helping of Grayford Valley Stilton or head straight back to the lab?

"Hang tight, guys. Trakz is on a mission!" He whizzed down the table leg, zoomed across the floor and accelerated up the office wall, around the portrait of the Queen, and entered the air vent.

50: Bidding War

The warehouse was deserted. Thin partition walls and windows, once housing small offices, had been vandalised and graffitied. Windar sat near the hangar entrance and watched rain-water seep through the roof, pattering into the docking bay where vans once parked. Now, in their place and thriving, were weeds and moss. Nature prevails, he thought, noting other varieties of flora and evidence of animal droppings. In the background the professor heard voices, three of them. They were in heated discussion.

"Professor Windar."

Windar turned and blushed. The biker, who had driven him away from the maddening pack of reporters and soldiers, was now dressed in a sharp suit to match her facial features. He recognised her as the double agent saved by Spikez during the Grayford operation.

"Milk and five sugars," she said, placing a cup of hot coffee by his side. Agent Dahab sat opposite him on a tired old chair and opened up a laptop. He gazed in admiration as she flicked glossy strands of fine red hair across her shoulders and addressed him in her sultry voice. "Professor, we don't have a lot of time." She signalled for her colleagues to enter the yard.

A well-dressed agent carrying two attaché cases was followed by an elderly man wearing silver rimmed glasses similar to Windar's.

"We're very grateful for the work you've done for your country," she continued. "And I'm personally grateful for the work you did in saving my life."

"Please, I can't take all the credit - my creations were acting on their own accord."

"Well, I hope that I can meet them one day and say thank-you."

"As would we," remarked the older of the two men, replacing his satellite phone. "And let's not forget the excellent work they did in London, either. But as you're well aware – all that is about to change."

Agent Woods tapped away on a laptop and Windar caught a glimpse of the MI6 crest on the screen.

"General Grievance has ordered the termination of Project Carrion. Tomorrow morning, researchers from London will arrive to take the specimens away where they are likely to be destroyed," he continued.

Windar held his head. "You can't let this happen – they're not machines, they're intelligent beings."

"Don't worry, Professor, they won't be . . ." Windar went to thank him. "Because our intelligence sources suggest that your machines are going to be stolen."

"What?"

"We think there might be a mole in the base."

Windar was confused. "No, there's no mole. I've only rebuilt a mouse, a pigeon, a hedge-"

"He means an inside man," interjected Dahab. "Professor, you have to help us recover the drones before the military have them transferred."

"Do you have access to my materials?"

"No, we'll need to find other ways," she stressed.

The older man limped back into view. "You can have whatever resources you need, Professor." He winced as he crouched down to Windar's level, staring deep into his rich blue eyes. "You have the full support of Her Majesty's Intelligence Services, Professor. Help us help your country."

Windar sat for a moment and thought about his options. If the outlook of his creations being destroyed was not enough, the vision of someone else stealing his technology and producing an animal army was an even more alarming prospect. "That won't be necessary."

Agent Dahab moved over to Windar. "I don't understand."

"I do. Take me to Montgomery's canal."

Being a mouse with an inbuilt map of the military base, Trakz meandered through the air conditioning ducts towards the laboratory.

Prickles pushed himself against the bars of his cage; he could detect the noise of tiny motors whirring above him.

"Trakz, is that you?"

"Right here, buddy. I've come to get you out." Trakz squeezed himself through the vent. "All that lovely cheese has put grams on me!" he said, speeding down the wall.

Trakz reappeared again on the lab table opposite Prickles. PIG30N flapped excitedly. They watched him wheel himself towards his docking station where he synchronised himself to Windar's machine.

Prickles listened as his cage unlocked itself and the door slid to the side. To celebrate, he took a running jump over to the table, joining his friend. PIG30N landed next to him. Trakz sped over to hug them both. "Ouch!" he said, pulling away from Prickles. "Guys, we need to get out of here ASAP before you end up in specimen jars."

"How?" Prickles asked. "You said yourself, without Windar we're pretty much prisoners here. If anyone sees us trying to leave the laboratory, that's it – we'll be caught and locked up separately."

"Then we think outside the box," said Trakz, directing them towards a computer tablet. He connected his tail to the USB port of the device. The screen flashed on and a map of the base appeared – Trakz talked them through his plan. "Prickles, we'll use your laser to cut a hole through the window so that PIG30N can escape by air. I'll use the aircon ducts to make my way towards the delivery bay."

"I'll come with you."

"I'm afraid that's not a good idea. Both of your locator chips are still active, and when Grievance shut down the operation you both became electronic inmates. Only Windar can disconnect these, so as soon as you cross the lab perimeter the whole base will be alerted. I know you're good at what you do, but I don't know if you're ready to take on the army just yet."

"So what's my other option, I need to get out of here and help my family."

"Well, I've been thinking," Trakz tapped his paw on the monitor and highlighted the sewage network. "There's an overflow waste pipe that pumps directly into a pond about a third of a mile from here. This is your best bet to avoid immediate detection - it'll just look like you switched yourself off."

"How long will it give me?"

"You should have at least half an hour before they track you down – will that give you enough time to find and disable Magatron?" Prickles shook his head. "Look, PIG30N can do the hard work for you – she can locate him in the air."

"What if I fail? What if I can't defeat him and the army capture me again?"

"Lighten up, Prickles. It's time to start believing in yourself, you know Greenacres better than any of the soldiers that'll follow you. It's going to work!"

Prickles looked deep into the eyes of PIG30N; even though she couldn't talk, he knew that she wanted to help. He was grateful to have one more shot at seeing his family again, something that the others would never be able to do. "We stay together as a team," Prickles said, "no matter what."

"Then let's do this!" yelled Trakz, racing off the table. Prickles and PIG30N gawped in amazement at the mouse's raw enthusiasm, inspiring them to do the same.

PIG30N flew up towards the window. Prickles fired his grapple hook, hoisting himself alongside her. Trakz zoomed up the wall to join them, watching as Prickles deftly clicked out his laser and began cutting through the glass.

The sparks and glare from the powerful beam ricocheted off Trakz' glasses whilst PIG30N welled up inside; she felt like she was ready to race again.

Bound with twine and plastic bags, the Hog family were being held in an abandoned rabbit hole. To his frustration, Mr Hog could not take his eye off a worm as it poked through the soil and wriggled precariously in front of him.

Big Mag commended Nutcase on an excellent job before he addressed the captive hogs. "I'm really looking forward to your son seeing you like this - it'll be like a family reunion at a funeral."

"You're a lunatic!" squealed Rosie.

"I remember you from the early days!" scowled Mrs Hog. "You used to hop around the woods promoting yourself as a thinker, a wiser alternative to the raptors. But look at you now, you're blinded by power."

Nutcase sidled up to Big Mag. "Mag, when the 'edgehog comes and you deal with him, will you help me find Hercules?"

"After you've rounded up the young."

"You what?"

"We are not in complete control until we have hostages from the whole of the Greenacres population. In the morning, you and your crew - along with Ringpull - will begin rounding up the fledglings and cubs."

"And do what with them?"

"Let me answer your question with a question, Nutcase. Do you enjoy looking for food?"

"Not particularly."

"Does it not frustrate you when you forget where you put your nuts?"

Nutcase thought for a second. "Are you trying to be funny?"

"Not in front of the hedgehogs."

"Well, then I guess the answer's yes."

"Good, then you will make the creatures work the forest for you. Eventually, I will need you and your gang to advance beyond Greenacres – you will need your energy for fighting, not foraging."

Windar arrived at a quiet stretch of canal, accompanied by agents Dahab and Woods. He led them towards a tattered looking barge, sheltered under a willow tree. The paint had lost its vibrancy and peeled away like dead skin, revealing a depressing grey hull. The windows, small and blacked out, were coated in a thick glaze of green.

"What is this place?" asked Dahab.

"This is my plan B," Windar replied, a triumphant smirk etched upon his face. "When you work for large multinationals and military organizations, you quickly learn to find a place where work can't find you. Due to the nature of my experiments, I sometimes choose to work out here all alone."

The three clambered onto the barge. Windar removed his keys from his pocket and unclicked several padlocks. "Shall we?"

Woods and Dahab ducked their heads as they descended into the boat's dark interior. Windar clicked the light switch to reveal an Aladdin's cave of technological wonders. Screens and lights were compacted along one side of the boat with several hard drives and thick bundles of coloured wires feeding in and out of scientific instruments; a small, silver operating table lay in the middle, complete with inspection lights and medical tools; three chrome fridges were cramped into a corner, and beneath them was a combination-safe with the bio-hazard symbol stamped upon it. The agents stood aghast.

"I'm here at least twice a week. My neighbours don't deal with noise very well." Windar removed his jacket and placed it on a small coat hook protruding amongst the hundreds of knobs and dials. He brushed past three cages and a docking device linked to a computer, which he switched on. "From here I should be able to contact my creations directly at the laboratory," he looked up and saw their bemused expressions. "Come, please, see."

"Professor, are you sure the military don't know about this place?" Woods asked.

"Well, you didn't – and if they did, it would have surely been cleared out already." He stopped and looked both agents in the eyes. "They must never know about this place."

"Professor, we'll help you keep a lid on this whole operation – just get those robots out of there."

The thick circle of glass fell to the ground. Prickles moved aside to give PIG30N a taste of freedom. She could see the silver moon arching in the sky - it was how she had remembered it.

On the ground, the clear-up operation was about to begin; sniffer dogs and soldiers equipped with tracking devices were assembling, ready to be deployed beyond the perimeter in search of Magatron; above, a military helicopter circled the farm, using thermal imaging to search for snooping journalists or animal rights activists.

"It looks pretty dangerous out there," Prickles said. "Wait here and go on our signal."

PIG30N nodded. Trakz sped down to the ground. Prickles followed - releasing his grip and letting his spiky bulk drop to the floor. They landed and sped past the kitchenette, towards the toilet. Trakz enjoyed racing Prickles, but even with motors instead of legs he could not match his friend's agility and prowess as he was beaten to the lavatory pan.

The toilet lid was already raised. Prickles balanced himself on the edge of the rim and looked down through the funnel of water, assessing if the pipe was big enough for him to fit through. "Are you sure this is going to work?"

Trakz stood above him, ready to wheel over the flush button. "Unless you've grown since I last measured you, there should be just enough room for you to plop through. Are you ready?"

"How will we keep in contact?"

"Without Windar running the show, we won't."

"Then how are we supposed to meet up again?"

"We'll find a way. I've managed to link you and PIG30N together wirelessly, but it'll only work within a certain range. I believe in you, pal – I'll see you when this mission is complete," pledged Trakz.

Drawing his spikes inwards, Prickles took a deep breath and saluted Trakz. "See you on the other side."

Trakz reciprocated the gesture and steered over the flush, triggering a tumultuous whoosh of foaming water.

Prickles held his snout as he jumped into the bowl, curling himself up tightly. He felt the water bubbles explode around him as he crashed towards the start of the S-bend. He rolled himself along as the stream of cold water pushed him clear of the turn and sent him surging towards the main sewage outlet.

Trakz, elated at seeing his plan work, shouted out for PIG30N to launch. She cooed excitedly before taking off into the clear night sky.

For a moment she was back with her friends, racing home.

Trakz heard the alarms sound. He was about to make his way back though the air vents when Windar's computer screen flickered on. An image of Windar and the agents appeared. Trakz saw the web cam rotate above the computer, searching the empty cages.

"Good heavens!" Windar cried. "We're too late. They're gone, someone's already taken them!"

"How is that possible?" asked Woods.

Windar shook his head – he had been outfoxed again.

"Is there any way that you can track them, Professor?" urged Dahab.

"Yes, Spikez and PIG30N have GPS locators. I should be able to track their movements from here."

As Windar began frantically loading his program, Dahab and Woods gave a startled yell. A huge pair of eyes glared at them from the other side of the screen. They were convex, alien looking with pupils that darted rapidly from side to side. Windar looked up with glee. "Trakz!"

Trakz plugged his tail into the computer so that they could interface. The professor tapped frantically on his keyboard – a mixture of scientific code and Standard English. Windar struck the return key:

`'Locate: SPIK-3Z and PIG30N?'`

Trakz' eyes flitted to and fro, as if reading the message before responding via text:

`'…despatched: sequence echo-tango-golf-hotel…'`

"What does that mean?" Dahab asked.

The professor brought his spindly hands to his face and rubbed them across his mouth – confused as they were. "They're . . . heading for home." Windar stood and traversed the narrow gangway.

"But I thought their home was the laboratory?"

"It is," Windar replied, turning – a spark of realization in his eye.

"Professor, if you're not controlling them then who is?"

"I think they're controlling themselves," he sat back down and explained. "On their last mission to recover Magatron, something happened to Spikez' memory. At first I thought that he'd simply malfunctioned, a problem with the programming, but when I recovered his memory files I found evidence that he can still remember what he is, something I hadn't anticipated. I think he's trying to get home."

"Where is home?" she asked.

"Greenacres."

"Professor – the military are looking for Magatron in Greenacres. If Spikez has gone there too, then he will be captured or worse, destroyed."

Windar shook his head. "This is all my fault!"

"Professor, don't give up. I think we can still help you get them back. You said you can track them?"

Windar nodded. "Yes, but you said yourself, the whole area has been sealed off. I mean, they have soldiers, sniffer dogs, helicopters and hi-tech surveillance equipment – how are we supposed to get round all that?"

"Professor," Dahab said, folding her arms together, "MI6 are with you on this one – this is what we do."

51: Furry Fugitives

A gaggle of geese were roosting on the grassy verge near a tranquil part of the pond where the water barely moved. Mum and dad were at peace, nuzzling their goslings, until a mighty splash of water shattered the silence.

"Who's there?" The mother hissed, waddling towards the water's edge and searching for any signs of a predator. A set of ripples had dispersed into faint tremors that hunted across the water's surface. She was joined by the dad who looked for danger in the reeds.

A burst of fine spray exploded next to them as Prickles came into view. The geese frantically flapped their wings and honked in alarm, shielding their young – watching as the hedgehog shook his spikes dry and wiped the muck away from his visor. He raised his hands defensively.

"Don't worry, I'm not here to hurt you. I'm looking for Magatron."

The geese reflected on his words. "Why should we help you? There's a rumour that you're going to turn us all into demons like you!" said the dad, trying to peck at Prickles.

"That's crazy, I mean you no harm," the hedgehog said, ducking under the water to evade each lunge. "I'm just trying to find my parents, you must understand?"

"That devil magpie friend of yours has them now," hissed the Mum, joining in on the frenzied attack, leaving Prickles no option but to retreat out of the pond and into the forest. As he did so, the hedgehog heard a loud bang and looked up at the night sky, now illuminated by red flares.

Perched on the tallest pine tree at the Eastern edge of the forest, Mag looked westwards at the erupting chaos. He identified the sounds and knew that the military were coming for him, but he was prepared. Stretching out his wings, Mag set a course to intercept.

PIG3ON had been taking thermal images of the forest, hunting for signs of Magatron. She could detect no trace of his energy signatures, nor could she identify large pockets of animals gathered together. But she could hear the commotion from the base and saw a helicopter hover ominously in the distance, its searchlight shimmering through the trees. She landed and transmitted the data to Prickles, who was busy scurrying through the undergrowth, away from the sounds of excited sniffer dogs.

Prickles emerged into a clearing, deep within the forest. There were signs of recent animal activity – scratch marks, scorched soil and droppings confirmed that a meeting had taken place recently. He knew he wasn't far from where his family had nested, but his gut instinct told him that they were no longer there. He had to keep looking.

Arim and Mira had learned of Nutcase's intention to find Hercules. They had been trying to nurture the mighty red kite back to health, but Hercules' condition continued to deteriorate. He would slip in and out of consciousness, murmuring the same words over again 'I can't feel my wings'.

Joy, now a bold and energetic fledgling, had no fear of Hercules, despite Mira's concern that he could lunge at her in his delirious state, devouring her.

"He's not going to make it," Arim said, risking his life to fetch water for the red kite.

"Baldwin says we must try to keep him alive - if the creatures learn that Hercules is dead then the forest will quickly succumb to Big Mag's control. We cannot let that happen – think of Joy!" Mira chirped.

"I am thinking of Joy. Mira, look at us – look at how we have to live. We could have gone nearly anywhere in Europe to have a chick, but we stayed here, in Greenacres. Apart from Baldwin, look at how they've treated us. We thought things would improve if we had a bird born here, but even still - all we get is abuse from the natives." Arim scratched the earth in frustration. "When the magpies were attacking us, no one offered us help or support, and now we are lumbered with Hercules because everyone is too afraid to help him."

He hopped frantically across the burrow floor, catching a worm in his claw. "I tell you, Mira, we owe them nothing. If Nutcase finds us here then he will do to us what they have done to him."

"Leave me here to die," Hercules croaked, roused by Arim's anger.

"Don't listen to him," said Mira, rushing to his side. "He is scared. We are all scared, but we cannot leave you – you are our only hope."

"I cannot defeat him," he continued. "Things have changed – this is not the future my parents talked about." He turned his head towards Mira, his eyes glimmering in what little light there was. "I don't know if we can win this war."

"You are not well," replied Mira. "He is just a bird, like us – he's been defeated once, he can be defeated again."

Hercules grumbled and moaned.

"Mira, perhaps we should listen to him. I have heard terrible, crazy things about what Big Mag can now do. You have to think of Joy."

Mira snapped. "I'm not leaving him - Joy is not ready to be exposed to the real world."

She was hushed by the sound of a helicopter passing over-head. Arim moved towards the burrow opening. "They're coming for him."

Several search parties had been deployed by the army, each unit was made up of two soldiers and a sniffer dog; one liaised via radio with other groups, the other operated the tracking device.

Captain Ripley, of team Alpha, was the first to pick up a faint signal a few hundred metres ahead of his position, heading in an easterly direction. He was quick to call it in. Two other parties also confirmed that they had detected the signal. 'Alpha team, moving in . . .'

Prickles continued to weave through the undergrowth towards of a set of deserted warrens. He got to an opening and, seeing a group of animals, froze. PIG30N had confirmed this, a pack of rodents and other mammals were bunched tightly together above burrow entrances. Rabbits and hares were being made to keep digging as fierce looking squirrels beat them with sticks. In the trees, magpies and crows watched the proceedings. Prickles also saw Baldwin slumped at the base of a tree with his legs tied.

The hedgehog studied the aerial images downloaded from PIG30N – three search parties were closing in on his position fast and if he was to find Magatron and rescue his family, he would have to act swiftly.

Prickles broke cover and ran towards the centre of the clearing, charging at the oppressive squirrels. But several of the squirrels had anticipated the attack and dashed out of the way, apart from one who reacted too late; Prickles swung his foot to the rodent's chest and sent the squirrel crashing into the undergrowth.

The rabbits and hares stopped, dumbfounded by what they saw. Prickles assessed the situation and looked over at

Baldwin; even from a distance, the hedgehog could still detect a faint trace of optimism glimmering in the badger's eyes. Two squirrels powered forward to confront Prickles. "You've picked the wrong place to come snuffling, hog!"

"Let the creatures go!"

A gruff voice bellowed from behind. "On whose authority?"

Prickles flicked his head to see Nutcase emerge from the shadows, flanked by numerous squirrels carrying sharpened sticks. "I don't want to hurt you," he said, tracking movement above him in the trees; magpies and crows were taking up diving positions. It was a trap!

"You won't even get close!" said Nutcase, signalling for his gang to attack.

Prickles swivelled and deflected a leaping squirrel's kick, sending him thundering into others. A magpie was next, shooting out of the darkness, only to be hit by a spike. It cawed in agony and flapped away to the black of the forest. Another furry adversary went to bite Prickles' neck, but he was also shown a bed of spikes and flurry of fists before being propelled head first into a deep crevice.

"More!" cried Nutcase, unimpressed by his army's dismal display of force.

Baldwin, a spectator, grew strength from Prickles' courage and broke free to confront his oppressors, biting a squirrel's bushy tail with his thick jaws.

Prickles received his first direct hit, a sharp swipe across the chin from an agile squirrel. He snapped his hands across his opponent's tail, span him and launched the rodent across the clearing whilst wrestling another into a headlock. Several corvids flew in to repress Prickles as squirrels surrounded him; the hedgehog was grossly outnumbered.

PIG30N could not sit back any longer. She circled high above to find an appropriate gap to dive through. With her feet electrically charged and her eyes fixed on the writhing mass of fur, feathers and spikes, PIG30N bombed to the ground with devastating effect. The shock was felt by all amidst the twirling scrum of flinching limbs and frazzled feathers.

Nutcase took great pleasure from seeing his mob continue to attack the hedgehog, but he did not see Baldwin creep up behind him. The Badger suddenly kicked him forward into the mud.

"Run, my brothers and sisters, seek shelter!" Baldwin cried.

Enraged, Nutcase bounced back up and looked over at Prickles who was still managing to hold his own, but only just. "You focus on the rogue pigeon," he told the crows and magpies. "I'll handle the hedgehog."

Prickles was not trained for such a fight. Neither Trakz nor he had considered such resistance – the squirrels were fast and unpredictable, almost mechanical and calculated in their method of attack; the hedgehog span round and deflected sharp blows from sticks and shielded himself from rocks volleyed in his direction. Eventually, a claw gashed above his visor and Prickles started to think that the rodents had been taught how to attack him and where his specific areas of weakness were.

PIG30N launched herself back up into the night sky, bringing with her a string of angry crows and magpies who would not be satisfied until they'd had a good peck.

Amidst the cawing and kissing of teeth, Prickles was adamant that he could hear his family – screaming somewhere in the burrows below – as he fought for his life. He desperately needed an escape plan.

The forest suddenly lit up.

Powerful flashlights shone from all around and the sound of raucous barking echoed across the clearing. The squirrels turned and snarled, hastily darting up the trees to safety. Prickles looked around to find all his exits blocked – his old ally was now his new enemy. The hedgehog could hear their voices across the intercom. 'Team alpha, approach with caution – use EMP as a last resort.' He watched as two soldiers knelt to the ground and removed a thick rifle with a customised net attached to the barrels. They slowly cocked the hammer and took aim. Prickles braced himself for impact but then several of the torch lights exploded and the radios fizzled wildly; the sniffer dogs barked as their handlers stumbled and fell backwards. They had all been hit by an invisible force.

The forest was plunged back into darkness.

The woods lit up again momentarily as the burning light from a small orb shot through the trees.

Capping their eyes to make out the object, the soldiers watched it float through the branches around them.

"Maintain your positions!" one of the officers commanded, re-aiming his gun back at Prickles. He went to pull the trigger when out of nowhere a bolt of brilliant blue plasma struck the base of a tree next to him.

Flaming hot embers splintered across the clearing.

Two of the dogs broke free and bolted back to base whilst the men shielded their eyes. "Initiate defensive manoeuvres!" Ripley cried, firing his machine gun at the rapidly moving light source. As his weapon discharged several rounds, another jet of light bolted at the men, sending shockwaves across the forest floor.

Electrical equipment exploded into chards of red and yellow burning metal. A soldier screamed as some of it scorched his bare skin.

Prickles had seen enough, he knew Magatron was somewhere above him and that he could be the next target. He saw an exit and sped towards it as fast as his robotically enhanced legs would carry him. Magatron clocked the hedgehog and blasted his primary weapon at the fleeing ball of spikes. A bulb of effervescent, fully charged ions impacted ahead of Prickles, temporarily blinding him and catapulting his body backwards against a tree. Momentarily overcome, Prickles rolled to his feet and fired an explosive spike in Magatron's direction.

The magpie had not anticipated such a quick return of fire and faltered. The branch he had been firing from effortlessly snapped in two and hurtled to the ground.

The military helicopter was hovering over the clearing within seconds as the soldiers retreated to fetch a more powerful array of weapons. Prickles was running out of options – he began moving again, all the time sensing that Magatron was over him, taking aim. But Mag's attention was now directed at a new adversary - the helicopter and two crew members ahead of him.

The pilot spoke nervously into his headset. "Er, we have a confirmed visual on the magpie –permission to engage, over ..." But before they could receive a response, the helicopter shook violently and was forced into an uncontrollable spin. Alarm buttons flashed across the instrument board as the electronics flared. "We've been hit, I repeat, we've been hit!" But his calls were useless, no one could hear through the interference.

Luckily, the crew had enough engine power to make an emergency landing. They span for several hundred metres, the rotors clipping numerous trees, before the helicopter became permanently grounded.

PIG30N had successfully evaded the magpies and was on a course to re-join Prickles when she felt her tail feathers stand on end. She glanced behind, enough time to see Magatron in close pursuit and about to fire a pulse of light from his chest. PIG30N took evasive action, dropping in an arc toward the ground. The bolt of energy missed her and continued forward, hitting the centre of a mighty oak, igniting it brilliantly in the night sky.

Van wheels skidded to a halt. From inside the vehicle, Agent Dahab and Professor Windar looked out and saw the chaos from the roadside. "Looks like we already have our diversion," she said.

Windar shuddered. "I'll need you to draw the military back to base. Use the decoy to channel all their resources away from the woods. It'll take at least twenty minutes for me to make contact."

Agent Dahab slid the van door aside and helped him out. "Good luck, Professor," she said, handing him his Kraken attaché case. "You have ten. Stay in radio contact."

The professor was dressed like the night. He activated the Kraken-300 prototype and synched it to his tracking device. "I know you're out there, Spikez," he said, pulling the black hood tightly over his head.

Prickles snaked between the warped roots of trees, watching out for signs of Magatron. PIG30N had also found cover and was busily scanning the area for signs of danger. They could both hear soldiers regrouping and military jeeps grinding to a halt nearby.

Kitted out with hi-tech weaponry, four soldiers coated in black armour emerged from the back of the vehicles. Captain Ripley ran over and briefed them on the last known location of Magatron. They fixed their night vision goggles on and agreed a plan of action: destroy all hostiles.

Trakz emerged out into the main courtyard of the military complex. He had carefully chosen his exit well, not covered by CCTV and within metres of a military truck – his ticket out of the base. Checking that the area was clear, the mouse sped over to the vehicle and attached himself to the undercarriage. Windar had given Agent Dahab a tracking module, allowing Trakz to identify how close he was to the target; all he needed was a reason for troops to rally towards the main gates.

The MI6 van stopped about a hundred yards from the military blockade which was heavily fortified by several guards. Agent Woods, who had been driving, got out and opened the rear door and waited for Dahab to activate Windar's decoy drone. She opened a large metal case, revealing a mechanical but anatomically correct model of a bird. It didn't resemble a particular breed, but it was black, would fly fast and had flashing LED lights dotted across its body. Hopefully it would do enough to create a diversion to allow Windar to enter the forest and rescue Spikez and PIG30N.

Dahab synched the device, Model number JAY-Z, to her PDA so that she could control the unit. She activated the drone, watching it propel itself into the night sky. Then, activating its flight sequence, the device arced like a firework and channelled itself towards the base.

Woods closed the doors and got back behind the wheel. "Time to call it in."

Flattery had just confirmed orders for his team to destroy all bots. He was about to make a cup of tea when the phone rang. He answered. "Is there a problem, soldier?"

"Colonel," the guard said uneasily. "You need to get down

here, sir. Two agents from MI6 have arrived and . . . there's something circling the base."

Flattery froze, checking his security monitors. "I'm on my way." He replaced the kettle and quickly radioed his field team. "Alpha team, target is now circulating above base – return for immediate support."

The special ops team quickly responded, returning to their vehicles and heading back to base, much to the relief of Prickles and PIG30N, who were hiding in the shadows.

Sensing that the danger had passed, Prickles decided to keep moving - a fatal mistake. The hedgehog sprinted past a set of burrows when an energy pulse hit the ground beside him, vaporising the soil. Prickles crashed along the ground, his leg blazing from the heat.

PIG30N saw the blast and scanned the area for signs of Prickles as clumps of dried earth pattered to the ground. She could see none. Her eyes quickly focussed on the feathered fiends surrounding her. She tried to escape, flying away from the forest, but even she could not negotiate the swarm of magpies and crows that obstructed her path. Claws hacked against her face and back, forcing her downwards into a crash dive.

A ring of magpies had already gathered where she hit the ground. Their chattering echoed through PIG30N's head, telling her she was 'done for'. Mag pushed through the mob, assessing the pigeon with his deep red eyes; to him, she was an anomaly like the hedgehog that he had just incinerated.

And now, as testimony to the other birds, Mag would continue to demonstrate his supremacy against any creature, man or cyborg that opposed his rule.

Flattery arrived at the main gate, accompanied by three other officers. Agents Woods and Dahab continued to argue with the guards about access rights, but their heated discussion was continually interrupted by the whirring noise of JAY-Z as it swooped above them at speed.

Dahab flashed her ID at Flattery. "Colonel, as a matter of national security, you must contain this weapon before it leaves the base."

"This is supposed to be an internal military operation – how do you know about this?"

"Colonel, half the population heard about it this morning – do you really think MI6 would turn a blind eye?"

"MI6 were consulted and approved the operation this afternoon. The situation is under control, and we have our teams taking up position now. I received no memo about extra agents being drafted in to support. Now, if you'll excuse me, you're not authorised to be here and must leave."

Soldiers escorted Woods and Dahab back to their van. As they were marched back, two jeeps skidded to a halt and the armour-clad commandos leapt from the back and quickly took up tactical firing positions. Dahab activated the battle simulation on her PDA and watched as JAY-Z circled the base and swooped in low.

The agents hit the floor as the drone glided only feet above their heads, listening to the sound of weapons being fired. It was whilst Dahab was on the ground that she caught a glimpse of a familiar looking rodent, hiding in the shadows.

Mag stood opposite PIG3ON, reading out her sentence whilst she continued to record data of the whole trial. The corvids were wild with fury, chanting for Mag, the executioner, to finish her off. She detected his energy signatures begin to rise.

PIG3ON charged all of her internal EMP pellets, ready for dispersal. Although they would not be powerful enough to destroy Magatron, all she needed was a small window of opportunity to escape. She closed her eyes and breathed deeply, measuring atmospheric conditions. She imagined that she was back in the cage with the other Racing Homers – with Hammond; visions of her keeper and the sight of a bustling loft filled her mind until she heard the words of comfort 'see you back home'.

As Mag fired his plasma cannon, PIG3ON propelled herself with all her strength into the night sky. The heat from the beam narrowly passed beneath her and aided her ascent. She left a trail of active EMP detonators behind in her wake. Mag's fierce light display temporarily blinded the magpies and they did not see PIG3ON escape - only Big Mag noticed - but before he could re-target, a succession of tiny electrical bombs exploded across the pack.

Windar saw the blue lights flickering deep within the forest and listened to the cacophony of angry birds squawking. He knew that Magatron was in there somewhere. He wanted to send in the Kraken-300 to recover him, but the professor knew it would not survive the encounter. Suddenly his tracking device started beeping rapidly, something was approaching at speed.

PIG30N gave an elated electronic coo as she landed on Windar's shoulder; she may not have made it to the loft, but she felt a step closer to home. Windar was delighted, but confused by his locator chip readings "That's strange," he said. "PIG30N, where is Spikez?"

The pigeon bowed her head. She was solemn, silently tipping forward in several directions at the scorched earth metres ahead of him. Windar feared the worst.

Arim continued to chirp ferociously at the intruder. "Stay back!" he would say, lunging forward to attack. Mira and Joy squawked with fright; Hercules did nothing.

"Wait!" Prickles said, trying to catch his bearings. "I'm not here to hurt anyone, I just . . ." he stopped as his night vision came back online. He saw past the frantic, frightened faces of the redwings and gazed at Hercules' broken body. ". . . He's not safe here. They'll surround you and take him."

"There is nothing that anyone can do," chirped Mira.

The rest of Prickles' primary functions rebooted, including his locator chip. He motioned towards Hercules, running a full analysis of his vital signs. "Unless we move him, he's going to die for sure."

The debate was disturbed by the ominous whir of a machine

drifting somewhere above them. The redwings huddled together and chirped softly at each other, fearing the end as tiny granules of soil dropped to the floor. "Stay here and don't make a sound!"

Prickles emerged from the burrow in full view of Windar and PIG30N, who were both relieved that he was still intact.

The professor leant forward. "Come on little fella, we've got to get you to a safe place." But as Windar tried to collect him, Prickles retreated. "What's the matter, Spikez – are you hurt?"

Prickles waved his arms and pointed into the den, then at the Kraken and back again. Windar frowned. "I think there's something down there," he said, relaying new directives for the rescue drone to search the burrow.

Hovering above the entrance, the Kraken slowly extended its long mechanical arms downwards. Windar could hear the twittering of alarmed birds reacting to the probing metallic appendages.

"Now before we do anything else, I need to deactivate your locator chips," Windar said, pulling out two large electrical leads. He wired up PIG30N and manually deactivated her chip. As the professor leant forward and deactivated Prickles' tracking module, the redwings shot out of the ground chirping wildly. The hedgehog stood by the hole, watching as the Kraken gently teased around inside the burrow.

Windar radioed Dahab. "I've got them!"

"We're on our way," she responded. Dahab watched out of the van as the JAY-Z continued to circle, simulating attack sequences under gun fire from the soldiers. "Time to finish this," she said.

Agent Woods watched her activate the self-destruct sequence on her PDA.

Flattery looked on as JAY-Z exploded in a ball of flames over the military base, fragmenting into shards of silver and orange. The soldiers cheered – they thought it was over. "Splendid work men!" he proclaimed on his megaphone. The colonel turned to his chief field operator. "How many more devices are you reading?"

"None, sir. Captain Ripley says that the specimens came under attack from the hostile bird, it's likely that they were destroyed in the ambush."

"Likely, but not definite - have your men sweep the area one last time. We'll return at first light and search for wreckage. The main objective is complete – we've destroyed Magatron."

Woods brought the van to a halt. Windar emerged from the cover of hedgerows with Spikez and PIG30N, placing them in the van. Agent Dahab stepped outside to assist Windar with the Kraken. "What is that?!" she said, seeing what the professor was carrying.

Windar looked down at the injured red kite. "I can't leave this beautiful bird to die."

"Get in Professor – we've a friend who'd like to meet you."

The van quickly sped away, returning back to Windar's floating lab.

Inside the rear of the vehicle, Prickles and PIG30N were in makeshift containers, watching as Windar held Trakz in his hand. Prickles was happy that they'd all been reunited again, but he was also very angry with himself: mission failed.

Windar placed Trakz in the container with PIG30N and Prickles. "Boy am I glad to see you both." The mouse looked alarmed as he studied the hedgehog's injuries. "You're hurt! What happened out there?"

Prickles looked down at his legs, some of the flesh had been burnt away to reveal hydraulics and metal. "Magatron happened."

"Did you get him?"

"I couldn't even get close – things are worse than I thought. He's controlling the animals, Trakz. I was outnumbered."

"But you're alive," assured Trakz. "You'll get your shot. Now, will someone please tell me what's in the box?"

Prickles looked over at Hercules. "He's the one everyone turned to when things needed sorting out."

"Judging by the look of him, it doesn't look like he'll be able to sort anything out."

Prickles was silent for a few moments. "I failed, Trakz."

Trakz gently wheeled himself forward. "No, you haven't. We escaped, and now we're all back together as a team again. The fight has only just begun."

52: We're Not Machines

D
eep in the forest, Magatron conferred with Nutcase and his newly appointed corvid generals. PIG3ON's EMP blasts had temporarily affected his power cells and caused his weapon's tracking system to remain offline, which did little to reduce his anger.

"Any sign of the pigeon or the hedgehog?" he asked.

"Negative, we've found no trace," replied Ringpull.

Nutcase added to Magatron's woes. "We've also lost Baldwin, he escaped during the ambush."

"Then find him!"

"Wiv all due respect, Mag, my comrades are not built like you. We don't run on lights – some are injured and need rest." Nutcase looked weary as Mag's eyes blazed at him. "We can be more efficient in the day."

If it had been any other day, Magatron would have publicly

reprimanded Nutcase for his flippant outburst, but he thought about the squirrel's words; his little setback with Prickles and PIG30N had rattled his army. "Fine, tell them to rest. But tomorrow we find Baldwin as a priority." He looked into the forest depths, knowing the badger was out there, plotting. "And when we do, we'll silence him for good."

Clambering back on to his barge with the MI6 agents, Windar switched the power on and lined his team up along a black shelf, giving them all refreshments. Trakz fervently munched through a series of protein sticks, but they did not match the marvellous taste of Grievance's vintage cheeses.

Windar pulled an inspection lamp from the ceiling and pointed it at Prickles' leg, tutting at the extent of the damage. He went to his cabinet to look for replacement parts.

"Professor," Agent Woods called, holding a box, "what do you want us to do with the dead bird?"

"He's not dead, I've sedated him – place him on the operating table please. I need to take an x-ray."

Dahab watched Woods carry Hercules over to the cold slab of steel in the centre of the barge. "Professor, now that you've recovered your ... devices, we really need to think about getting you all to safety."

"But I'm not done here," he replied. "Magatron did this to Spikez and still remains a threat to other animals, and to the general public." Windar put on some surgical gloves and his operating goggles. "I have to put things right."

"Professor, if they haven't done so already, the military will be back to finish the job in the morning. Three of their weapons are now missing and so are you. I can only cover our tracks for so long."

"Agent Dahab, I appreciate all the help that you have given me, but I must finish this. It's all my doing - it was me who called Farmer Cullem and asked him to look out for any corvids on his farm." He looked at them both, reflectively. "I was pushed into a corner. Grievance wanted something aggressive and that's exactly what he got, because I rushed - I cut corners, and worst of all, I went against all my moral principles, creating a weapon with the sole purpose to kill. Now Magatron is out there wreaking havoc because of my mistakes. Your best gift to me is time." Windar pulled out a series of test tubes filled with bright ionic liquids and metals. "When I'm done, I'll go far, far away from Greenacres."

"Very well," she replied, "we'll be watching closely, just in case things don't quite go to plan. Call me." Dahab handed him a satellite phone and beckoned agent Woods to follow her. "Good luck, Professor." She looked past Windar and down at the injured hedgehog. Finally she had time to gaze upon the remarkable creature that had saved her in the restaurant. "Thank you."

"No - thank you," Windar replied, unaware she was expressing her gratitude at Prickles.

The agents left the barge.

With Hercules sedated, Windar began analysing his internal systems. Trakz and the rest of the gang looked on quizzically.

"What do you think he's going to do, make him into one of us?" Prickles asked.

"Wake up!" Trakz said. "He doesn't have the time or the resources for a bird that big here, he's probably going to fix him up for another day."

"So then how are we going to defeat Magatron?"

"Judging from the state of you, it looks like we're not."

"Thanks pal," Prickles scoffed.

"I'm sorry, that came out all wrong. What I meant was that, now your locator chip's been disabled, he definitely won't miss again. What happened out there?"

"I was . . . too slow," Prickles shook his head in frustration. "I'm programmed for covert operations, not all out offensives. There were too many squirrels to fight off, and as for Magatron – he can fly."

"Listen, buddy, I know it's hard to believe but there are ways to fix that. I've seen what Windar is capable of and if you let me, I can give you some training in how to fight off rodents."

"You can?"

"Hey, just because I'm attached to these tracks now, doesn't mean I wasn't able to defend myself before my little accident."

"But you said so yourself, we don't have time."

"Spikez, Prickles, buddy, pal – where we're going, time doesn't exist."

Prickles was puzzled by his friend's words. He turned away and watched Windar diligently tend to Hercules' wounds. "Perhaps you're right, maybe Windar does hold the key to defeating

Magatron. All I want is a chance, an opportunity to prove to the creatures of Greenacres that hedgehogs still have a purpose."

Two hours passed. Hercules slept in a cage, carefully bandaged in several places across his wings and along his back from where Windar had operated. The professor returned from the deck, leaving the boat's controls in the hands of the Kraken. He lifted up a large key-pad and entered a fifteen digit code.

Trakz and Prickles sat up. It felt like they were sinking. As the vibrations from the boat's engine churned rhythmically, the floors and ceilings also began to hum with it and move. They watched as the floors of the barge deepened by two feet before grinding to a halt. There was now more headroom, and beneath the original floor level was a series of cylindrical gas chambers.

Windar looked at the team and smiled. Even though he trusted the MI6 agents, he had learnt the hard way - some secrets are best kept hidden. He walked over to PIG30N and gently stroked her collar, inspecting her with a magnifying glass. On finding no signs of heavy damage, Windar replaced his tools and made a note of what needed restocking. His thin, pebbly hands then moved towards Prickles and Trakz. He carried them over to the main console table where an egg shaped pod was glowing. "I'm going to let you both relax whilst I make a few modifications," he said, connecting them to the device.

Trakz looked over to Prickles. "Relax," he whispered, "you're gonna enjoy this."

Prickles felt tingles of electricity surge through his legs and slowly trickle up his spine as Windar sent them into an electronic hibernation. The lights in the room pixelated and the sound of the boat's rumbling motors gradually slowed, to the point where he could hear each spray of diesel fuel ignite, pushing the engine piston upwards; he sensed the kinetic energy travelling along the crankshaft and through to the propellers. But before the next compression could begin, Prickles had passed over with Trakz.

MI6 INBOX:

From: Agent_701 (DAHAB)

Windar has care of SPIK3Z and PIG30N. Declined offer to be taken to safe house until confirmation that SPYM-A9 has been destroyed or recovered.

Have secure lock on Windar's position (10244.65326), request that all other Military protocols searching these co-ordinates be redirected so that he can execute mission.

This should make cooperation more likely in future MI6 objectives at home or internationally using SPIK-3Z.

53: Inside The Mainframe

The room was a brilliant white – it was hard to see if there was any end or beginning to the walls around them. The ground felt real but there was a perfect silence as Prickles walked in his new environment. There was no echo, no sound of his claws scraping against the floor, and not even a hint of the chugging barge. He stopped for a moment, studying his leg – it looked like new, completely repaired, re-covered in his own flesh and fur like he had remembered it. He scratched his head, was Windar really that quick? But as he processed the thought, Prickles realised that he no longer had the visor strapped across his face. In fact, nothing about him gave away any clues as to his robotic interior.

"You look as confused as I was," said a voice from behind.

Prickles turned to see Trakz, standing upright without his tracks; his eyes were smaller without his goggles, but still as genial as they had always been. "Your legs!" Prickles gasped, gazing at two perfectly formed rodent feet. "What's going on?"

"We're inside a computer program. As we speak, Windar is busy making important hardware upgrades to us and repairing the damage you sustained in the attack. I'm here to install updates and introduce you to new programs, stimulate your mind and recommend some cool apps."

"I don't understand – why have you got your legs back and how come I'm completely hog-like again?"

"This is how our mind perceives us, understands us." Trakz walked over to Prickles and stared deep into his eyes. "Just because what's left of our physical self is not natural, doesn't make us any less the creature we were meant to be. I am still a mouse and you will always be a hedgehog, don't let any other animal tell you differently."

Prickles thought about Trakz' wise words. "But the animals are scared of me. They think I'm cursed, even my parents found it hard to accept me – I'm not sure my father even has."

"Animals are naturally resistant to change, Prickles, but if you give up on them, then you give up on animal-kind."

"Maybe." Prickles studied his hands, clenching them into fists. "I still don't know how I'm going to defeat Magatron."

Trakz shuffled backwards, pretending to shadow box. "Windar will find a way for us all to defeat him, it's what he does – he finds solutions to problems, no matter how challenging." He span round and performed an aerial kick.

"But you don't understand," Prickles said, turning away in

frustration. "Magatron has an army of other birds. And then there are the squirrels - when I fought them at the barn, I could beat them - in the forest, I felt that they could predict my next move. They were too fast for me."

"You can thank Magatron for that, which is also why we're here," Trakz clicked his paws and raised his tiny arms. From the horizon of white space spun a landscape of green trees, the floors crinkled beneath their feet and became a bed of dead wood and damp leaves. "This is a training program."

"Training for what?"

"To get to Magatron, you will first have to get past his army. I'm going to teach you how to fight squirrels."

"You're kidding, right?"

"Prickles, I don't kid."

"Yes you do, you do it all the time."

"Okay, so maybe I do – but not inside the mainframe. Are you ready for the simulation to begin?"

Prickles shrugged his shoulders and pulled his quills into place, surveying his new surroundings. "Sure. So what happens, do squirrel avatars jump out at me or something?"

"No."

"Then who am I training against?"

"Me."

Prickles laughed. "C'mon, Trakz – I said stop pulling my leg."

"I'm serious. I may not be a squirrel, but we're descended from the same family." Trakz took up a defensive stance. "Now hit me, if you can."

"But you're my friend. I can't fight you."

"It's because I'm your friend that I want you to fight me."

Prickles shook his head. "No, I can't. I won't."

Trakz dropped his guard and crept towards him. "Listen, that wound on your leg was a lucky warning, next time he locks his sights on you – it'll be hog roast for tea!"

"I don't want to hurt you."

"But in this training program, Prickles, you can't hurt me." Trakz walked away to where he stood before. "Because you won't be able to hit me."

"That sounds like a challenge." Prickles eased up and stretched his arms and legs. "No hard feelings?"

"How about I make it easier for you," Trakz said, raising his paws once more. Prickles watched as Trakz slowly and digitally transformed into the effigy of a harsh looking grey squirrel; only his teeth were unmistakably recognizable as his own. The makeover complete, Trakz turned and launched himself up a virtual tree. "Stay focused!" the rodent cautioned.

Prickles watched in awe as Trakz disappeared, up and out of sight. He found the whole virtual process entertaining. Suddenly a leg came crashing into his side, knocking him across the forest bed. Prickles got back to his feet and looked over at Trakz with a shocked expression.

The rodent smirked and flicked his bushy tail as he called out to him. "The same laws of nature still apply in here. Squirrels are fast – what you have to do is learn to be faster."

Prickles ran at him, but Trakz bounced out of the way and accelerated up another tree. "You can't keep running away!" he sneered as he watched him leap to the opposite branch behind him and drop down. Prickles twisted, just in time to parry a few scrappy blows. "For a mouse, you've certainly got a few moves," he said, absorbing a kick in the chest. He went to throw a punch at his friend, but it was half-hearted. Trakz took his arm and threw Prickles across the floor. He tumbled along the leafy bed and rolled to a stop, then quickly flicked back to his feet.

"Come on, you're faster than this!" Trakz cried, hurtling an acorn towards him. Prickles snapped the nut in his hand and crushed it. "Impressive," the mouse said, running in for another assault.

Balancing himself, the hedgehog tried to predict Trakz' next move – unsuccessfully. As the rodent leapt past him, his hind feet flicked dirt into Prickles' face, causing him to shield his eyes. Trakz then pinned the hedgehog firmly to the floor. "Perhaps we need to up the stakes," he said. Prickles looked to the side and saw another squirrel emerge from the trees, followed by another, and another. Trakz released his hold on Prickles and stood with the other rodents, preparing for another attack.

Prickles flipped himself back on his feet – he understood that this was no longer a game. Trakz was preparing him for survival in the animal world, for a possible life beyond Windar and the lab.

As each squirrel launched their attack, Prickles managed to deflect each limb, but he failed to counter other attacks and bites with equal aggression of his own. He grew frustrated, and his guard dropped again. Trakz and the other simulated squirrels fixed Prickles' arms and legs to the ground. He was powerless.

"Stakes still not high enough, huh?" one of the squirrels said. Prickles did not recognise the voice or the face, he grew worried – and then he heard Rosie's muffled voice.

"Rosie!" he cried, trying to break free from the pack. He could feel electricity buzzing around his muscles as the squirrels strained to hold him down. He let out an almighty grunt, sending each rodent tumbling aside. Prickles rolled to his feet and, ahead of him, saw his sister tied to the base of a tree with a plastic drinks lid pulled over her face. Beside her was Magatron, his chest glowing intensely.

Seconds later a series of energy blasts peppered past Prickles, shooting bracken into the air and exploding against the trees. Prickles rolled forward and then began a fierce sprint, weaving through the vegetation. Squirrels dropped in front of him, but Prickles dealt with each one, butting them to the side or running through them, pounding their scrawny bodies into piles of dead leaves. He kept charging towards Magatron. He had his sister in his thoughts, and sights. The hedgehog was untouchable; each ambushing rodent was hammered with hog ferocity as Prickles came to the final few metres, the home run. Magatron turned to fire, but before he could release gigajoules of energy, Prickles had channelled all his anger and anxiety into a solid, rounded fist which sent Magatron hurtling towards the stump of a tree and into a black plume of smoke.

Feathers drifted back to the earth as Prickles watched the body of Big Mag slowly rematerialise back into his friend. "Trakz!" He ran towards him, apologetically.

"Hey, no worries Spikez – you've just passed your first level of training."

Prickles stepped back and turned to the image of his sister, who dissolved away before he could touch her. "But . . . how did you do that?"

"I didn't, that was you," Trakz said, standing back up. "We're both connected to the computer, but I never said that I was in control." The mouse shifted over to Prickles and looked at the spot where Rosie stood. "The mind can hide our deepest fears, but when you step up and confront these demons, you can cast yourself free of all doubts. You can defeat Magatron and save your family, you just have to believe in yourself." Trakz stood in front of his friend. "You will save Greenacres."

"Maybe," Prickles said, "but it's not going to be easy. I mean, I can't even fly."

54: Pieces

As his car entered the Greenacres Base, Grievance noted fewer protestors and news teams than the previous day. There was little sign of military activity and he felt more at ease knowing that Magatron had been destroyed. The general was also proud that the latest military drone technology could not match the training of skilled British soldiers under his command.

Flattery was scheduled to meet with Grievance at 08.00 for a full debrief on the operation. He would leave directly from his meeting with Military Forensics, who had been working through the night gathering debris from the destroyed drone.

"Does it match?" Flattery asked, watching the chief analyst inspect fragments of metal and spliced wires under a large, electronic microscope.

"Well, it's hard to tell since we're still sampling the wreckage

– but it's made from the same material Windar uses to create his other machines. I'm not finding any traces of magpie DNA, though."

"You let me know when you have conclusive evidence that we destroyed that damn bird. What about tracing the other cyborgs, Spikez and PIG30N."

"I've been looking through the transmission logs from last night, trying to figure out where and how they breached the complex. It looks like they had inside help."

"Have all military personnel been accounted for?"

"Yes." The analyst looked a little uneasy as he spoke. "The evidence suggests that these devices broke free themselves."

"Give me something explicit," Flattery urged. "You've stopped making sense and I've got a meeting with the general very soon - he's going to want real answers, not hypotheses."

"Well, communication records show that someone remotely broke through the firewall and dialled into Windar's laboratory."

"Windar?"

"Possibly, but we couldn't trace the source. Whoever hacked in had technology far superior than ours. But, Colonel, this was two minutes after they broke free."

Flattery shuffled nervously. "What does the CCTV show?"

"That's what I've been itching to show you, sir. We pulled these images from the laboratory at the same time that the connection was made." He clicked the play button on the LCD monitor.

Flattery watched: the footage showed an empty lab; for

a moment no-one was in sight, until a scurry of movement appeared on the computer desk. Flattery drew breath and shook his head as he identified the blue rodent with the tank-track feet, effortlessly connecting itself to a computer and aiding the escape of Spikez and PIG3ON.

The analyst stopped the tape. "Colonel, can you please tell me exactly what we're dealing with here, sir?"

Flattery was seething with anger. "Not a word to anyone about what you've seen until I speak with the general, I need everything you've got - right away."

The general's secretary was waiting for Grievance to walk through the door. The kettle had boiled and she had warmed the teapot. "Good morning, General. Shall I bring your tea through?"

"Please, Miriam." Grievance tapped the keypad lock on his door and walked in. He set his briefcase down and opened the blinds, filling the room with glorious sunshine. "Rise and shine comrade," he said, strolling over to the cage. He scoured his desk for any trace of the blue mouse. "Hah! Playing hide and seek are we?"

Miriam walked through the office door, carrying a tray of tea and biscuits. Grievance saw her and held out his hand. "Hold it right there, Miriam. We've got ourselves a fugitive."

"General?"

"My mouse, Miriam. I think he's gone AWOL!"

Miriam screamed, dropping the tray of tea on the floor. Her heels kicked together at the thought of a mechanically enhanced mouse whizzing between her feet. Grievance bolted upright and barked at her: "For goodness sake, woman – pull yourself together!"

"My goodness, I'm so sorry General. I just don't like mi ... I do apologise, General, let me call someone to clear up this mice ... I mean mess." Miriam scurried back through the doors, pulling them tight.

Grievance tugged the coarse strands of his moustache upwards to help sniff out the elusive rodent. "I'm going to find you, old chap!"

The sun was slowly gaining strength in the morning sky. Windar stood at the bow of his boat, checking his position on a map. He had moored the barge at a covered section along Montgomery's Canal, as close as he could possibly get to Greenacres – near enough to launch an operation.

Prickles and Trakz had been well rested and were hibernating in their respective pods. Hercules remained sedated in his cage. PIG30N was the only one naturally awake, cooing at the sunrise as she watched the professor. Windar turned and looked at her. "Time to run a couple of tests," he said, disappearing below deck.

Windar returned with Trakz and Prickles in hand. He placed them both upon a miniature helipad, which jutted out to the rear of the barge. Trakz wheeled himself forward and Prickles sleepily followed him, stretching his arms. "I feel different," he said.

"Yeah, your leg looks great. He did a good job," replied Trakz.

Prickles hadn't even noticed the leg, but on inspection found that Trakz was right, Windar had worked wonders – barely a stitch was in sight. But he felt heavier, like he was carrying an extra half a pound in weight and his shoulders felt knotted, probably from all the tension he had been feeling ahead of their final mission.

The helipad rose upwards until it was level with Windar's chest. He bent forward and observed them, unclicking a set of instruments and computer controls from beneath the platform. Prickles and the others watched their creator tap away on a keyboard as they assessed the weather conditions.

"Beautiful day for a liberation," commented Trakz.

Windar struck the 'action' button. PIG30N and Trakz reacted quickly, but not as fast as Prickles - two aluminium-alloy rods sprung outwards from the hedgehog's spines. "What the . . ."

Trakz wheeled in to inspect each bar, watching as thin strands of metal separated; they were joined together by a thin, metallic mesh to form a wing, which was linked to each of Prickle's shoulder blades. "Nice upgrades!"

"Please tell me we're still in the mainframe," the hedgehog said, rotating his wing attachments. PIG30N bobbed closer to inspect the underneath, focusing her attention on the protruding circular fuel cell, which was glowing amber.

"I told you Windar would find a way!" exclaimed Trakz, watching him adapt to his new limbs.

"I just hope I don't get airsick."

"Listen, Prickles, a few words of advice from a mouse with

tank track feet, when you're up there using your new wings – try not to get distracted."

Windar ran a diagnostics test on Prickles, happy that the upgrade had installed successfully. "Time for a little test flight," the professor said, his smile at full capacity.

"I think he wants me to try them out."

"Well, what are you waiting for?" Trakz replied.

Prickles knew what to do and activated his fuel cells. Powerful jets of concentrated hot air fired out from each one as he slowly began hovering above the pad. Trakz and PIG30N moved away as Prickles steadied himself.

Windar nodded approvingly to himself. "The latest in thrust vectoring technology," he said. "Courtesy of Her Majesty's Royal Air Force, of course." He stepped back and looked at the hedgehog. "You're clear to launch, little fellow."

Prickles took one final glance at his wings, rotating the jets sideways. Surprisingly he didn't feel scared; he understood that whilst he was training with Trakz in the mainframe that Windar had uploaded the appropriate software needed to fly. Looking upwards at the brilliant blue sky, Spikez pulled his arms inwards, accelerating off. The G-force pushed his snout tight against his visor as he gained altitude, shooting higher and higher, leaving a fine vapour trail behind him.

Windar and his team looked on in both amazement and admiration as the distinct shape of a winged hedgehog became a small blip racing skywards. Windar looked at his monitor measuring altitude, airspeed and power consumption. Trakz also had his own screen to examine Prickles' stress levels.

In the sky, Prickles was in control – he was able to direct the amount of thrust and pressure with ease and even rotate his wings, creating wonderful loops. With vector thrusting, Prickles could also hover in a single spot and pull off defensive manoeuvres by snapping his shoulders together. As he ran through each of Windar's test scenarios, Prickles wondered whether it would be enough to counter Mag, a native to life in the skies.

Several minutes later, satisfied that the upgrade had installed successfully, Windar instructed Prickles to return to the boat for a final debriefing.

Prickles confirmed his orders and flipped downwards, heading home for the barge. On his way down he could see Greenacres, barely a couple of miles away. He thought about his family, about all the creatures and how they must be feeling. Beyond the forest he saw the base, creeping across the land along a web of cables, wires and roads, ready to entrap anything that ventured beyond its perimeter, like it had him.

Since his memory repair back at the lab, Prickles had remembered everything from that dreadful night, several months ago with Rosie. Oh how they should have believed the rumours that 'what went in never came out'. But he also reflected on how his life had changed, considering whether it was fate - perhaps he had found his purpose in life? Other than Rosie, he never had any friends, but now he had Trakz, PIG30N and a compassionate human to care for him. As the thoughts processed in his mind, his right wing jolted and spun unexpectedly.

Windar's monitor flashed red: a section of the hedgehog's shoulder was highlighted on a skeletal image with the message 'MALFUNCTION'. His eyes dashed towards the altimeter which was rapidly decreasing.

Prickles had entered into a wild spin. The landscape and pastures of lush green lands were now a whirlwind of yellow and silver as he spiralled out of control. He desperately tried to counter the spin with an opposite movement of his left wing, but all that did was cause him to tumble faster and more wildly.

Trakz radioed in. "Buddy, this doesn't look good – I thought I told you to keep a clear head."

"What can I do?"

"Anything, and fast, you don't have much time before you drop a hole in our new home!"

Two thousand feet. Prickles turned off his fuel cells and attempted to steady the spin, but it wasn't enough, his wing was still locked. Eighteen hundred feet. Windar tried to control Prickles manually from his computer but was unable to alter the hedgehog's flight path. Sixteen hundred feet. Prickles restarted the left jet which, for a moment, reduced the rate at which he fell, but without control of his right wing he was still powerless. Fifteen hundred feet. Windar ran below deck to fetch materials for plan B. Fourteen hundred feet. Prickles could see PIG30N flying away from the barge. Twelve hundred feet, one thousand feet, eight hundred feet. Trakz is relieved that Prickles will not land directly on top of him, but is still alarmed at his friend's rate of descent. Six hundred feet, five hundred feet. Windar emerged on deck, throwing a buoy into the water. Four hundred feet. From the corner of his visor, Prickles watched PIG30N race towards him, crashing against his right wing in an attempt to loosen it. Three hundred feet. After colliding with PIG30N, Prickles is spinning more wildly than ever. He braces for impact. Two hundred feet. The buoy explodes in the water, becoming a huge floating raft, as wide as the canal. One hundred feet. Prickles sees the raft but cannot get close enough.

Impact.

The ducks and coots erupted in a chorus of wild quacking and hooting. Water fountained at least thirty feet into the air, generating large waves for a small hedgehog. PIG30N sheepishly returned to the barge and scanned the water for signs of Prickles; Trakz and Windar also surveyed the canal in horror and waited for the commotion to settle.

After a minute, Windar activated the Kraken. The machine, with its gangly metal arms, sprouted from the hull. Whispering silently above the water, it glided past the life-raft and to the point of impact, skimming back and forth, searching with mechanical efficiency but to no avail.

"Prickles, buddy, if you're out there, I could really do with a sign that you're okay," said Trakz.

Just then, a wire shot out from the water like a fishing line cast with deadly accuracy. The Kraken rotated itself, examining the thin cable attached to one of its arms, and began to pull.

PIG30N erupted in a loud coo of relief as she saw Prickles' fist punch through the water holding the line. His spikes and wings were caked in mud and thick, green weed.

Trakz waved his arms, looking for a signal. Prickles gave it – his arm raised upwards with his thumb-claw pointing skywards. The hedgehog had proved his resilience once again.

Flattery entered the Officers' foyer and saw Miriam shivering nervously. "Is the General in?"

Miriam nodded, her face scrunched up. "He's in the office. Go right in, but please close the door," her shoulders flicked upwards, "he's having problems with his mouse."

"Aren't we all?"

Entering the office, Flattery was greeted by an unfamiliar sight. On all fours, his posterior pointing at Her Majesty, Grievance was searching for his trophy mouse under a cabinet. Flattery coughed.

Grievance growled as he picked himself up off the floor and checked his uniform. "Flattery, close the door old chap, my mouse seems to have done a runner."

Flattery obliged. "General, I need to talk to you about the operation."

"Yes, yes – I hear we got the blighter, I'm just glad it's all over. Perhaps we can reconvene in half an hour or so once I've captured the little rascal."

"General, the operation isn't complete. I'm here because of the mouse."

Grievance angled towards Flattery. "Well go on then, Colonel, spit it out!"

"We have evidence to suggest that the mouse helped Spikez and PIG30N escape last night."

The general erupted into a fit of hearty laughter. "Don't be ridiculous, Flattery – we're talking about a mouse with no legs locked in my office."

"We think he had help, General – from the outside."

Grievance waved his hands and fingers at Flattery, directing him to the chair opposite him. "Go on."

Flattery sat. Trakz' empty cage rested on the general's desk between them. "Sir, I think you need to see this for yourself." He turned to Grievance's computer and connected a memory stick containing the video footage. "What you're about to see was taken last night in Windar's laboratory."

Grievance put on his glasses and watched the screen. His eyebrow rose as he watched Trakz appear within frame, connect his tail to a computer and free Spikez and PIG30N from their cages. The general's ears began to burn, as did his cheeks, nose and neck. "Damn mouse," he said, rising from his seat and pacing towards the window. "Who put him there?"

"No-one, sir, we believe he was acting alone."

"But you said he had help from the outside – did Windar get back on site?"

"We've still no trace of Windar, sir."

"Colonel, listen to me," Grievance hunched across the desk, pushing the cage aside, "I left you in charge of the operation to find and destroy Magatron." The cage crashed to the floor.

"Yes, General."

"And you believe that you have successfully done this?"

"Yes, General."

"Yet, at the same time, you're telling me that the remainder of the Carrion project escaped right under your nose?"

"It would appear that way, Gen-"

"IT WOULD APPEAR THAT WAY!" blasted Grievance, infuriated that his base had become the laughing stock of the armed forces. He held his head - deeply annoyed that his decision to keep the mouse had miraculously backfired. "These devices," he continued, "have tracking modules, do they not?"

"Yes, General."

"Then have your men go-fetch!"

"We did, General – we had Spikez surrounded but it would appear. . . it seems that he was destroyed by Magatron."

"Colonel, are you making this up or is this what's going to go into your report."

"I'm not making it up, sir. During the recovery our team was attacked by Magatron, who fired indiscriminately. Several minutes later, our field operatives lost GPS signals for Spikez and PIG30N, moments before Magatron engaged our men at the base."

"And you have satellite images to confirm this?"

"Well, we are currently having some technical difficulty retrieving these images."

"Bah!" Seething with anger, Grievance looked out across the pastures of Greenacres. "What's happened to the world, Flattery?"

"Sir?"

"I remember what it was like when I joined the army. Every new recruit was young, clean and able to speak the Queen's English. None of us had degrees or qualifications, just a desire to serve our country. We fought wars on the ground and in the air, soldier versus soldier, across the world to protect the Commonwealth." He turned his attention to an antique war map, hanging above his golfing trophies. "We had men behind the controls – in command of the very machines we built with our bare hands." He directed his speech at Flattery. "Now the battle is conducted from the comfort of an office, in a comfy chair using drones steered by men in white coats - thinkers rather than doers."

Flattery felt proud to be sharing a moment of patriotic nostalgia with his boss.

"And then there's us!" he snapped, spittle gathering at the corner of his mouth. "We go one step further and resurrect roadkill to do our dirty work. Project Carrion will be our legacy, Flattery – the government's going to shut us down, for sure."

There was a moment of piteous reflection as the two men stared down at their medal ribbons. Flattery coughed up enough courage to speak. "General, what would you like me to do, sir?"

"Once you have all the data you need, I'd like you to file your report and put an end to this chapter before it becomes a saga."

"Yes, General," Flattery rose. "Will that be all, sir?"

"How long's it been since you were Corporal, Colonel?"

Flattery didn't answer immediately, recounting in his head the battles and operations he had fought. "I believe some fourteen years, when I was stationed in the Middle East."

Grievance looked Flattery dead in the eyes and saluted. "Make the report a good one, Colonel. We don't want history to repeat itself, do we?"

Flattery wavered, saluted and then exited the office – Grievance's words pulsating in his head.

55: The Window of Opportunity

Back at the barge, Prickles lay on Windar's operating table once more. Windar tutted at himself, identifying the problem. Fortunately for them all, the injury to Prickles was minimal, but the fuel cells designed to power Spikez' wings had sustained permanent damage - he would have limited flight time available. Trakz and PIG30N were by his side, talking about the mission that lay ahead.

"Listen," Trakz said, "apart from the glitch, you looked pretty confident up in the air this morning. Magatron has met his match today."

"Trakz," said Prickles, troubled, "to save Greenacres I'm going to have to destroy Magatron."

"Right, it's the only way we're all going to get back to some degree of normality."

"But I've never killed anything before," he replied, removing his visor. "I don't know if I've got it in me to obliterate him."

"Prickles, don't forget what you're dealing with here. If you don't destroy him, he will destroy you and many others – cyborgs like that can't be reasoned with."

"You're so sure that this is the only way? I need some options, Trakz - perhaps there's a way to neutralise him without killing him."

Trakz thought for a moment. It was easy to be objective as a mouse on the ground, but having not been directly involved in any of the military operations, perhaps Prickles had a point, maybe fighting fire with fire was not the way forward.

Windar repaired the fault to Prickles' wings and snapped them back behind his shoulders. The hedgehog flinched as he felt them fold inwards, pushing against the bone, a bearable but necessary twinge. Windar then motioned over to Hercules who was beginning to stir.

"Okay," said Trakz, leading Prickles over to a small epad. "I've been thinking about what you said and have been studying Magatron's schematics." A 3D image of Magatron revolved on the screen. "He was designed as a weapon, so anywhere on the front of his body is tightly armoured and you'd be directly in his firing range. The weakest point of his body is here!" Trakz pointed at Magatron's neck and the two pipes that fed directly into it. "These are the tubes that regulate his body temperature and help displace heat created from his weapon. If you can damage one of these, then you can disable his primary weapon – rendering him powerless."

"Sounds feasible, what can I use to do that?"

"Windar never intentionally built you as a weapon - you were always planned as a defensive machine capable of stealth, disabling computer systems. Your laser, however, is powerful enough to cut through his pipes - you just have to find a way to get on his back."

"Well that sounds easy," mused the hedgehog. "Why don't I just ask him for a ride?"

PIG30N studied the schematics thoroughly, wondering what hers looked like. Like Prickles, she was also never intended to be used as a weapon, but nonetheless Windar had given her basic defensive systems, the EMP pellets which were now replenished and her electrical generator was fully operational.

Windar was examining Hercules, to see whether the operation had been successful, when Dahab's phone started to vibrate in his pocket. He withdrew the device and read the text:

New SMS:

Planned military clear-up operation to commence 09:00. Make sure you are clear of your current position by 11:00 as intelligence operations will be closely scrutinising the area – we can only scramble signal for so long. Agent Dahab.

Prickles and the team turned to see Windar's reaction – they didn't need to read the message, they knew it was time.

56: Calm before the Storm

Deep inside the woods there was silence; a stillness that signalled uncertainty and struck fear into any living being that stopped to notice it. Most animals remained out of sight, only coming out at night to feed and avoid detection. Arim and Mira were an exception; they had remained in the burrow with Joy for the whole evening, too afraid to hop into the open for fear of capture. Tiredness held them both, but Joy had other plans. The young fledgling saw it as an opportunity to explore her surroundings and find her own food. She wanted to surprise her parents and show that she could be independent.

Magatron and his army had been active since dawn, finalising a strategy to cleanse the woodland of all raptors and gather up the young. The magpie had also sent teams of squirrels to various outposts across the forest to monitor for any sign of danger, animal or man.

Nutcase still believed that he would find Hercules, but until that glorious moment came, ambushing birds of prey in their pine nests would suffice. They would then be brought back to Mag, who would act as the exterminator, eradicating the raptors as a glorious spectacle for all animals to witness. The supreme magpie believed that instilling such fear would guarantee manageable woodland.

Joy was metres away from the makeshift family hideaway, but to her it felt further. She watched wonderful rays of sunshine beaming through the thick forest canopy. Dust and pollen danced and swirled like the entrails of a spirit, bouncing off heavy leaves and sprinkling over coarse bushes. Joy chirped with delight. Everything seemed glorious, until she heard a nerve-jangling chatter behind her.

The redwing turned, searching for signs of movement. Joy hopped across the soil, trying to get a better look when she spotted a bushy grey tail dart up a tree several metres ahead of her, screeching to the birds that lurked in the shadows.

Joy quickly regretted her decision to leave the burrow and hurried back, only to have her path blocked by a fierce looking magpie. It was flanked by two others, both towering over her. "Well, well – look what we have here," they said.

"A pretty little thing like you could get hurt twittering around on your own."

The squirrel dropped down behind Joy, jerking his tail left and right. "You don't seem to be doing much here, best come with us where you'll become more productive."

Joy chirped wildly with fear. Arim and Mira awoke, expecting the worst. They shot out from the burrow and into blinding sunlight, seeing Joy surrounded by a mob of grey fur and black and white feathers. Arim charged in, trying to break a hole in their wall, but he was met with aggression, batted to the ground and held by a severe looking magpie. Mira was more successful, funnelling in to land beside Joy, shielding her with her wing.

"Well look who it is," they cawed, "Greenacres' favourite immigrants." They cackled wildly to themselves, oh what fun this was going to be. "Mag says there's no place for foreigners in our society - 'e reckons you've nuffin to offer."

One of the squirrels bore his yellow teeth. "How do you plead?" he asked, cracking his knuckles. Mira did not answer, instead she continued to shield Joy, singing gently to block out Arim's screams as a magpie plucked feathers from his chest.

"Hey!" a voice called. The magpies and squirrels stopped and turned.

Emerging from the darkness, Prickles swaggered forward until the sun glared off his visor.

"It's him," one of the birds cawed.

"The anomaly - what do we do?" asked another.

The squirrel spoke purposefully. "He's just a hedgehog. If it bleeds, we can kill it." The pack dispersed from the redwings and surrounded Prickles.

"Listen, I really don't want to hurt you, I just want to know where you're holding my family."

The pack erupted with raucous laughter. "Mag told us all

about you, he told us what you'd be like. The boss said that if we catch and kill you that we'll never have to hunt again!"

"And if you don't?" Prickles asked. There was a stunned silence, they hadn't really thought about that. Prickles studied his assailants and mapped the area of the forest floor; in the cover of branches, PIG30N covertly streamed live footage to Prickles and Trakz, who monitored events back at the barge.

A squirrel attempted to fly kick Prickles from out of the blue, but his attack was deflected and Prickles held the squirrel by the foot, span him round and launched his assailant directly at the two magpies, who hissed wildly as the rodent whacked against them. The magpie hen was next to have a turn, she cast Arim aside and went for Prickles' visor – a tactic learnt from Magatron. Prickles was prepared, erecting his spines and presenting her a wall of spikes. Two other magpies attacked the hedgehog with their sharpened beaks, but Prickles snapped each bill in his hands and twisted the birds over onto their backs, subduing them by swiping his fists across their heads.

A mob of squirrels charged towards him, targeting his feet and legs, but Prickles had already fired his grapple hook at them. He watched as the wire wrapped itself tightly around their limbs before he yanked hard, bringing them all to the floor. The last two of the remaining corvids saw sense and attempted to flee the fight scene and caw for help. Prickles rolled forward and fired two tranquilising darts in their direction. They hit one, who dropped to the floor, leaving the other breaking for freedom, but he had not counted on PIG30N being so bold. The pigeon swooped, her feet charged with electricity, and struck the magpie cleanly in his chest. He let out a squawk and plummeted to the ground in a swirl of white and black.

PIG30N landed beside Prickles and surveyed their handiwork. In the shadow of an elm tree, the redwings were shouldered together, chirping in gratitude. Squirrels spat insults at them all whilst magpies flapped across the forest floor, dazed and confused. Prickles marched over to one of the females as PIG30N held her to the ground. "Where is he?"

"Do you know what he'll do to me if I tell you?" she cackled.

"It'll be far worse if you continue to support him."

"No, we will all share in the fortunes of his victory!"

Prickles looked deep into the magpie's eyes and took an ultrasound reading, detecting that she was carrying a clutch of eggs. "But your fledglings will grow up in the shadow of his evil. A victory for him does not mean a victory for the magpies. Far from it, no-one will trust your kind ever again."

The magpie mused over his words for a moment, gazing at her reflection in Prickles' visor. Was it fair to be stereotyped as a menace for life? Since she was a fledgling, she had watched the magpies' population grow in strength, and it was because of the carrion that they had survived the harsh winter months. Mag was the one who wanted to change things further; he wanted the magpies to become the master race.

Her salvation was interrupted by the foul rhetoric of the squirrels. "Don't tell them, he'll kill us all!" they yelled.

"I know where they are," a voice called. Prickles turned to

see Arim perched behind him. "Baldwin told us. He plans to lead a resistance over at the main rabbit colony by the eastern edge of the forest. That is where Mag is based - he has your family captive there."

Prickles thanked Arim. PIG30N ascended through the canopy, hoping to find Baldwin. The hedgehog turned back and addressed the squirrels. "Just for the record, I want you all to know that I'm not going to kill anyone," he said, replacing his utility tool. "Not even Mag. But when I see him, I'll tell him that you all tried your hardest."

With his belt replaced, Prickles unhinged his wings to the amazement of the magpies. The stared in awe at their shininess as the hedgehog angled his body in the direction of PIG30N and rocketed skywards.

57: Martyrs

Eliza was dragged before Mag by and a host of other corvids who would form part of his dictatorship. The great magpie hovered and addressed the crowd. "Today you will witness the beginning of your future. No longer will we have to succumb to the will of the raptors, and no longer will they pollute our skies with their arrogance."

Packs of squirrels and magpies cheered as others arrived for the rally- carrying unhatched eggs, ushering young cubs and fledglings into burrows. Mag continued. "By controlling the population of Greenacres, we are in full control of our destiny, deciding who can stay and who must leave." He directed his attention at Eliza. "You and your kind have prospered from us all, watching us grow tired and hungry – but now you will see how a forest should be run."

"I've heard enough of you chatter," Eliza remarked, "No matter what you do here, or whatever you do to me and my kind, you will never be able to truly control anything. Even man cannot control us fully. You aim to rule by fear and terror, but a forest will not thrive in that sort of climate. Chaos cannot be controlled. I implore you - release the young back to their families."

As Mag and Eliza continued their heated exchange, PIG30N and Prickles watched from a secure looking post high up in thick trees. Using PIG30N's excellent vision and his own thermograph, Prickles identified the most probable den where his family were being held. The challenge was how to enter by foot and out of clear view of hundreds of corvids and rodents.

Trakz radioed in. "I hate to rush, but you've got little over an hour to complete this mission."

As Prickles thought of a way to get in, his spikes instinctively flinched; something moved on the branch behind him. He spun round, ready to fight.

"I was hoping you'd come back," Deacon whispered, beckoning the hedgehog over.

Prickles shimmied along the branch, drawing closer to the owl. "There's too many of them."

"Yes, but there are still creatures prepared to fight - as we speak, Baldwin is rallying his most loyal supporters to make a final stand against Mag and his army."

"But you can't, Magatron will kill you all."

"My dear hog, we have all had long and colourful lives. Many of us are on borrowed time, as are you – we cannot sit back and allow him to carry on with this dangerous autocracy. If we pay with our lives, it shall be a small price for a worthy cause - the freedom of Greenacres."

"I can help you," Prickles said, "I know a way to defeat him, but it's not going to be easy. He has my family captive."

"And many other families," added Deacon, "and this latest tactic is proving highly effective."

Prickles thought for a moment, processing ideas. "Leave Mag to me – I think there's a way we can safely lead the young to safety and rescue your elected Queen."

"We will support you in any way we can, hedgehog. What do you need of us?"

"Do you have any diggers in your team?"

Deacon smiled. "A few." The owl turned and led Prickles through a hollow in the tree.

58: Network of Fear

"I see my prayers have been answered," said Baldwin, resting his paw upon Prickles'. "Thank you for returning." The young hedgehog smiled briefly; it felt good to be accepted.

"Where are the others?" Prickles looked past Baldwin at two elderly hares and Deacon.

"Many have already left Greenacres, fearing for their lives – others are too scared to stand up to Mag for fear of what he'll do to their young. We are the resistance." Baldwin glanced at the faces around him. "After the great battle in spring, we thought that our generation would never have to fight such a battle again. And because Mag has become like no other adversary we have ever fought - they won't. We need your help."

Prickles looked into their eyes, past the thick film that coated each eyeball – they were deluded if they thought they could win the war on their own. However, they were veterans who were prepared to die for their home – his home, and the hedgehog concluded that if there was ever a time to step into adulthood, this was his moment. "What's your tactic, Baldwin?"

"If we can get to Magatron or even injure him, others will begin to believe that the war can be won – we just can't get close enough. I lost three of my best rabbits in the night."

"Then we dig underground, into the network of tunnels. Once we find our way in, you lead as many fledglings and cubs to safety as you can. I'll keep digging until I can get close enough to Mag."

The hares, who knew the tunnel networks better than any squirrel or magpie, led Prickles and the resistance towards a small burrow entrance, hidden between broad tree roots. "You lead," they said to him. "The main tunnel will take you directly above the magpies' main harvest store. Beyond it you will have to choose carefully where you dig."

Prickles' visor lit up and neon light encapsulated the rim. He squeezed himself through the tunnel, closely followed by the others; they were burrowing into the heart of Mag's terror network.

In a darkened chamber, Rosie sat bound and gagged next to her mother and father, awaiting their cruel fate. They were hungry and cold – Rosie felt numb. The squirrels mocked them, telling them that Prickles had been killed by Mag in a bungled rescue attempt. Rosie hoped the rumours were lies, not because of the pain it caused her, but the suffering it inflicted upon her parents. Her father spent most of the time sleeping, trying to conserve energy, but Mrs Hog did nothing but worry – she could not sleep and refused to eat what little scraps they were given, growing weaker by the hour. Rosie knew that her mother risked slipping into early hibernation and that she might never wake up unless they escaped.

Eliza screeched as Nutcase ripped another feather from her wings, much to the laughter from Mag's supporters. She tried to finish the work of Hercules by leaping on the squirrel, but her feet were tethered. The queen of the raptors was a prisoner and now, it seemed, entertainment for the fiendish masses.

Mag was radicalising a small group of hardened followers, including Ringpull, about how they must kill the remaining birds of prey for his cause. Just then, an abrupt cacophony of cawing and cackling broke out. Mag swivelled, targeting the figures that burst through the forest canopy. A pack of magpies and carrion crows landed before him, bowing their heads. "Master, the hedgehog lives!"

Mag frowned. "You have seen him?"

"We have fought him – he was with the redwings."

"The redwings! You see, just as I suspected, these foreign freedom fighters are polluting our land. Where is the hedgehog now?"

"We thought he would be here already, we came as quickly as we could after a patrol set us loose."

Mag angled and did an electronic sweep of the trees high above, catching a glimpse of PIG30N. "Intruders!" he yelled, firing a bolt of energy directly at her.

PIG3ON leapt from the branch as it exploded.

Prickles froze in the tunnel as his live video feed died. "They know we're here. It won't be long until they start searching the warrens." Prickles looked at the burrow wall – he detected no clay, it was pot luck where they would end up. "We dig here!" The animals gathered next to him and began clawing frantically.

PIG3ON was pursued by a pack of agile and blood-thirsty magpies desperate to please their leader. She was confident she would out-manoeuvre them, but only for so long.

Eliza smirked to herself. "You're seeing a glimpse of what's to come. Whoever you kill or destroy on your way to power will become a martyr - the creatures of Greenacres will never give up the fight."

Mag marched over to her. "Don't think for one moment that I want to make you one - if I wanted you dead you'd have joined your friend Hercules already. I'm keeping you alive so that you can watch your species become extinct! And when I'm through with you, I'm going to have you stuffed with the feathers of your old friends."

"Be alert, there could be more of them!" shouted Nutcase, sorting the squirrels into platoons. "Spread out and don't disappoint me, I want that hedgehog found."

A black cloud of angry birds fought to stay airborne as PIG3ON continued to climb. Sensing that the magpies, rooks and crows were slowly tiring, the pigeon deployed a cluster of stun-pellets. Each one she ejected burst into a flash of blinding white light, sending ripples through the irate mob. PIG30N turned sharply and dived back to earth at great speed – no bird could get close to her.

Trakz radioed PIG30N. "You need to draw Magatron out – we're running out of time." But PIG30N already knew what she had to do, it was risky and meant facing her biggest demons, but it was a gamble she was prepared to make.

Rosie looked at the wall of her earthy cell. Her nose twitched, then the hairs on her snout stood on end as she fearfully watched clumps of soil crumble before her. Her father woke from his slumber, also sensing the vibrations. Harold began to stutter and yell deliriously as a juicy worm wriggled in front of him.

Rosie's mother stirred and called to her daughter. "Rosie, what's happening?"

"I think the roof is collapsing. Mum!" she cried. "I'm so sorry about everything – about the lies I told you both, and for running away. I really love . . . mud!"

The wall of earth caved in, coating them all in clumps of brittle dirt. Mr Hog was quick to shake his head free and gave a triumphant cry as the worm was finally within reach. He quickly snapped his jaws around its tail and sucked it up, only to choke on it when he saw four figures standing before him, veiled by a gentle neon light.

Rosie shook herself free of the dirt and looked at her rescuers, yelping with delight. "Prickles, you came back!"

Prickles stepped forward and shovelled the mud away from

his family with his claws. Baldwin and the hares helped him, chewing through the twine that bound the hedgehogs together. Rosie leapt up, cupping her brother's cheek. "I knew you'd come back for me."

"I came back for all of you," he said, helping his mother to her feet. "For Greenacres."

Henrietta looked up at her son and smiled. "My little Prickles," she said, nuzzling his cheek. The hedgehog savoured the moment, recording it in his mind; she was warm and soft like her voice, just as he remembered. He felt his biological heart pound frantically inside him for the first time in months.

Harold motioned behind him and muttered under his breath. "My boy, you've done well."

Prickles could hear Trakz sniffling on the intercom. But amidst these teary moments of joy, he knew they would become distant memories unless he stopped Magatron. "You need to go!" Prickles directed Baldwin and the hares. "Take them away from here, away from danger."

Rosie stepped between Prickles and Baldwin. "I'm not leaving you again!"

"It's time you started to listen to your older brother for once. I want you away from here - I'll meet you by the river. Now go!"

Before Rosie could argue, Baldwin ushered the hedgehogs away. "Your brother's right, it's not safe here." He instructed the hares to call for reinforcements to help rescue the young.

"It's going to be dangerous out there, you could get hurt," warned Prickles.

"Don't worry about me," grumbled Baldwin, "there's plenty of fight left in the old badger, yet. You lead, I'll cover."

Prickles turned and ran towards the daylight above, Baldwin in support behind him.

59: Spikez' Fight

Two squirrels guarded the burrow entrance, their attention directed at the forest perimeter, searching for any signs of the hedgehog. They were too slow to react to the speed and force of Prickles as he butted them both outwards.

As the rodents lay sprawled across the floor, Prickles stopped to adjust his visor and saw his target: Magatron. The magpie was clearly taken aback by the hedgehog's boldness. A group of hardened squirrels, led by Nutcase, quickly charged at Prickles. "All yours, Baldwin," he called, firing his grapple hook at a branch above him.

The squirrels watched Prickles ascend into the branches. As they marvelled at the hedgehog, Baldwin burst from the depths and ploughed into them like a juggernaut.

Mag directed his weapon at Prickles and prepared to fire. Eliza saw this and, with every last ounce of strength, flew at him

- sinking her beak into his back. It did just enough to pull him off track as the shard of energy fired upwards, missing Prickles and amputating a large tree branch from its trunk. A bundle of squirrels leapt for cover, but Stoatey was too slow – the bough hammered him deep into the burrows, splintering all his bones.

Mag turned on Eliza. "I'll take my words back, Eliza. You can die a martyr for your pathetic cause." He struck her with the back of his wing and directed his plasma canon at her head. Mag went to fire when something struck his back, hooking one of his coolant tubes. Before he could react, the magpie found himself being forcefully pulled through the air at speed.

Prickles used a branch as a pulley, leaping downwards to mount Magatron halfway. But Mag would not play along - he spread his wings and fired up his propulsion system, and Prickles suddenly found himself on the wrong end of a leash, shooting skywards.

A young rabbit dashed over to Eliza and frantically chewed through the twine that bound her talons to a tree stump. Baldwin continued to fight the squirrels but he was being slowly overrun, battered and bitten into submission until he could not move.

The squirrels soon surrounded Eliza and the young rabbit, who'd successfully managed to gnaw through, but Eliza feared it was all in vain. They were outnumbered by ten, fifteen, twenty to one. Nutcase pushed forward and bawled at the top of his voice. "So, the Queen likes it a bit of rough and tumble, does she? Then let's give her a right-royal battering!"

As Nutcase swung his stick upwards, PIG30N burst through the trees with a following of raptors: kestrels, buzzards and a fearsome peregrine falcon. The pigeon carpet bombed the squirrels with an electric charge, sending them all howling wildly into the woods.

Nutcase studied his new adversaries, looking into the fiery yellow eyes of the falcon. He knew when he was beat. "You aven't seen the last of me, Queenie!" he snarled, slinking through the bracken.

"My Queen," the kestrels called, "what would you have us do?"

"We must support the hedgehog – lets end this war once and for all." Eliza led the charge with a mighty battle cry, accelerating skywards with a volley of vengeful raptors by her side.

Magatron was fervently trying to shake himself loose from Prickles' grapple hook by swooping, diving, and halting in mid-air. At any opportunity he would fire at Prickles, but the hedge-hog swung wildly. However, Mag was soon supported by other corvids who dived at Prickles, attempting to knock him from the sky. Prickles desperately held on, slowly reeling himself in towards Magatron so that he could strike. And still, more enemies began to attack. But despite his spikes and fast reflexes, Prickles eventually lost his grip and hurtled back to earth.

Mag and the others cackled wildly as they watched him plum-met, but their laughter was short lived. Prickles coolly steadied himself and hovered in one spot, facing them defiantly.

Circling above, the corvids contemplated this strange phe-nomenon, a hedgehog with wings! And as they pondered, a wave of raptors ripped through the pack, tackling bundles of white and black feathers.

Mag fired a blast of energy at Prickles with steam erupting behind him as the pressure was released. Prickles veered sharply to the right and flew at Mag.

Eliza had her eye on Mag also, wanting to avenge him for all the misery he had inflicted. She was within a swoop away from sinking her claws into his back when she was gripped by an equally unpleasant face. Ringpull, fuelled by hate, clipped her and left her tumbling downwards. "Give it up, prey!" he squawked, hammering her again.

PIG30N shot past and zapped the magpie with an electrical charge. His fizzy drinks tab spun away from his head as he cackled wildly, trying to regain his balance. Ringpull watched as Eliza caught a thermal and propelled herself upwards.

Diving towards Prickles, Mag fired indiscriminately. The flying hedgehog initiated evasive manoeuvres. The magpie veered to the left. Prickles followed in hot pursuit, but it was soon clear that he was being drawn into another trap. A fleet of black feathers encircled him. Prickles countered with a sudden change in direction, rocketing upwards at speed.

Now it was PIG30N's turn to attack Mag – she accelerated at top speed, arching above Magatron and releasing a series of highly volatile pellets that would disable any electronic device, and corvid, that they touched. Mag saw this and shot clear, narrowly missing the capsules; his followers, however, were less fortunate. Three magpies were hit, flapping uncontrollably as electrical pulses exploded across their nerve endings.

Mag retaliated by firing at PIG3ON, hitting her tail feathers which burst into flames. The pigeon retreated, cooing wildly from the sting as her feathers smouldered leaving a black trail in the sky.

Trakz was busy monitoring vital signs. "Guys, this doesn't look good – time to be a bit more inventive!"

Ringpull headed for a collision with Eliza. As they struck he felt the raptor's claws tether to his chest, piercing and crushing the air from his lungs. The magpie tried to caw for help as they tumbled, but Eliza bit hard into his neck, ripping through muscles and arteries and tearing open his throat. Then she released his lifeless body to earth. It was a merciful death, quick and painless – but despite Eliza's wrath, she would have it no other way. The sparrowhawk looked round at the kestrels as they skilfully weaved between adversaries, purposefully clipping corvids across their heads and wings; the peregrine was fierce, lunging into crows and magpies with such speed and force that he left a cloud of feathers in his wake; and then Eliza watched as Magatron pursued Prickles higher and higher through the clouds. She wanted to support him, but this was their battle.

Prickles had limited flying time left – minutes! Mag fired, narrowly missing him, ripping a hole through a cloud by the heat generated from it. Prickles saw his chance and entered before the gap sealed itself back up. Mag pursued, firing at will, but the hedgehog had vanished from sight. He did a thorough scan but found no trace. Cautiously, Mag ground to a halt below the clouds and surveyed the battle below him; he was losing, the raptors were on the cusp of another victory.

Prickles dropped from the cloud like a silent angel, locking himself to Magatron's back. Mag spun violently, but despite the incredible G-force, Prickles did not let go.

Trakz' voice buzzed in Prickles' head. "You've got him, take the shot!" With one hand, the hedgehog removed the laser device from his belt and began cutting.

Mag hissed wildly, firing haphazardly at the birds below – vaporising some of his own. Each time he fired, jets of steam erupted from the vent behind Mag's neck, scalding the flesh from Prickles' hand until nothing remained but titanium wrapped bone. Mag suddenly accelerated downwards, planning to use the trees to scrape Prickles off. But the hedgehog held on for dear life until the laser finally severed the pipe, rupturing Mag's coolant system.

Prickles was blown clear by the explosion.

The birds stopped fighting and watched both adversaries tumble downwards.

Falling back to earth, Mag began to overheat. His eyes burned. Internal systems began shutting down. Wings locked. Second by second he slipped further out of consciousness, plunging earthwards in a ball of steam. And then, for a split second, he was back in Greenacres on a spring morning, the warm egg in his mouth. Blackness followed.

The magpie's body dropped into the River Charon. Mag was quickly engulfed by the heavy currents which splashed over him, pulling him to the depths.

Prickles hovered in the air above, watching, waiting for Mag's wings to start thrashing back to life. Instead he saw the cold waters consume his enemy, carrying the magpie out of Greenacres to a watery grave in the icy depths of the sea.

Trakz cheered on his intercom. "You did it, you lasered that sucker!"

The magpies had seen Mag fall from the sky, as did the crows, jackdaws and rooks. Their leader was gone. Prickles held their attention now - a prickly statuette of liberty for the raptors; sun beams burst through clouds behind him, making him a silhouette of hope for animal-kind.

The battle had ended. Several of the corvids cawed for a retreat.

"Prickles..." Trakz sounded alarmed. "Do you want the good news or the-"

Without warning, Prickles' fuel cell's died instantly. He plummeted from the sky.

PIG30N turned and flew at Prickles in an attempt to hold him, but it was no use – he was too heavy. She watched him follow the same perilous path as Mag, hurtling at speed towards the meandering river, a serpent waiting to swallow him up.

Windar glanced across his screen and relayed new directives: 'hang in there Spikez'.

Eliza and the kestrels watched the hedgehog fall helplessly when their attention switched to an object swooping high above them. "It can't be!" they said as they watched it launch into a frenzied dive.

Prickles did not know what came from the sky to save him. He felt talons hook around his artificial wing and heard the hum of a hydraulic motor.

"Impressive work for a hedgehog," a voice said. Prickles turned his head to see a familiar face. "I would have liked to have had a piece of Mag myself, but I think you did a tidier job," remarked Hercules.

The red kite soared across the horizon with Prickles in his grasp. PIG30N flew in their slipstream. They slowly descended, approaching the floating runway - Windar's barge. Prickles could see Trakz and the professor waiting for them.

"Hold tight, I hear you haven't quite perfected the art of landing yet." Hercules fanned out his wings further, slowing himself right down so that he could drop the hedgehog to the ground with great accuracy. Prickles ejected the broken wings from his shoulders and hit the barge roof, rolling to a halt.

Trakz whizzed towards him. "You did it!"

"No, we did it," Prickles said. "Your plan worked. Do you think he's dead?"

"Whether he is or not doesn't matter – he can't use his weapon anymore without blowing himself up, which is probably what he tried to do. If that's the case, then his death was self-inflicted – suicide - your conscience is clear!"

Hercules landed on the steering wheel behind them. Prickles noted a delicate, skeletal wire frame swathed around his wings, and strapped to his back was a small hydraulic engine linked to neural wires that rested above the kite's blazing yellow eyes. "A temporary fix," Hercules said, stretching his wings out for all to see. "They'll be good as new soon."

Prickles' celebrations were short lived. "Baldwin!" he cried, as the barge chugged down-river. "I said I'd meet them. Trakz, why do we need to leave now that Mag is gone?"

"We were never staying, buddy. It's not safe for us anymore – with or without Mag. Windar's still a wanted man and we're his accomplices."

Prickles asserted himself, addressing PIG30N, Trakz and Hercules. "No, we have to stop - I need to see my family one last time!"

"Hey, I'm just a mouse – Windar is the one controlling the boat, maybe you should speak to him."

Prickles glanced at Windar, who was sorting through his tools; he knew it was useless to try and communicate with him – the programming wasn't there yet. He peered over the side at the water – as refreshing as it looked, he didn't have the know-how or energy to start swimming. "Hercules, did you see anything along the river when you left?"

Hercules looked up and gave a piercing cry at the raptors, who were circling ahead to the left of the river bank.

"What are they doing?" Prickles asked.

"Maybe they've found Mag's body?" Trakz suggested.

"Allow me to investigate," bellowed Hercules, pushing himself into the air.

"Look, I know you can't tell Windar what to do," Prickles said, "but if you can break us out of a top secret military lab, then I'm sure that you can make an old boat accidentally crash into the river bank."

Trakz paused for a moment. "I'll be right back," he said, disappearing down a hole.

60: The Promise

Windar was proud and reflective as he steered the barge down the river. He had his cyborgs back, had successfully prevented Magatron from creating further mess, and received a text message from agent Dahab informing him that the military had completed their sweep of the area and found no anomalies. He was in the clear, for now.

A gentle breeze drifted across the canal. Windar inhaled, the fresh air rejuvenated his senses and gave him clarity - perhaps it was time to choose a new career path? His creations would keep him company for several years to come, but he knew that he would outlive them – being a cyborg didn't make you immortal. Windar thought back to the work he did in Africa, wishing he had never given up so quickly on his Rabb-04 mine clearance devices. The professor intended to return to doing charity work in war-torn regions across the world.

The Sun's rays continued to warm his face as he mulled over endless possibilities, but Windar's dreams were quickly put on hold - the engine shuddered and the barge veered violently to the left, heading towards the river bank.

"Blast!" Windar fumbled with the controls, trying to steer the boat away from the bank. He cut the power to the engine, hoping the drag from the reeds would minimise the impact, but the barge clipped the side. "Curses!" He tossed a rope over portside so that he could moor up and investigate.

Trakz re-emerged next to Prickles, who was gazing into the trees. Parading before them was Baldwin, the hares and his family. Queen Eliza and Hercules were perched regally on a branch above as other creatures slowly began to appear from the undergrowth.

As Windar tussled with some rope, Prickles seized his opportunity and leapt overboard.

"You came back," wept Rosie, watching her brother walk to greet them.

"I said I would," Prickles replied, embracing her. He looked at his parents who watched with admiration.

"Welcome home, lad," his father said, offering him some insects to munch on.

Prickles looked down at the bugs and pondered the word 'home' as Baldwin approached to share his gratitude. "Rosie, I'm so glad that I got to see you all again. . . but I can't stay. I have to go."

"Don't be silly," she replied, "why do you need to go, the danger has passed?"

"We would be honoured if you would stay," remarked Baldwin, gripping Prickles' robotic hand.

"It's for the best," Prickles said. "I've been thinking about it for a long time, about a lot of things." He looked around at the creatures, at his family, at Rosie. "I've finally realised that I can never go back to being who I was."

"That's not true," hushed Rosie.

"But it is, sis. Things have changed, Greenacres has changed – I've changed. I'm safer with Windar. You are all safer without me."

Rosie grabbed his hands and held them against her face, she didn't care that they were metal and hard. "You can't leave us – I won't let you!"

Baldwin turned to the creatures that had gathered around them, and looked up at the redwings - they also looked set to leave Greenacres. "We cannot ask any more of you, Prickles. If you decide to leave then we will understand your reasons, the freedom you fought for has bought you that choice." Baldwin addressed the animals. "The wise hedgehog has made a good point. Things have changed and it will take time to restore balance to these woods. Man has not learnt to give up his possessions so easily – this we know is true."

There was silence amongst all the creatures as they reflected on the suffering and loss during past months. "On behalf of the Animal Council, I thank you – we are all indebted by your bravery. You can leave here with your snout held high."

Prickles motioned over to his parents and gave them one last nuzzle.

"You don't have to do this," his mother said.

"I'm not a hoglet anymore, mum, this is what's best for everyone - what's best for me."

Rosie cried. "You can't leave me!"

"Yes I can, Rosie. It's my choice."

"But you said you'd never leave me," she sobbed.

"Then come with me. You always said you wanted to become an explorer, to go beyond Greenacres with me at your side. We can still live that dream."

Her spikes tingled and twitched across her body as he said those words. Go with him where? All she knew was the forest and the animal way of life – the thought of what she didn't know was terrifying.

Eliza called down from the tree. "Greenacres will always be your home, hedgehog."

"Thank you." Prickles gave Rosie one last kiss, turned and walked back towards the barge.

Trakz and PIG30N watched in stunned silence, their eyes watering. The mouse saw his cue to disappear back down the hole to the engine room, whilst Windar remained below deck out of sight.

Rosie was rooted to the spot. "I've lost you once, I'm not losing you again!" she called, turning to her mum and dad. "I'm going with him, but I will return one day. I promise."

She said her final goodbyes before running after her brother.

Prickles helped her clamber on to the boat along the thick, heavy rope. "I'd best introduce you to the rest of my friends."

The boat engine rumbled and started running again. Windar returned on deck with a puzzled look on his face. He looked at the riverbank to see creatures slowly dispersing back into the wilderness. Then Windar looked at Prickles and noticed, with great delight, the newest addition to the team.

Prickles and Rosie were together again, like they had always been. "Where are we going?" she asked.

"On an adventure."

61: The Incident at Greenacres

Windar made good time along Montgomery's Canal, eventually arriving at Grayford. During that time he received another message from Dahab, informing him that MI6 had arranged protection for him over the coming months whilst further investigations took place.

During that period, the professor made many discoveries. His most significant came whilst installing upgrades to Trakz: a series of interesting video files recorded in General Grievance's office. They made their way to Harry Brown at the Daily News and it went some way towards restoring Windar's name.

```
                              MEMO


      TO:     General Grievance

      FROM:   Colonel Flattery

      RE:     The Incident at Greenacres


      General,

      Please find enclosed my official report.  I have also
      attached  a  summary,  which  I  hope  will  keep  those
      magpies at the press office busy.

      I  would  also  like  to  thank  you  for  the  five  years
      of  service  we  had  together.   I  hope  that  you  enjoy
      your  retirement.   I  have  been  redeployed  to  oversee
      operations in the Middle-East.

      I will be thinking of you.
```

Beneath the murky waters of the estuary, waiting to be dragged by the tide into a cold abyss, Mag's body drifted between muddy channels. Crayfish and crabs competed to pull at what little flesh remained amongst mechanical components and muscle sinew. All the while, tiny electrical signals continued to pulse within Mag's brain, as though something or someone was trying to send a message to wake him up.

That evening, as the sun finished its blazing retreat towards the horizon, Morag stood by the riverside, chanting to the moon. She held her damaged wings to the stars and made hideous cries through her decaying lungs. The raven witch repeated this process continually for minutes, which turned into hours as darkness cloaked the sky.

In all the howling and reciting, Morag did not see her killer approach. Deprived of a good meal, slinking out from the undergrowth, Fagin thanked his lucky stars as he watched the raven flapping by the river. He saw her broken wings, tattered and ruffled as she hobbled along the water's edge.

The fox had learnt lots from his encounters with the hedgehogs, one of which was not to laugh until he had secured his meal.

Fagin did not go hungry that evening. None of Morag's magic could protect her.

Spikez in Schools

The concept of Spikez was something I came up with at a very early age. I loved insects and robots and used to draw all types of weird and wonderful insect cyborgs - it was only a matter of time before I branched out to animals.

We've included a range of themes and textual references to great novels and films within Spikez for you to explore. There is also scope for cross curricular study at KS2 or KS3.

Our aim was to regenerate the animal fable genre, making it relevant to today's world and more appealing to a modern audience. We really hope you enjoyed reading it as much as we loved making it – now's the chance to tell us what you think!

There are plans to take Spikez on more exciting, dangerous missions. Why not create your own animal cyborgs that might help or impede him. If we like them we'll showcase them on our website.

Follow us on twitter for all the latest news and to get in touch!

Glossary

AI	Artificial Intelligence (the science and engineering of making intelligent machines
COBRA	British Government military intelligence unit
CORVID	A collection of birds from the Corvidae family (crows, rooks, magpies, ravens and jackdaws)
CYBORG	A being with biological and artificial parts (also known as Cybernetic Organism)
EMP	A burst of electromagnetic radiation (can destroy electronics)
LED	Light Emitting Diode
GIGAJOULE	Equal to one billion joules of energy (watts of power per second)
GPS	Global Position System
MoD	Ministry of Defence
NANO-TECHNOLOGY	Closely linked to Nanorobotics, the study and manipulation of matter at an atomic and nanoscopic scale
RAPTOR	A naturalist term for a bird of prey
SYMBIOSIS	Interactions between different species
THERMOGRAPH	Device for measuring temperature visually (hot and cold regions)
USB	A port used to connect electronic devices together (computing)

Wild Weblinks

British Intelligence Service **www.mi6.gov.uk**
Educational Science and Tech **www.howitworksdaily.com**
Royal Society for the Protection of Birds **www.rspb.org.uk**
Tiggywinkles Wildlife Hospital **www.sttiggywinkles.org.uk**
The National Trust **www.nationaltrust.org.uk**
Wildlife Trust **www.wildlifetrusts.org**
Future Technology **www.animalcyborgs.com**
Computer Science for Fun **www.cs4fn.org/ai/**
Animal Watch UK **www.animalwatchuk.com**

British Hedgehog Preservation Society
www.britishhedgehogs.org.uk
Charity organisation supporting mine clearance
www.apopo.org/home.php

Be sure to visit **www.spikez.co.uk** and become a fan

Look out for Spikez' next exciting adventure;
Spikez: 紅龍